SAVANNAH SLEUTH

VIGILANTES FOR JUSTICE BOOK ONE

ALAN CHAPUT

First Paperback Edition: January 2018

Library of Congress Control Number: 2017916583

Paperback ISBN: 978-1-947295-01-8

E-book ISBN: 978-1-947295-00-1

AUTHOR NOTE

While I have used some actual Savannah places in this story, Falcon Square, Saint Gregory's Cathedral, and The French Bakery are entirely fictional places.

CHAPTER 1

*P*atricia lifted her blond hair to cool her sweat-soaked neck. April in Savannah was normally more tolerable.

She took a deep breath, cut short by her close-fitted armored vest. For the third time, she pounded on Faith Pinckney's door.

Faith had called at noon, a couple of hours ago. She had said she was ready to go to the shelter, had confirmed her husband was at work, and had agreed to be picked up at two. They were on time. So where was Faith?

Patricia touched the holstered Kimber 45 on her hip and made sure the safety was off. She glanced at Judy, the newest member of her team, on her right, and Meredith, her closest friend, on her left. Both were grim, coiled, and pale as ghosts. Patricia supposed there was safety in numbers, but they were still vulnerable. And if the situation became life-threatening? Well, none of them had ever shot anything but paper targets.

"I don't like this," Judy said, her hauntingly pale blue eyes methodically cataloging the environment. "It's taking too long. This is a rough neighborhood. We're too exposed."

Meredith, a woman more comfortable with financial ratios than cold steel, gestured over her shoulder toward the curb and the idling SUV. "Don't worry, Alisa has our backs."

"Meredith, check that front window. See if there's anyone inside," Patricia said, trying to speed things up.

Meredith put her face to the window. "Can't see anyone."

Patricia pounded on the door again. No one responded. Had Faith changed her mind about leaving? It wouldn't be the first time that had happened.

But Faith had made the call to the rescue line and had said she wanted to leave. Patricia, the shelter's voluntary emissary, was here at Faith's invitation to provide transportation.

Patricia pulled her smartphone from its hip-mounted case, scrolled to Faith's number, and pressed the call icon.

Ring. Ring.

Patricia shifted weight.

Ring. Ring.

Come on. Answer the phone. Heightened concern for the safety of her team flooded Patricia. The three of them, armed and dressed in black tactical gear, were on an abuser's porch in a dangerous neighborhood. A rundown realm with its own rules. They were easy targets.

Patricia snapped her gaze left and right, checking the wraparound porch once again for threats. If Faith's husband wasn't inside, had a neighbor called him and told him they were at his door? Was the abuser on his way back to his house? Did he carry a gun? How long did they have before he arrived to defend his property? It had happened before, and the thought it could happen again today made her jumpy.

The phone kept ringing. *Where the hell was Faith?*

"Hello," finally came a weak female voice from Patricia's phone.

"Faith?"

"Yeah."

"It's two o'clock."

"Oh."

Patricia let out an impatient breath. "We're here. At your door. You wanted a ride to the shelter, didn't you?"

"Yeah."

"It's time to go. Where are you?"

"In bed. I got tired. I suppose it was them painkillers they gave me down at the hospital. Just a sec. I'll be right out."

"Is your husband home?"

"No. He's workin'. Won't be home 'til after five, if that man comes home at all."

A couple of minutes later, the weathered door eased open on squeaky hinges.

Patricia dropped her shaking hand to her gun.

Pungent air poured from the house. The smell of decay registered. A tiny, thin, middle-aged Caucasian woman stood in the shadowed foyer.

Patricia's heart sank at the sight.

Large purple bruises puffed the woman's pale face and forearms. Her mousey hair was pulled back into a ponytail accentuating sad brown eyes. Though clearly a victim, Faith stood straight, projecting determination.

Good for her.

"Faith?"

"Yeah?" The woman's voice trembled.

"I'm Patricia from the shelter." Patricia gestured to either side. "These are my friends, Meredith and Judy."

Faith nodded at each.

"Are you ready to go?" Patricia asked.

"Guess so."

"Okay then. Let's do it."

Faith picked up a stuffed garbage bag and a limp teddy bear.

3

Patricia stepped aside, and the woman shuffled unsteadily out onto the wide wooden porch. In the outside light, some of her wounds seemed more recent than the chaplain at Falcon Memorial Hospital had described. She must have been subjected to tremendous pain, severe enough to require prescription painkillers.

Faith looked around nervously as if ready to bolt at the slightest threat.

"You're shaking," Patricia said, more abruptly than intended.

The woman looked down. "It ain't easy to leave."

"I know. You're very brave." Patricia wanted to speak more words of comfort and reassurance. She wanted Faith to be happy. But the right words didn't come. So, Patricia sighed and eased her arm around the stale-smelling woman. No more beatings for poor Faith. Ever.

Just as they moved toward the steps, heavy footfalls hammered the porch where it wrapped around the side of the house.

The Escalade's horn erupted from the curb, signaling that Alisa had seen danger.

Patricia's fingers fumbled for the handle of her weapon.

"Hey, bitch," shouted a coarse male voice.

Patricia spun, put her body between Faith and the spine-rattling voice, and eased her hand off the gun. Experience had taught her that confrontation required calm focus, not panicked stiffness. She turned and looked up into a charging man's flushed face. He stopped less than a yard away. His breath reeked of alcohol.

She shot a glance past him to see if he'd brought others. He appeared to be alone, and his stubby hands were empty.

Okay. The three of them against one riled-up drunk. Good odds.

She returned her attention to the man's creased face.

Their eyes met. His eyes were black and hard like coal. His unblinking stare bore into her.

She tensed. She hadn't seen cold, piercing eyes like his before. Though drunk, this brute was likely as dangerous as he was ugly. She kept her face blank. "You talking to me, mister?"

"Yeah, you. What y'all doin' on my porch?"

His porch? Must be the husband. "Your wife asked us over," Patricia said as mildly as possible considering the situation.

His dark eyes narrowed. "Like hell she did. Sure 'nuf she don't know folk like y'all. Besides, you got armor on and a gun on your hip. You a cop?"

Patricia let out a long breath then shook her head. "No."

He stepped near, gripped her arm, and squeezed hard. "Then get the hell off my property."

Keeping her face an impassive mask, she peeled his stiff fingers from her arm, then turned to Faith. "Okay Faith. Stay beside me while we walk to the car."

"She ain't goin' nowhere."

The spit from his spewed words splattered the side of Patricia's face. She fought the screaming urge to wipe her cheek; a reaction that would convey weakness.

Summoning all the authority she could muster, Patricia squared her shoulders and pivoted to face the abuser again. He towered over her, inches away, poised like a grizzly bear ready to fight. Smirking. Close enough to intimidate.

The Neanderthal swung an arm behind him.

Patricia's instincts screamed, *Gun!* Her hand darted to her pistol, but she hesitated. Before she could decide to show her weapon, he fumbled out a small pistol of his own and shoved the barrel toward her face.

"This here says y'all are leavin' right now, and my precious little woman is goin' back inside."

Patricia's chest seized so tightly she could hardly breathe.

Heart thudding, she stepped back, getting distance. The husband had given her ample warning fumbling behind his back. She should have drawn her gun. She should have maintained control; guns were about control. Now he was in charge. This wasn't the ending she'd imagined. If they left now and came back tomorrow, would Faith be alive? And if they didn't leave—

Click.

The man's eyes bulged. His jaw dropped.

Judy, standing behind the man, had her gun barrel pressed against his head. "And *I* say," Judy said coldly, "we let Faith make her own decision about where she's going this afternoon. Now put your peashooter on the floor and back off."

He laughed the harsh laugh of a defeated man trying to regain some pride as he placed the gun on the porch floor and stepped to the side. "Sure. Whatever the bitch wants. But, Faith, you leave, don't bother comin' back."

Patricia took a couple of deep breaths. *That was close.* She gestured, palm up, to Faith. "So what is it? Go or stay?"

Faith wrung her hands. "I can't take any more of this life. Not another minute." Faith's eyes danced. "Um, I gotta go." She stretched her bruised arms toward the man. "Honey, I'm sorry."

He scowled and swept his hand toward the street. "Go, you ungrateful bitch, and don't even think about comin' back."

Judy retrieved the man's pistol and kept her gun on him as Patricia and Meredith led Faith to the street. Once they reached the SUV, Judy backed off the porch and down the sidewalk, all the while keeping her gun trained on the man. At the curb, she placed his pistol in the mailbox and then pointed at the scowling man standing on the porch. "We know about men like you. You think harass is two words."

Alisa covered her mouth with a hand, stifling a giggle.

Faith tossed her garbage bag into the Escalade, then, teddy bear in hand, stepped inside. Once seated, she cuddled the teddy bear like a child.

"I know you don't have any children. Is there anyone else in the house he might hurt?" Patricia asked.

"No. Do you have kids?"

"Just one." Patricia's eyes followed Judy as she got into the car. "She returned to college this morning."

"Spring break?"

"Yes. She was here for just a few days. Too short to really reconnect."

"Is she a good girl?"

Patricia nodded.

"Don't let you baby get mixed up with scum like my old man."

"I hear you." Patricia knew too well that her headstrong daughter, Hayley, was in a different world. Out of reach. Beyond control. There was no telling what she was up to.

When everyone was buckled up, Patricia gave the okay, and Alisa pulled the Escalade away from the curb. Out of habit, Patricia turned and looked back. Good. They weren't being followed. For the first time in an hour Patricia's tension eased.

The trip to a better life had begun for Faith, just as it had begun for countless other souls Patricia and her colleagues had transported to her mama's shelter. Battered women beaten to the point their survival instinct finally overwhelmed their fear.

* * *

AFTER DROPPING FAITH AT THE SHELTER, AND MEREDITH AND Judy at their cars, Patricia found herself parked in her driveway on Falcon Square, staring at her Kimber 45. Her heart hammering, she ran her thumb over the grip. Three years of helping those unable to help themselves. Three years of making a difference by stepping out of her comfort zone to do the right thing. But today it all went wrong. Very wrong. She shook her head.

Today was the first time anyone had pulled a gun on her. She'd hesitated when she should've reacted. She'd been uncertain when certainty should have been instinctive. It was a chilling tactical lesson she'd failed and hoped she'd never forget. She'd survived, but only because Judy intervened.

Her small arms training had been extensive and effective. Her husband, Trey, her granite cornerstone, had seen to that. She was as prepared as a person could be. Yet she'd hesitated.

Over the years, she'd shot a lot of things, paper targets, cans, bottles. She'd hunted successfully with her husband, mostly small game. Trey boasted she was a good shot. But could she actually shoot a person? Since marrying Trey, she had a gun with her all the time at his insistence. If she couldn't use it when necessary, why bother?

Getting women out of abusive situations was important, but was she really meant for that work?

That work? Who was she kidding? This job wasn't the reason she was armed. She could walk away from the transport job, but she could never walk away from the very real dangers that came with being a member of the Falcon family and the wife of a Cotton Coalition director.

She was proud of the demanding, dangerous work the Coalition and her husband did to keep Savannah safe. Work above and beyond that done by sworn authorities. Work done in secret.

And whether targeted because she was a Falcon or utterly at random, the dangers to her were real. When confronted with deadly force she had to shoot to kill, or die.

Heavyhearted, she slid the gun into its holster. Maybe if she trained harder, longer, next time she wouldn't hesitate. What would she have to do, what new training would she have to endure to convert her instinct from defensive to offensive?

When she stepped out of her car, the sharp aroma of freshly cut grass permeated the air. Overhead, birds chirped against a background of rustling leaves.

Scanning the thick oak canopy as she went to the front of her house, she couldn't see the birds for the long strands of gray Spanish moss that swayed in the afternoon breeze. Tangled, bloom-laden azalea branches rose up toward the moss. Pink azaleas, gray moss and dark-green oak leaves—glorious chaos.

Patricia climbed the stairs, crossed the wide porch and clenched the brass doorknob. She paused. The house had been so alive over spring break. Hayley had flitted from room to room all week like a restless hummingbird. Now that vibrancy was gone along with Hayley. Vivid memories of Hayley were everywhere, as they should be, but the house simply wasn't the same without her beloved child.

She went in and entered her security code.

A rainbow of light reflected off the beveled edge of the mirror on the foyer wall. The piece was one of the few family heirlooms her father had allowed her to take when she married Trey. The mirror's provenance dated it to the late seventeenth century when her English ancestors arrived in Virginia. Now the treasure, with all of its family history and Southern heritage, hung proudly in her home.

The reflection that greeted her in the mirror was but a vague resemblance of the former beauty queen. Her structure remained, though softer and fuller. The oval face, the wide eyes, and small nose were there, but her green eyes lacked luster.

She turned her head to the side. Faint but noticeable lines led to her temples. Though her mascara was smudged, her lipstick was even and her once-uncolored blond hair was still in place. She waved a general dismissal to herself and went to her office, where she put her armored vest, holstered gun, and spare clip on a table in the walk-in safe.

She stared at the gun. She was a failure. Not just any failure, a colossal failure. Well, at least the pickup was over. Done. She was home, safe, and ready to relax. If only—

Her phone rang. The landline. She closed the heavy safe door, spun the dial and grabbed the office handset, glancing at the caller ID. *Her mother.* Perfect timing. As tightly wound as she was, she could use Mama's quiet voice and calm manner.

Ever since Patricia left home for college twenty-five years ago, Mama called each day around three or so, and they chatted until they ran out of topics. It was a daily routine that brought joy to Patricia, and she certainly needed a shot of Mama's joy.

"Hello, Mama."

"Hello, sweetheart. Did my precious granddaughter get on her way back to college okay?"

"Sure 'nuf." Patricia bit down on her lip. "But Hayley's spring break was too short. I'm already missing her a bunch."

"I had a marvelous time with her too." Her mother sighed. "My but she's growing into such a fine woman."

"Most certainly. Independent too." Patricia had tried to establish the daily call routine with Hayley at college without success. Hayley claimed she was too busy studying.

"Would you like to go to a movie later this afternoon?" Patricia went into the study at the front of the house. She thought about sitting down, but she was too keyed up. She paced instead. "I'm truly sorry, Mama, but I'm not up to it today." She slumped onto the overstuffed sofa and kicked off her tactical boots. "How about tomorrow?"

"Tomorrow is my weekly tennis game with Judy."

"Oh yes. How could I forget that?" She stood, her feet finding precious comfort in the plush carpet, stepped to the window and looked out. Wind lifted the long stands of moss that hung like gray curtains from the huge oaks. A storm was on the way. "How about the following day?"

"That works. I'll drive."

"That's not necessary, Mama. I can pick you up."

"No, I insist. I want to show you my new car."

Patricia removed a plump strawberry from the fruit bowl. The boy at the farmers' market said he'd just picked them that morning. She took a small bite. Her mouth filled with the intense flavor and juicy sweetness. "A new car?" she asked. "You already have three cars. What on earth would you need another one for?"

"I still only have three. My financial advisor, Sonny, suggested I get rid of the Escalade. I haven't driven it much since your father passed, bless his heart. It was too much car for me."

"With a sterling reputation like yours, Mama, I don't understand how you can do business with a blatant womanizer like Sonny."

"Sonny may have shortcomings, but he's a damn good accountant."

"What did you replace the Escalade with?" Patricia asked, watching the tea olive bushes that lined one side of the driveway. They were handling the rising wind well.

"A vintage Mustang convertible."

"Red?"

"You betcha."

Patricia chuckled. "You're such a red-hot mama."

Her mother's raucous laughter could probably be heard all the way to Jacksonville. "I'll pick you up at three."

"I can't wait."

A horse-drawn carriage of tourists eased by Patricia's front gate.

"What's got you down today, honey?" Her mother always seemed to know when she was troubled.

Patricia tensed as her thoughts returned to Faith's porch. It would be unthinkable to lie to Mama. "A problem with a pickup."

"Oh my. What happened?"

Patricia took a breath and slowly let it out. "Things got out of hand."

"Are you okay?"

Her gaze drifted from the tourists to the tree-shrouded city square they'd stopped to admire, one centered with a statue of her husband Trey's great-grandfather. Falcon Square. There were so many squares in Savannah the tourists probably didn't care what they were called. But she did. She was proud to be a member of the Falcon family, and to be part of a Savannah heritage dating to colonial times. But had her failure today marred the Falcon name? Would Trey's family, or better yet her own reputable family, consider her a coward?

"Patricia, are you okay?" her mother repeated.

"No." Something inside Patricia ignited, then her frustration exploded like a shaken bottle of champagne. "The husband showed up. He was supposed to be at work. He got the drop on me. He reached behind his back..." She paused to catch her breath, then her unbridled mouth resumed its babble. "I hesitated. The creep shoved his gun in my face."

"That's horrible," Mama said.

"No, that wasn't the horrible part." Patricia sighed. "When he reached behind his back I had a good idea what he was likely to be doing. He even fumbled while doing it. I had plenty of time to draw my weapon and maintain control, but I froze. I froze and put my friends and the poor abused woman in harm's way. Thank God Judy was there."

"What did Judy do?"

"Came up behind him. Jammed her gun against his head. Took control. Bless her heart." Patricia took a moment to gather herself. "I hesitated. I ... I failed the team." *Mom must think I've lost my mind.* Patricia clamped a hand over her mouth to stop rambling.

"What made you hesitate?"

"My first reaction when he reached behind his back was he was going for a gun. It was just like I'd been trained. But then I thought, if I pulled my weapon and he produced a gun and aimed it at me I'd have to shoot him. Probably kill him. And even though he's a woman-beating jerk, did he deserve to die? And who made me judge and executioner? And that hesitation put my entire team in jeopardy."

"Oh honey, I understand. You're only human. You had a natural reaction to potentially killing another human. Of course it's overwhelming. Maybe it's too much. Do you want to continue picking up these women, or do you need a break?"

Patricia let out a sigh. "Do you want me to stop?"

"You can't ask me that. I'm your mother. I don't want you ever in danger, but it's your decision. Entirely yours. And I'll support whatever you decide."

"I really believe in this cause, but what if I'm not cut out for it?"

"I believe you are. That's why I asked you. And you did so well in your training. But you were lucky today. Not everyone gets a second chance when they have a gun pointed at them. I definitely don't want you or any of your team getting hurt, or ... I couldn't stand that."

"I do want to continue, Mama. I can't imagine doing anything else. I know I'd miss the satisfaction I experience when those poor souls enter your shelter and get some measure of safety for the first time. I'm in one hundred percent. But I think I need more training, more assurance that the next time I won't endanger my teammates by hesitating. I'm going for more tactical practice."

"You sure? Do you think more training will not only make you draw your weapon without hesitation, but also make you use it next time? Make you a killer?"

"I guess I won't know until either I or my team are threatened again. Did you know you could shoot someone before you did?"

"No. You have to be tough or crazy to shoot a person. And neither you nor I are crazy. Though I thought I was when I first shot someone."

"Could you shoot a person again?"

The phone was silent for a moment. "Under the right circumstances? Yes, indeed."

"How do I get there?"

"Honey, as a Falcon you have no choice."

Patricia shivered. "I need to conquer my fear."

"Yes you do, but be careful, child. Having a gun is a huge responsibility."

That was the problem. She'd been too careful. "I understand. And I know what being a Falcon demands." Patricia sighed. "I have no choice but to carry a gun, and if I carry a gun I must be able to use it. Right now, all I can think of is more training. So that's what I'll do."

"I pray you'll never have to use a gun, honey, but if you must, you will for my sake and your team's sake. Patricia, my personal trainer just arrived. I'll talk with you again tomorrow. Love ya."

"Love you too, Mama."

After the call, Patricia took a shower, dressed in a pink floral shift, then returned to the safe and picked up her handgun. The grip fit her hand perfectly. The gun felt right. Like a part of her. A lifesaving tool she needed because her world was dangerous. Trey's legal profession, his inherited responsibilities at the Cotton Coalition, and their wealth all attracted criminals. As Mama said, she had no choice. If she wanted her independence, she'd have to be able to defend herself.

Arm extended, she sighted down the barrel. Power eroded her doubts. She could do this. She *would* do this.

CHAPTER 2

$\mathcal{T}$en hours later, in the darkness of early morning, Patricia turned her Escalade onto a dimly lit, cobbled side street. She eased the large SUV to the curb and killed the engine.

After the uncertainty at Faith's house, Patricia wondered why she'd let Judy talk her into doing this job. And, more importantly, why in God's name had she brought the damned gun? She wasn't ready to use it, not yet. She needed more time.

Worn down by self-doubt, she wiped her forehead with the back of her hand. She regretted promising Judy she'd help her. True, the probability of having another life-threatening situation was remote. In the three years they had been transport abuse victims, yesterday afternoon was the only time she'd looked down the wrong end of a gun barrel. She shuddered. The small caliber pistol had looked like the mouth of a cannon.

Going on another mission tonight was like venturing back on a frozen lake you'd just fallen through. But a promise was a promise, and loyalty meant sucking up the discomfort and moving forward.

Not another car in sight. No pedestrians. Somewhat unusual for two in the morning in the entertainment district of historic Savannah, but entirely suitable for their purpose.

"You ready for this?" she asked Judy, though she was really asking herself.

"Hell yes, I'm ready." Judy gave a wide smile.

"What are you smiling about?"

"I'm thinking about how good it's going to be to get the goods on my cheating husband."

"If we get caught, you won't be smiling."

"I've practiced my lines." Judy tilted her head. "Why, Mr. Officer, we ladies weren't doin' nothin' wrong. This is my husband's office. My friend and I were out socializin' and I realized I had forgotten my house key. He keeps one here. And well, I didn't want him to know how late we were out."

"Is there a house key in his office?"

Judy turned her palms up. "Hell if I know."

Patricia shook her head. "You realize things could happen?"

"Things?"

"Savannah has a high crime rate. Someone might try to mug us. The tracking device I put on the guard's car might malfunction. Someone might see—"

"Patricia, stop fretting. Your tracking device is working just fine, thank you very much. And look around. Do you see any muggers on this street? Homeless? Party animals? Anyone?"

"No."

"Then let's get moving."

Patricia grabbed her bag and stepped out. A typical spring night in Savannah. Nothing finer. The warm, jasmine-scented air settled her. She could do this.

Judy slipped from the car, and the two headed toward the corner. At five feet nine, Judy not only towered over Patricia by three inches, but her eager stride had Patricia on the verge of running.

Patricia's ankle suddenly turned on a broken slab of concrete sending a sharp pain through her ankle. She mumbled, "Damn," as her leg buckled and threw her off balance. Stumbling, she grabbed Judy for stability.

"What?" Judy asked.

"Slow down. I've never known anyone who can run in heels like you. I nearly broke my ankle on that crack. Watch your step. There's bound to be more. Slow down, OK? We don't need a trip to the hospital."

"Okay. Cautious it is. Are you all right, sweetie?"

Patricia extended and rotated her foot. Full range of motion. She weight-tested her ankle and then took several tentative steps. No pain. "Seems so."

She and Judy turned the corner at The French Bakery. The restored building that housed Beau's medical offices loomed halfway down the block. Farther down the street, two guys were walking away from them. No problem there.

Their biggest issue would be the security guard who did rounds of several properties in downtown Savannah. If they were caught in Beau's office they had a cover story, but there was always a chance something bizarre could occur. The guard might overreact, might pull his gun, might shoot. Patricia's heart thudded. Her mind was flooding with 'what ifs.' She was on the verge of panic with no reason but fear of the unknown. *This is crazy.* She sucked in air. They absolutely *had* to avoid the guard.

They knew the properties he patrolled, but because he visited the properties randomly they couldn't know his exact route tonight.

At the entrance to the building, Judy fumbled with the

key in the dark while Patricia removed the wireless receiver from her purse and turned it on. "He's four blocks away," she announced without glancing up.

She stuffed a wisp of blond curl behind her ear and pushed back a sleeve to view her watch. This wasn't her first clandestine entry, but repetition didn't ease her tension. As soon as Judy opened the door, Patricia punched the timer button. "All right. Let's do this thing."

Judy headed straight to the security pad and punched in the code that disabled the office's security system.

Patricia was amazed Judy had ferreted out the numbers so easily. One of her many skills. Judy had it all—deportment, natural beauty, education, and more curves than a mountain road. She also had a handsome husband who slept around.

The two strode noiselessly down the hall to Beau's office and went inside. The office was tasteful and modest, except for the photos of him schmoozing with dignitaries, catching big fish and skiing in the Alps. There wasn't a single picture of him and Judy. Patricia pointed to a fishing photo. "As big as that swordfish is, I don't think it's a big as his ego."

Judy chuckled. "Right on."

The space was more a small conference room than an office. A circular table functioned as a desk. Patricia's hyper-alert senses caught the sharp hint of incense in the air, something she hadn't known Judy's husband to use. "What does he use this office for? I've only seen his hospital office when I've taken my mom to see him."

"He keeps this for consultations."

"I'm surprised there's not a Murphy bed in here." Patricia looked at her scanner. "The guard is three blocks away. If Beau's office is next on his route, we have ten minutes max to clear out," Patricia said. She stretched to close the blinds overlooking one of the town's original squares while Judy turned on her husband's unsecured office computer.

Two minutes later, Patricia asked, "Are you in yet?"

"It just booted up. Hold on."

Light from the computer screen illuminated Judy's sober face. Her green eyes, a shade darker than Patricia's, were wide with what might have been alarm. Judy sucked air through her teeth and mumbled, "My Lord."

"Is it bad?" Patricia asked, coming around the table to comfort her friend.

"Oh my, it's worse than I had ever imagined." Judy cupped her face, her eyes mapping, reading, and recording. "He has a house in St. John. It's all here. Names. Places. Notes on what they did. The creep even grades the poor deluded women."

Patricia touched Judy's hand lightly. "Oh, I'm so sorry, honey. He doesn't deserve you. What a snake." Patricia's watch beeped. "Seven minutes. We've been in here for three minutes. Time to go."

"I need a copy of this calendar," Judy said.

"Hurry."

Judy took her smartphone from her pocket and snapped a photo of the screen. Glancing at the display, she said, "This will do for now." She shut off the computer.

A deafening clap of thunder erupted, and then another clap exploded too close.

"Out. Now," Patricia said. "Oh, damn. I forgot to open the shades."

"No time," Judy said.

"We have to make time. The closed blinds are a giveaway someone was in here."

Judy tapped her fingers on her watch. "Make it quick."

One by one, Patricia elevated the blinds.

The desk phone rang. They both looked it. *Did someone see*

us come in here? Patricia looked closer. It was a blocked number.

"Maybe Beau is expecting this call." Judy's eyes widened. "Maybe he's on the way?"

"Maybe it's just a booty call."

Judy scowled at her.

"Too soon?"

Ring. Ring.

"Let's ignore the blinds and get out of here," Judy said as she headed for the hall.

Patricia grabbed the last cord and yanked it, but the shade stayed in place. *Dammit, wrong cord.* With shaking hands, she fumbled with the other cord, tugged, but the blind wouldn't rise.

"Come on, Patricia."

Ring. Ring.

Only two cords, neither worked. Oh yes, release the catch. She pulled the cord to the side. As she hastily raised the last blind overlooking the square, she gasped and went for the gun she'd left in her purse.

A man, a stranger, stood anchored like a statue right outside the window, facing her just a pane of glass away.

She jerked. Gasped. Coldness hit her like a blast of arctic air, freezing her muscles and overpowering her desperate need to run. Patricia's heart thumped frantically.

Startled, round eyes as large as palmetto bugs loomed on the other side of the window. A bulky man with a prominent scar in his eyebrow, his long dark hair dangled in disarray. His eyes narrowed.

Ring, ring.

"Come on, Patricia, let's get out of here."

Patricia glanced at Judy then looked back at the window. He was gone. "There was a man right here."

"Where?"

"On the other side of the window."

"That does it," Judy said. "Out now."

They ran back to the lobby.

"Alarm is reset," Judy said.

"Okay." Patricia glanced at the tracking device. "Guard is a block away. Let's go."

They stepped out. Once Judy had locked the door, they headed for the Escalade parked around the corner.

A fire truck with sirens blaring and red lights flashing turned onto the street. Caught in the truck's headlights, the two froze.

If the guard was close by, he'd see them. And anyone who looked out their windows to see what the commotion was about would see them as well. Patricia fought back rising panic. Her mind spun as she tried to digest the situation. "Girls' night out," she shouted to Judy.

The two entwined, laughed, and staggered like drunks toward the corner. Judy, bless her heart, started to sing "Dixie."

The fire truck, wheels thumping over the cobblestones, rushed by.

The two turned the corner and closed the distance to the Escalade. Patricia ducked into the SUV just as a veil of rain descended.

"Phew, that was tense," Patricia said.

"Yeah, but I got exactly what I needed. Best of all, nobody will find out we were there."

"I don't know about that."

Judy blinked. "What do you mean?"

"When I opened the blinds, I swear there was someone on the other side of the glass. He was big, burly, and he was looking in at me."

"Well, we are in Savannah. Maybe it was a ghost."

"I know what I saw, Judy."

"If he was there, who was he?"

"I don't know, but I'm afraid he might have recognized me. My picture is in the paper all the time. And if he recognized me, he's someone who could create problems for us if he talks to the wrong people."

CHAPTER 3

*I*t'd been merely a day since Hayley, Patricia's only child, had returned to college to complete her freshman year, but to Patricia the time seemed much longer. She sipped her second cup of coffee and gazed down from her second-floor bedroom window at the city square where she and Hayley, as a child, had spent countless hours lounging on the benches feeding the pigeons and squirrels. So long ago, before Hayley's world stretched beyond family bounds.

Patricia noticed a big burly man with a cap pulled down over his face standing on the edge of the square staring at her home. She knew most of the regular vagrants, but didn't recall seeing him before. She did a double take. *Oh my God. He so resembles the man from last night. He did* recognize me. *He found me.*

No, she assured herself, just a coincidence.

She walked away, checked her smartphone for messages, and returned. He was still there, still studying her house. Was he casing the place? Looking for vulnerabilities? *Good luck, buddy!* The house had the best available security.

He leaned against the light pole as if he owned the square. A broad smile filled his affable face. His black hair hung limp at his cheeks. He stooped to scratch his bare foot.

Patricia tensed. Shoeless in the city, walking barefoot on cracked concrete, broken glass, and rocks. People shouldn't have to live like that. Not in *her* city. She'd helped the down-and-out before, of course she'd help this time as well. Besides, it would give her an excuse to learn what he was up to.

She turned from the window and went downstairs, where she removed her gun from the safe. After slipping the weapon into her purse, she went to the mudroom and pulled an old pair of Trey's flip-flops from the beach supplies bin. In the foyer, she hesitated in front of the hall mirror, making sure her floral print day dress and hair were tidy enough to be seen outside.

When she stepped onto the porch, she was pleased to see the man was still standing in the square. She descended the wide staircase to the courtyard, where she lifted the latch on the wrought-iron gate and crossed the cobbled street.

She stopped in front of the man. Not too near. A foul, unwashed odor closed the distance.

His head was down.

She waited for him to glance up and acknowledge her. He seemed lost in thought as she looked him over. Big body. The broad shoulders of a laborer. Tangled, long black hair hung over his face.

She coughed.

He raised his head and brushed hair from his eyes. A distinctive scar hovered over his right eye. Breath left her. *He was the man in Beau's window.* She'd known he'd seen her. Probably recognized her. But she had no idea he'd find her so quickly. "What do you want?" she asked cautiously.

He remained silent, motionless. If he remembered her, he

didn't show it, but she certainly recognized him. Patricia let her shoulders drop. Took a deep breath and then another. *Stay calm.*

He might have been in his mid-twenties, but it was hard to say. And while he was shabbily dressed, his teeth were straight and white. Though his sad eyes tore at her, she kept coming back to the scar like a tongue to a chipped tooth.

"Do I know you?" she asked.

"Don't believe so." He smiled, wrinkling the tanned skin around his eyes.

Her neck hairs bristled. "I couldn't help notice you've taken an interest in my home."

"Not really." His deep, syrupy voice was proud.

"You from around here?"

He shook his head. "Just passing through."

She held out the flip-flops. "You can have these."

He raised his eyebrows and gave her a bewildered look. "I don't want to go to the shelter."

"I don't know what you're talking about." She brought the shoes up higher. "These are for you."

"What's the deal?"

"Deal?"

"There's always a deal."

"I'm not looking for anything in return." She stepped closer, placed the flip-flops on the bench, and turned to leave.

"My name's Rhett, Mrs. Falcon."

She froze. Her vision sharpened to catalog the shadowed sidewalks, old homes and cobbled streets. There was no one else in view. Just him and her. Knowing better than to show her fear, she touched her purse with the concealed gun and turned to face him. "You know my name?"

He spread his thick arms. A smug smile crossed his face. He nodded. "That's your house over there."

"How do you know my name?"

He grinned. "Everybody knows the famous Falcons."

But he'd said he was just passing through. "Why are you here?"

"Last night. There was rain. There was an overhang. I went to it to get out of the rain. Suddenly the blinds opened, scaring me to death. And I think you were startled too. I'm sorry I scared you. I wanted to tell you that and to make sure you were okay."

"That's very thoughtful of you."

He took the flip-flops and slipped them on. His heels hung over the back a bit, but they looked like they'd do. "Thank you for your kindness. Won't nothin' happen to your place as long as I'm here."

"Do you think I need protection?"

He raised his shoulders. "Who doesn't?"

"You know you can't loiter around here."

He nodded.

Unable to find anything else relevant to say to him, she gave a proper gracious smile and strode back across the street, leaving the young man and his mystery behind her. At least for now.

Just as she entered her home, a chime from her cell phone jolted her. She walked to the front window while she consulted her phone and read the text message from her husband. *Meeting at Chatham Club tonight. Won't be home until after supper.*

She texted back *OK* just as the phone rang. *Judy.*

"We need to talk. It's urgent." Judy's voice was uncharacteristically somber.

"Are you okay, honey?"

"After last night, what do you think?"

"I think we need a long talk, but don't you have tennis with my mom?"

"Yeah. In a couple of hours."

"Do you want to stop by on the way to the club?"

"You don't mind?"

"No, not at all. I'll put on a fresh pot of coffee."

WHEN JUDY, DRESSED IN TENNIS WHITES, ARRIVED SHE SEEMED distressed, not unexpected considering last night's revelations. They greeted each other with a double kiss on both cheeks then went to the kitchen where Patricia poured coffee.

Judy sat at the table and let out a long sigh.

"Hard day?" Patricia asked.

Judy rolled her bloodshot eyes. "I want it over."

Patricia took her friend's hand. "Divorce?"

Tears formed in Judy's eyes. "I want him and all this drama out of my life."

Patricia patted Judy's hand. "He has a successful practice here. He's not leaving Savannah and neither are you."

"I want out of this sham marriage."

"You two should be able to do that."

Judy squinted. "We can't talk."

"Lawyers?"

"Too confrontational. I'd just like to get the divorce details settled with him, then have the lawyers write them up."

"You'll need an intermediary."

Judy's eyebrow elevated. "You?"

She knew them both, but this was asking a lot. "I, ah, if you like."

"You sure it's no bother?"

"What are friends for, particularly in time of need. If he's available, I'll speak with him this afternoon."

Judy smiled. "Meanwhile, let's keep this to ourselves."

After Judy left, Patricia called Doctor Beau Simpson, Judy's lying, cheating husband and Patricia's mother's doctor, and asked to see him immediately. He agreed. She walked to his medical office, just a few blocks away.

"I appreciate you seeing me," Patricia said as she took a seat in his office. The computer with the incriminating information loomed on the right of the credenza. The azalea bushes outside his office window where the stranger had been were laden with red flowers. It all seemed so innocent, but she knew better.

Beau, a noted cardiologist and marathon runner, wore his brown hair long. Like the incense that still lingered, he was both an unusual as well as an intimidatingly huge man.

He settled his six-foot-eight frame into his chair and smiled. One of those face-lifted, permanent, unnatural smiles. "What can I do for you, Patricia? Is this about your mother?"

"No. I know you're a busy man, Beau. I'll get right to the point. You've been cheating on Judy."

A strained look briefly crossed his well-tanned face. He avoided her eyes. Silence gathered for a moment and hung like a storm cloud over the circular office table they shared. Then his lips curled up and he brought his eyes to hers. "You damn Falcons, you're all alike. Old money with no self-earned credentials. Now you're butting into my business. The apple doesn't fall far from the tree. Yesterday your mother tried to tell me, a Harvard med graduate, what medications she should be taking. You're all fools, operating on unfounded information. As for Judy, she's the one who is cheating, not me."

"It's not about my family. It's about you. Your infidelity is a fact, Beau. You're not helping the situation by denying it."

She cleared her throat. "I'm here as Judy's friend to help you two deal quietly with this matter and come to an equitable settlement, a divorce resolution."

He shook his head, swaying his long hair. "That's ridiculous." He didn't appear to be concerned. He consulted his watch and stood up. "I'm due at the hospital in fifteen minutes."

She dug her nails into her palms. "So, you'd prefer public divorce proceedings and the attendant media coverage that socialite divorces always get in our city?"

He gave her another crooked smile, but his brown eyes were frigid. "There won't be any divorce proceedings. Not in this city. Not anywhere. Now get out of my office or I'll call security and have you thrown out."

Incredible. She leaned forward. "You might want to think this through. You're taking on more than your wife."

"You think I'm intimidated by you and your silly bridge group?"

Patricia clenched her teeth and stood. He was powerful, well connected, but could he really block divorce proceedings? Nah. He was bluffing. "Judy has names, dates and places. She has receipts and video surveillance footage."

He elevated his wide, tapered chin a tad. "She has no such thing, because I've done nothing."

"Beau, believe me. She can take you down."

"Let her try." He rounded the table and stooped face-to-face with her. "This discussion is over."

She walked to the door.

"One more thing, Patricia."

She hesitated. *Now what?*

"Tell Judy I have photographs too."

CHAPTER 4

*A*fter three hours of back-to-back meetings with clients, Trey Falcon's working day was only half over.

He pushed back from his desk, stretched his six-six frame, and headed into his private bathroom where he changed into a fresh shirt. He needed to look dapper for his lunch meeting with Alton at the club. There would surely be clients at the club this time of day.

He tucked the shirt in and buckled his thirty-six-inch belt using a new notch. It was time to buy a bigger belt. While knotting his tie, he noticed his graying hair needed a trim. He'd often considered having it cut on a regular schedule, but his chaotic life was neither routine nor predictable enough to schedule haircuts.

Trey left his office on Falcon Square and strode west on the brick sidewalk. The overcast sky took the sting out of the sun. A jasmine aroma filled the air. Historic buildings with wrought-iron balconies loomed over the sidewalk. The magnificent structures were a testament to Savannah's wealth, an opulence that had grown and been passed on over centuries by a small group of merchants and their offspring who looked after such things. He was proud to be a member of that group.

An ornate antique clock stood on a brick pedestal in front of the bank. Eleven-thirty. He nodded. He had just enough time to get to his meeting with Lucius Alton. Trey would have preferred working through lunch, but Alton, who wielded extraordinary political and economic power in Savannah, was a close friend.

Trey would never be able to repay his debt to Alton. Years ago, Alton had shared inside information that had proven essential to several inter-related high-profile cases Trey was handling. Winning those cases had established Trey's legal bonafides. He owed Alton big for his extremely successful career.

A midday rain started up. Had his lunch guest been anyone but Alton, Trey would have ducked for cover, called, and cancelled. With fat raindrops spilling down his neck, he threw his navy sports coat over his head and dashed to the entrance of The DeSoto hotel. Once safely under the portico, he blew out a breath and looked out.

Five years ago, when he was forty and running for exercise, he wouldn't have been winded, nor would his quads have been on fire. Such were the unintended consequences of prioritizing work over health. He patted his midsection. And too many fast-food lunches.

There was something ominous about the surprising downpour. His spirit dampened along with his sports coat, he wiped rain from his face with his handkerchief and strode into the hotel. Eyes on the lookout, a habit spawned from painful confrontations with ex-clients at this popular gathering place, he crossed the lobby to the private elevator for The Chatham Club.

As Trey exited the elevator at the fourteenth floor, Alton was waiting in the foyer. Alton's hunched back was permanently bent at a right angle to his legs by scoliosis. When he walked, he leaned so far forward he seemed about to plunge headfirst into the carpet. His small dark eyes, like two finger holes in his white bowling ball head, locked on Trey's.

Trey enjoyed time with Alton and looked forward to a pleasant working lunch with a man he loved like a brother.

"Trey," Alton said. No nod. No offered hand. No smile. Alton never smiled.

"Alton," Trey said with a nod, then gave his wet jacket to the maître d', who went to the club closet and returned with a dry one and a face towel.

After scrubbing his face and hands dry, Trey donned the fresh jacket and followed Alton and the maître d' into a paneled private dining room. One table, near the window, two chairs. Trey remained standing until Alton sat.

Seated across from each other, they placed drink orders. Red-rimmed eyes were the only color on Alton's pale, drawn face. He seemed to have lost some weight.

Questions about this unplanned meeting bombarded Trey, but respect for his friend restrained him. This was Alton's meeting.

Alton folded his pudgy, pale hands. Heavy lines etched his brow. He took a deep breath and let it out slowly. "I'm dying." He sighed and looked down and away. "Terminal cancer."

Trey shuddered. His stomach knotted. An awful, awkward silence ensued as Trey searched for the right words. Alton was a dear friend. Life without him was unthinkable. "I am so very sorry to hear that." Trey shook his head. "You know that I'm a God-fearing man, but I ... Damn it. Life's so unfair. I don't want you to leave, ever."

"I apologize." Alton's oval face had a look of intense focus.

"I didn't want to burden anyone with my condition, least of all you. But it couldn't be avoided."

Trey nodded solemnly. Alton wouldn't meet him just to tell him about this, there had to be more. Eyes locked on his friend, Trey brought a finger to his lips and remained silent.

"I've been taking stock of my life and have made a few important decisions, one of which I want to share with you. Before I depart, I would like the Cotton Coalition to rethink the subject of my replacement."

Trey straightened. The request caught him by surprise. Alton, like Trey, had no male heir. Under Coalition rules, at Alton's death his seat would be awarded to a deserving gentleman from an unrepresented historic family. Trey dreaded the day the Falcon family would lose their representation when he died.

"I'd like my seat to go to my daughter, Isabel." Alton's jaw tightened. "Since you don't have a male heir either, I thought you might lend your support for a rule change to permit female successors."

Trey gritted his teeth. It wasn't the first time the subject had been broached, nor was it likely to be the last. Trey had considered bringing it up himself a couple of years ago, but decided to wait until Hayley was older.

Trey thought of his only heir, his daughter Hayley. Could she mature to the point of being responsible for a city, including executions when necessary? Would he want her to take on that burden? Would the Cotton Coalition be weaker or stronger with women represented? Without a strong, decisive Coalition, would Savannah's economy deteriorate? The Coalition had been successful for centuries under the existing rules. Maybe the forefathers' males-only wisdom shouldn't be challenged.

But this was about Alton, his supporter and confidant.

Trey focused his attention on his friend, who had put forth a dying request.

"Have you discussed this with any of the other directors?"

"No." Alton's bald head gleamed in the light from the chandelier. "You're the first."

"Each time someone has proposed accepting female heirs in the past, the directors have quickly and soundly rejected the idea." Trey took a deep breath. "What makes you think they would accept it now?"

"Trey, listen to me." Alton cocked his head. "The reason the Coalition has a rule change provision is because our founders understood that sooner or later some, if not all, of our rules would have to be changed in order for the Coalition to remain effective. It's time we bring women into this organization. Well past time. Surely you understand that."

Trey leaned back in his chair and thought for a moment. Alton was right, times had changed. Plus, he owed Alton. And as Hayley's father, he owed her as well. Hayley certainly had the brains to do the job. The raw material was there and he could coach the substance into her. But membership would change her. And the work would make her hard. Did he want that? If the succession rule changed, membership would become her birthright. She'd at least have a choice to join or not when the time came.

The more he thought about it, the more a rule change made sense. He wished it could be simple to implement, but he knew it was, at best, a long shot. A shot worth taking for his friend and for Hayley. "We'd need a quorum. Four of the five. You and I would be two. We'd need two more. Any ideas?"

An awkward silence ensued. As usual, Alton's face gave no clue as to what he was thinking.

"I don't know, Alton." Trey swirled wine in his glass and took a drink "Who do you think we could draw in?"

"Hempfield is a long shot," Alton said "That leaves Simpson and Potter. Potter owes me. I'll see if I can bring him on board. Do you mind plying Simpson with your considerable skills?"

Beau Simpson was young, progressive and logical. He and Trey saw eye to eye on most Coalition matters. Simpson might be willing to consider a rule change. "Sure," Trey replied. "Last year I represented him in a wrongful death case. We spent weeks together preparing. He owes me because the prosecutor had convincingly strong arguments and I had to call in some favors."

* * *

SHORTLY AFTER PATRICIA RETURNED HOME FROM BEAU'S office, her cell phone rang. She checked caller ID. *Beau. Has he come to his senses?* She answered the call.

"Patricia, I'm sorry we quarreled. My personal life is so emotional and, well, never mind. I, ah, I have some terribly bad news."

Patricia tensed. "Yes?"

"Your mother passed away moments ago."

Patricia's knees failed her as she dropped into a chair. Vivid emotions tangled like seaweed. *This couldn't be.* She gasped for air that wouldn't come. *Not Mama. I just talked with her. Not gone. Not my mama. No!* Patricia's heart boomed in the sudden emptiness inside her. *Mama can't be gone. Mama has always been there for me. Always.* Patricia stared at the carpet, seeing nothing but Mama's sweet, endearing face.

"Patricia, are you okay?" Beau asked, his tone elevated with concern.

She struggled to find words, and a voice to convey them. "She ... she was in perfect health. This can't be."

"Patricia, her passing surprised us all. I've attended to her for years and, for her age, she was the picture of health."

"What happened?"

"Heart attack. She was on her way home from tennis. Plantation security found her in her car slumped over her steering wheel. Apparently, she went quickly."

Patricia's emotions clotted into panic. She grabbed her purse. "Which hospital? I'll come right over."

"Falcon Memorial," Beau said.

She glanced at her wristwatch, a thoughtful graduation gift from her parents. More tears gathered. "I'll be there by two o'clock."

"Is there anything else I can do for you, Patricia?"

She took a deep breath and shoved the stray strap of her summer dress back into place. "Not at the moment. Thank you for calling."

Now both Daddy and Mama were gone. Forever. Completely alone, Patricia buried her face in her hands and burst out crying.

How would she tell Trey? A sound caught in her throat halfway between a breath and a sob. She grabbed her phone and punched in his speed dial. Hopefully she'd have the strength to tell him without becoming a babbling idiot. She loathed babbling, as did her mama.

Trey answered with a business-like 'hello' that signaled she'd interrupted something important.

She took a deep breath, then paused to find the courage to mouth the words she dreaded.

"Patricia, is that you?"

A feeble 'yes' was all she could force out.

"What's going on?"

"Mama …" She couldn't do it. She just could not say those words.

"Is your mother okay?"

"No, Trey." Patricia gasped. "She's ... she's gone."

"Oh no. Hang up the phone, honey. Go lie down. I'll be right home."

* * *

PATRICIA CHEWED HER LOWER LIP. LIGHT FROM THE SUN SHONE through the study's casement windows and sparkled off the crystal chandelier. Usually, such beauty would have uplifted her, but sadness burdened her.

The front door banged shut, followed by slow, heavy footfalls. Trey's entrance clunked in the hallway. She glanced at her watch. He'd made it in five minutes. Bless his heart.

Any moment now. Though her life was in shreds, she didn't want Trey to worry. She stood, faced the door, and forced a smile. No. Smiling was wrong. She couldn't pretend. Not about this.

Wrapping her arms around herself, she turned and looked out the window at the pink azaleas in full bloom. Mama ... gone. Unimaginable, but true. Tears of sheer grief trickled down her cheek. She wiped them away. But the grief remained.

"Patsy." He came up behind her and gave her a bear hug.

Goodness gracious, how she loved that. She turned and pulled him to her, savoring his closeness.

He kissed her neck.

A shiver ran down her spine.

He deepened the hug. So warm. So secure.

More tears threatened.

"Do you want to talk about it?" he whispered.

No. She didn't *want* to talk about it. A future without Mama was incomprehensible. Why did...? How could...? What would...? She pushed the questions aside. She wasn't ready to talk.

But delaying wouldn't ease the disclosure. It had to be done. Now. She stepped back to face him and looked up, hoping to keep the rebuilding tears from spilling.

Care filled his deep-set, dark eyes.

Her throat tightened with dread.

He reached out and touched her cheek. Stroked it. His touch was soft and ever so gentle, like his heart. His tenderness tugged at her. Tears poured out. She took a deep breath and put her palms on his muscular chest.

He covered her hands with his, sharing his strength. His eyes pleaded.

"Ma … Mama's gone." She convulsed. Sobs spewed. Hardly able to breathe, she gasped.

Trey's shadowed face furrowed. He clutched her tightly and swayed with her. Exactly what she needed, and so like Trey. She snuggled against him.

After a few moments, he stepped back, his eyes filled with so much concern her chest tightened. His lips pinched together. He brushed hair from her eyes and gave her another wordless embrace.

Pierced with grief, her brain wouldn't function. She wanted to thank him and show her appreciation for his love, but the pain of grief over Mama's death mixed with sorrow was too encompassing. She didn't have the words. The grief held her hostage.

"She's already in heaven," Trey whispered in a kind, caressing voice. "She's reunited with her husdand, parents and grandparents. She's happy, Patsy."

"I know, honey. But her death still hurts terribly."

"She's in a better place."

"She's still gone." Mama was so very important to the direction and tempo of Patricia's world. A guide. A friend. A mentor. A companion. Patricia clenched her jaw, swallowed against the lump in her throat. The future would be like slogging through a tidal swamp in August. "What was wrong with Mama staying here with me?"

"I suppose her work was done." He stepped back from her and brushed a strand of graying hair from his eyes. "She did so very much for the community. The shelter for abused women and the residential maternity home for underprivileged unmarried women were her ideas and her money. Neither would have happened without her. And the no-kill animal shelter. And, well, the list goes on."

"Her work wasn't finished. She had more planned."

"Then I suppose you'll have to see those plans through for Henrietta."

She shook her head. No one could take Mama's place.

"We'll get through this. With God's help, peace will come."

Spiritual reassurance wasn't what she wanted. Her forty-three-year-old joints ached. Emotionally bruised and exhausted, she just wanted the day to end. She hung her head and massaged her eyes. "We need to go to the hospital."

* * *

TREY AND PATRICIA, HER PALMS SWEATY AND MUSCLES TAUT with apprehension, paused in the hallway outside Mama's ER room. She clenched her jaw. *This will be terrible.*

"I can't do it, Trey. I can't have my last memory of her tainted."

"Patsy, I'll carry this burden for you, but right now you're in shock, and if you don't see Henrietta with your own eyes it will be harder to accept. I know. It happened to me with my father." He took her face in his hands, wiped her tears with his thumbs, and kissed her forehead.

She knew he was right. Viewing her mother was necessary. Mama would call it proper protocol. Old-school people would call it closure. Either way it was her duty. Responsibility conquered her apprehension as her hand griped the doorknob. Patricia took a breath, and despite the tremor in her knees, pushed the door aside.

Mama's body reclined on the bed under a white blanket, like she was resting. In slow, numb steps, Patricia drifted to the bedside. She touched her mother's disconcertingly cold forehead, thought of the lovely woman who used to inhabit the lifeless body, and made a cross on the strangely foreign skin. "Dear Lord, please shower Mama with Your love."

Mama is with Daddy again, and in the company of all those who preceded her. Patricia wiped her tears. She pulled a chair to the bedside and sat. Trey stood behind her, his hands on her shoulders.

Her mother's spirit was gone, gone forever. Just like Daddy's. Nothing of importance remained. A chill went through Patricia.

More tears flowed and blurred her vision. She brushed them aside and bowed her head. She had a huge void to fill. The structured life she knew so well had suddenly disintegrated.

She thought of God's words, the Bible. Scripture might ease her distress, might calm her. The Bible had provided solace before. She took the Bible from the bedside table and read Psalm 23. "The Lord is my shepherd, I shall not ..."

When her voice faltered, Trey took the Bible and continued.

Verse by verse the spiritual tide of the lovely Psalm enveloped her and eased her despair. Though her trauma wasn't gone by the last verse, her distress had become manageable. Hope glimmered. *Thank you, Lord.*

Patricia leaned closer to the bed and touched her mother's shoulder. "Thank you, Mama, for giving me life and for guiding me. Thank you, Mama, for loving me unconditionally. I'll do my best to make you proud."

When the nurse came in, Patricia told her that Mama had requested cremation. Then Patricia inhaled a long breath, stood and turned from the bedside. Trey took her arm. At the door, she paused and looked back, knowing it would be the last time she would see Mama. When it was time, Patricia left with Trey at her side.

CHAPTER 5

*P*atricia couldn't recall ever noticing the brick sidewall of the hospital before. The reclaimed brick seemed the very symbol of endurance, the soft hue calming. She had no idea how long she'd been seated in Trey's idling car. Didn't care to measure time. She needed comfort, solace, the very things her mother had always given her. Now, who would provide that soft lap, those warm arms, and the rocking chair healing?

If Mama were here, what would she do?

The church bells chimed three. Saint Gregory's. Her church home. Meditation. *That* was what her mother would do.

"I need to meditate, Trey."

Five minutes later, Trey pulled into the lot behind the church. Warm air washed over her as she stepped into the bright spring sunlight of the church plaza. The afternoon molten sun seemed close enough to touch. Wisps of clouds streaked the vivid blue sky as she approached the church with Trey at her side.

Her legs involuntarily stopped. Rhett. Again. At the end

of the vine-covered building. Dressed in a white apron of all things, he was arguing with an older, hard-faced man in a chef's coat. Rhett's hunched, subordinate posture surprised Patricia. He seemed so sure of himself earlier.

The older man's fingers drummed his thighs. His features, bearing, and close-cropped hair shouted ex-military. He seemed as out of place in this quiet spiritual oasis as an alligator crossing a busy highway.

Suddenly, Rhett swung his arm in a contemptuous sweep, turned and stalked away. Toward her.

She and Trey moved to the edge of the sidewalk.

Rhett, his black hair shimmering in the sunlight, approached in a determined stride, removed the apron, and threw it into a flowerbed.

She wished she could discard *her* problems so easily.

"Afternoon, Mrs. Falcon," he said in a deep timbre. Almost a growl.

Trey stepped toward Rhett. Patricia stopped him mid-stride, then gestured to Rhett. "I know him. He's okay."

"You sure."

She nodded.

Trey stepped back.

Rhett's sweat-sheened face was grim. His tobacco eyes, wide and watery, projected hurt. The scar over his eye blazed bright red. She suspected that deeper scars lay within.

"Are you okay?" she asked, masking her own emotions with concern.

He stopped, looked off and then at her, studying her. She didn't mind his scrutiny. She had nothing to hide. Seconds ticked by.

He brought his right hand up, pointed his index finger toward his temple like a gun, and pulled the trigger. "I just lost my job!"

As a man who didn't own a decent pair of shoes, he

clearly needed work to survive. And because he had injected himself into her life, she needed to find out more about him and what he was up to. Daddy seldom used clichés, but he loved to say, "Keep your friends close and your enemies closer." Rhett might not be an enemy, but he sure as heck needed watching.

Watching and help. Mama had never been one to sit idly by in time of need. The man was out of work. A craving to help him came. Certainty surged over her like a tidal wave. She would do something for him. No, she'd do it for him, her, and Mama.

"We have some shrubs that need pruning and a whole garden that needs continuous love and care," she said. "Would you be interested?"

His body tensed. Confusion swept his eyes. He tapped his chin, then gave her an easy smile, sending creases to the corners of his eyes and exposing his dimples. "Thank you kindly, Mrs. Falcon. When would you like me to start?"

THE REST OF THE DAY WAS A BLUR. TREY HANDLED TELLING Hayley. Patricia napped off and on in the study. She spoke with Isabel Alton, who handled legal affairs for Patricia's mother, about funeral arrangements and asked if Henrietta had left any instructions. Isabel said there were no instructions and just a simple will.

Patricia and Trey skipped dinner and spent the evening cuddled on the sofa. Around nine, Trey brushed his lips over her neck. A rush tingled her skin. He tucked one arm around her back, placed another under her knees, and lifted her. Lips trembling, she tucked her wet face into his neck.

He carried her up the stairs to their bedroom, laid her on the duvet and, as her eyes fluttered open, kissed her forehead. A magical man. A man she loved so much it scared her.

She curled up, turning her back to him, praying for the peace of sleep.

Trey, his breathing slow and steady, eased against her back and draped his arm over her waist. So thoughtful. So giving. She loved him with all the heart that remained after Mama's death.

She lay in silence for a few minutes basking in his love but, though spent, she couldn't fall asleep. She feared an endless, fathomless night.

As if sensing her worry, Trey whispered, "I'll take care of you, Patsy."

His thoughtfulness, closeness, and warmth finally calmed her tension. Mended what was broken. Soothed.

"Thank you for your understanding and support," she said.

"I'm not much support during the day."

"You are." She turned over, cuddled close and gave him a kiss. "You're always here in my heart."

Her skin tingled when he started to caress her shoulder. A soothing warmth eased through her. She yielded to it, the man's limitless compassion.

CHAPTER 6

*P*atricia awoke groggy, vaguely aware that Trey was still in bed with her. But it wasn't the weekend. Was he ill? He'd been okay yester—

Reality slammed her like an immense black tidal wave. She gasped as the terrible pain returned in full measure. She turned away from Trey, curled, and sobbed into her pillow.

Trey snuggled behind her, draped an arm over her and drew her into his torso.

PATRICIA AWOKE AGAIN. TREY WAS STILL CUDDLED UP TO HER. She pulled her phone from the nightstand and checked the time. Just after eight in the morning. She couldn't stay in bed all day. Patricia turned to Trey. "Trey, honey, are you ready to get up?"

"I'll get up when you get up."

"I'm ready."

"You sure?"

She nodded.

Trey rolled to his side of the bed.

After punching the remote to open the shades, she went to the front bedroom window, pushed the sheers aside, and looked down at the beautiful square with the pink azaleas in full bloom. Spring in Savannah. Pink perfection.

She gave a gasp. Rhett was back, standing by the light pole directly across the street from her home. Trey's home to be exact. His family had lived in Falcon House since it was built for his ancestors early in the nineteenth century.

She could almost see Rhett's scar from here. She put her hand on her hip and wondered where Rhett had called home and why he was a vagrant.

* * *

SHORTLY BEFORE NOON, TREY PARKED HIS '61 BENTLEY S2 Continental in the club's private lot, donned his double-breasted gray suit jacket, crossed the oil-stained asphalt, and walked up the concrete steps to the entrance of the one hundred sixty year old building. The Oglethorpe Club, by far the oldest men's club in Savannah.

He pulled open one of the massive mahogany double doors, greeted the petite blonde receptionist, and took the half-circular stairs to the second floor. There he checked with the British-born maître d' who indicated where Beau Simpson was seated. Being lunchtime, most of the other tables were occupied.

Simpson stood as Trey approached. He was dressed in tan slacks, a crisp, light blue shirt and a navy blazer. Simpson's manicured hand clasped Trey's. The two men exchanged greetings, took opposing seats at a small two-person table, and ordered.

"I'm so sorry about your mother-in-law," Beau said.

"She seemed in such good health. Was something wrong with her?"

"Her last visit she was in perfect shape. I've looked back at my records and I can't see that I missed anything, but you never know what can happen."

"You graduated from The Citadel, didn't you?" Trey asked. He already knew the answer, but he wanted to get Beau focused on a different subject.

Simpson smiled and nodded.

Time for the setup. "What do you think of women attending The Citadel?" Trey asked.

Simpson tilted his head down a bit, then looked at Trey from beneath his obscenely perfect eyebrows. Plucked? Probably. "The adjustment was huge for all parties and not smooth."

"Women in combat, who would have guessed?" Trey paused to get Simpson's reaction.

Simpson hunched his shoulders. "Why not?"

"They're everywhere these days," Trey added.

"As they should be."

"Times have certainly changed. I suppose we change with them or we risk obsolescence. What do you think, Beau, about opening the Cotton Coalition to women?"

Simpson's jaws locked and eyes widened, then narrowed. His focus on Trey was as intense as a bass eying a worm. "No. No. No!" he said, his tone raw. He raised his glass of port and swirled it. "You're cagey, Trey. I'll give you that. But what we do isn't women's work. For sure it isn't."

Trey pulled back as if surprised. "Didn't you just say women could be in combat? Be anywhere men could be? How can you take that stance and immediately reverse it?"

Simpson sneered. "Well, ah—"

"Women *are* everywhere." Trey's eyes bore down on Simpson's. "There are women in Congress. Women run Fortune 500 companies. Women serve in command positions in the military as well as grunts in combat. They fight fires and police our neighborhoods. And I don't need to tell you how many are accomplished cardiologists."

Simpson's uncommonly symmetrical face contorted. His eyes blazed. "This is Savannah, Trey. Proper women do *not* engage in this kind of work."

"Are you saying what we do is improper?" Trey asked.

"I'm saying we do work that a civilized woman should not be subjected to."

"Not to be disagreeable, but Lucius Alton and I are both proposing the rules be changed to permit women members, our daughters. Would you consider my daughter uncivilized?"

Simpson's fingers turned white around the stem of the wine glass. His lips pinched. "Your proposal is a disgrace to your daughter. It's not right to even consider the subject. You're wrong to ask."

"Obviously Lucius is supportive, and he believes he can get Potter on board."

Simpson's face darkened. "Well I'm not."

The man's hostility shocked Trey into momentary silence. "Attitudes have changed. It's time you and the organization realize it."

Simpson's brown eyes narrowed. "Don't lecture me."

Trey took a moment to settle, trying not to give away his rising agitation. "What can I do to get you to change your mind?"

Simpson shot Trey a glare as sharp as a heron's beak. Simpson was not the sort one wanted as an enemy. He had killed in the operating room for the Coalition. Cardiac arrest the authorities had reported, but Trey knew better. "Let me give you a warning," Simpson said. "Drop this and save yourself from embarrassment."

Trey wanted to argue, but he choked back the words. "Your mind's made up?"

"Damn right it is. I'll never countenance changing the Coalition. And by the way…"

"Yes?" Trey fixed on Simpson's glaring eyes.

"Tell your wife to keep her nose out of my business."

What? Rather than gape, Trey closed his eyes and sucked a slow, deep breath. Patricia hadn't mentioned any trouble with Simpson. Perhaps the Coalition rules weren't really the issue here. Trey opened his eyes.

A crooked, self-assured smile filled Simpson's face.

"She handles her own business," Trey said.

Simpson shook his head. "Shame you can't control your woman."

"I wouldn't if I could," Trey shot back.

"Consider yourself warned. Nothing personal."

Under the fine linen tablecloth, Trey's fist clenched. He'd hit men for less. He glanced around. Not the place for an altercation. But he was far from dropping this subject. There would be another time, another opportunity to settle this, one way or the other.

"Noted," Trey said. Noted indeed. He wouldn't forget. Beau would pay.

CHAPTER 7

*H*ayley had arrived home a half hour ago, unpacked, and though she'd said she was weary from the drive from Atlanta, she was now seated across the table from Patricia devouring a late-night snack of salsa and chips.

"What exactly happened to Grammy?" Hayley asked between bites.

"Plantation security found Grammy in her car early in the afternoon. She was unresponsive. EMS transported her to the hospital. Doctor Simpson was summoned. He declared her dead."

Hayley wiped her bloodshot eyes. "Had she been feeling ill?"

"Doctor Simpson said she was in perfect shape. You saw her at spring break. Did she look ill to you?"

Hayley shook her head. "I just want to cry about Grammy."

"Trust me," Patricia said, "all I've been doing is crying."

"I wish I'd spent more time with Grammy over spring break."

Patricia nodded. "We all have the same kind of wish."

Hayley's sad eyes met Patricia's. "I miss her so much."

Patricia reached across the table and patted Hayley's hand.

"It's so hard to believe she's gone." Hayley blinked.

"She's not so much gone as in a different place, and someday we'll be reunited with her for eternity."

Hayley let out a long breath. "Family is so important. I shouldn't have gone away to college. I should have stayed home and gone to college here in Savannah."

"Emerald is an excellent school," Patricia said.

"I don't think so." Hayley took Patricia's hand. "Mom, I'm dropping out of school."

"You're dropping out of college?" Patricia repeated to her in utter shock. "You seemed so happy at spring break. Did something happen?"

Hayley twisted her hands. "No, nothing happened. But after the campus bombing last fall, I've just been hanging on. I can't take it anymore. I'm just dropping out for a while."

"I know that terrible bombing disturbed you, but y'all found the terrorist cell responsible and the authorities shut them down."

Hayley shook her head. "You don't understand. I can't walk that campus without being reminded of Ramona's death and thinking of what might have happened if Shawn and I hadn't stuck our noses into that business."

"How about attending another school?"

"No, Mom. I just want to drop out for a while."

"Though I'm having a hard time understanding you, I know this—you're staying in college. Period."

"Mom, it's not a great time for me. I loved Grammy. I just drove five hours from Atlanta to get here for the memorial service. I'm exhausted and I'm grieving. You don't want to talk? Fine. But I'm not going back to school. As you say, period."

Hayley's sharp insistence sent a shiver down Patricia's spine. "Honey, it's unwise for a woman with a mind like yours to waste it. You have a responsibility to develop your God-given talent."

Hayley braced both hands on the table and leaned toward her. "It's also a waste to spend time and energy doing something I have absolutely no interest in. Life is too short to waste. I could die any day. I want to have some fun before that. I detest college. I can't stand it."

Patricia gave a head waggle and sighed. *Where is Trey when I need him?*

"Mama, I'm serious about this. I'm going in the wrong direction. I need time to figure out what I really want to do. I need to find myself."

"Child, that's the purpose of college."

"There's no time for self-exploration at school."

"Make time."

"How can I make time? Being an honors student is a full-time job. I need to get away from school to think."

"Don't go fretting so." She patted Hayley's hand. "Stay in school. Things will work out."

"Mama, I *have* to leave. College is stifling. I need to retreat, to rethink. I need to be here, not there."

"You're running away from your responsibilities," Patricia said. "That's not the Falcon way and you know it."

"No. I'm turning away from a no-win, hopeless situation."

"This is insane. You put all that time into those courses, and you're not going to stick around for a few more weeks to get credit for them?"

"Credit?" Hayley's brow furrowed. "Those courses are irrelevant." Her cheeks flamed bright red. "It's insane to waste time in college."

"Dropping out of college is unacceptable. I know college is hard, sweetie. That's the point. You learn to handle the challenges. If you don't like Atlanta, move back to Savannah *after* the semester is done and go to a local college."

"It's not the challenges. I'm getting excellent grades. It's just ... I'm not motivated."

Patricia cringed. Her stomach knotted. Why couldn't Hayley understand? "If you drop out, you'll have to get a full-time job. Is that what you want?"

"No." Hayley clung to herself and bit her lip.

Patricia rolled her eyes. "Then finish the semester. It's just six more weeks. Take the summer break to figure out your future. We'll go overseas. I'll show you Paris, Rome, Madrid. Getting away will help."

"I don't know."

"Trust me. Finishing the semester is best."

"It doesn't feel right. Everyone is so focused, and I'm so... ambivalent. I feel like a fraud. I'm taking a place in college from someone who really wants to be there. It's wrong."

"Give it time. You'll find yourself this summer. Meanwhile, stay in school."

"I can't."

"You can and you will." Patricia laced her fingers. "End of discussion."

Hayley raised her hands in surrender. The chair legs scrapped on the stone floor as she stood and stalked out of the kitchen, slamming the door behind her.

Patricia's heart hammered as she sat at the kitchen table staring at her daughter's retreating back. Hayley's news had been a shock. Patricia's fingers were laced together to avoid trembling as thoughts raced. The selfish part of her wanted Hayley home. But what was best for her daughter was paramount.

Why hadn't she seen it coming? Hayley had seemed

sincerely interested in college at winter break, and again at spring break. But not now.

Hayley a quitter? A dropout? More importantly, what could she do to get Hayley back on track?

Patricia shook her head, took a deep breath and turned to glance at the clock. Eleven and Trey wasn't home yet from the Coalition meeting. The Coalition elders had been getting together a lot lately, plotting ways to deal with the outsiders and speculators who were trying to edge their way into Savannah's historic district. Her stomach had been tense all evening and was beginning to ache. How much more could she take? Mama. Hayley. Trey. She so wished he was home.

She was aware of a sense of foreboding. Trey and the Coalition would handle Savannah. As they always had. And always would. Her job was to take care of Hayley, bless her heart.

Deciding she'd wasted enough time, Patricia took a deep, shuddering breath and went into the media room. The widescreen television boomed with a music video. She grabbed the remote and punched the mute button. The dimly lit room went silent.

Hayley looked up from the plush chair, surprise on her pixie face.

"I want you to sleep on this decision of yours," Patricia said. "Tomorrow, after the service, let's discuss it with Daddy and get his input. Take it slow. Think it through. And we'll go from there, together."

* * *

THE FOLLOWING MORNING, PATRICIA, WITHDRAWN INTO HER memories of Mama, rode in silence to the memorial service. An excruciating, aspirin-resistant headache clung like a barnacle, piercing and compressing her skull. She and Hayley remained in the claustrophobic limousine while Trey got out and held the door for them.

She couldn't escape what was ahead. Avoidance would be unbecoming and would dishonor Mama. She surveyed the crowd and the cathedral. The gray clouds. The mottled pale sky. It was important to take it all in. She wanted to carve this day into her memory, the day she said her final goodbye to Mama. But it was a bitter sight. As bitter as the bile rising in her throat.

She took a breath, eased her legs out and stood, trembling in the sultry air. She hooked Trey's arm for stability.

The neatly trimmed, luscious grass and butter-yellow daffodils surrounding the cathedral stood in sharp contrast to the muted dresses and dark suits milling around the courtyard.

Sheila, a close friend who owned the corner florist, pinned a dainty forget-me-not on Patricia's lapel and gave her a long, warm hug. "I'm sorry for your loss."

Patricia, though wanting to languish in the warmth of her friend's hug, stepped back, patted Sheila's arm, and took a deep breath.

"Are you ready?" Trey asked.

She nodded, though she wasn't. *How could anyone be ready for something like this?*

He led her and Hayley, whose straight brown hair obscured much of her face, toward the entrance.

A jasmine-scented breeze rippled the Spanish moss hanging from the live oaks. No doubt, a farewell gesture to Mama. Those iconic trees were Mama's favorites, as was the ocean and everything in it. Patricia folded the moment into her memory.

The sea of souls in front of the church parted to make way for Trey, Hayley and her.

Everyone seemed to be watching.

Her cheeks burned.

Blurred faces mumbled bland condolences. She acknowledged each as best she could.

Judy Simpson smiled. Meredith embraced her. Alisa seemed stunned. Her band of sisters, there for her as always.

Once through the gauntlet, she paused. The concrete stairs to the church entrance appeared steeper and higher than ever before. Her knees seemed weak and ready to buckle forcing Patricia to will her legs to climb the steps and cross the landing to the open doorway.

Filled with sorrow, she gripped Trey's arm tighter, entered the cathedral and anointed herself with holy water. The cool air inside was so heavy she had trouble breathing. Her chest tightened. Her head throbbed. She paused and, stooped-shouldered, gasped for air. As her suffocation subsided, she stiffened her spine and moved forward with determination. She would ride out this storm with dignity.

Patricia genuflected as she entered the pew, made the sign of the cross over her chest and sat, relieved to be off her unreliable legs. Incense tainted the air. When she was ready, she knelt and prayed as Mama had taught her. In the background, people shuffled in. When her prayer was over, she returned to her seat.

Her eyes settled on the large, framed portrait of Mama at the front of the church. Patricia blinked away the tears. The crucifix over the altar taunted her. Jesus had taken Mama, and she didn't know why. 'The shadow on the face of God,' Father Mark had said at other funeral masses. It wasn't much of an explanation.

Father Mark, a young copper-headed man, stood and the congregation hushed. A boy priest. Did he know firsthand of death? Of loss? Of grief? Of sorrow?

Then she saw the urn. Mama. Her mother was truly an angel. God's masterpiece. Memories competed for attention like confined children. Mama, Daddy and her as a young teen on vacation at Myrtle Beach. The void Daddy's early death had left and how it brought her and her mother so much closer. Picking strawberries with Mama. Making Hummingbird Cake with Mama. Planting a tree in the live oak allee when Grandma died. Mama sitting with her in the rocking chair. The vegetable garden they grew one summer. And a collage of festive holidays. *When I was young and afraid of the dark, you read to me every night, Mama. And when I was sad, you sang to me.*

Mama. Gone forever. Her touch. Her hugs. Her open-ended love. Gone. Patricia shivered. In the presence of death, life was but a vapor. She blessed herself, folded her hands, and whispered, "Dear Lord, help me. Help all of us through this."

Trey covered her hands with his. His firm touch was reassuring. The distress faded. Somehow, they would get through this together.

She turned to him.

He gave her a reassuring look that stilled her further, and mouthed, "It's going to be okay."

CHAPTER 8

hey returned home following the memorial service and reception. Patricia took a short nap and awoke feeling somewhat more at ease, Trey sitting at her bedside. Not wanting to rehash the service, she briefed Trey on Hayley's decision to abandon college. He seemed to take the news in stride. He suggested, as she had, that they together speak with Hayley about the matter.

They found Hayley sitting at the kitchen table paging through a copy of *Town & Country*. Hayley looked up as they came in the room, a stern expression on her face.

Apprehension welled as Patricia pulled out a chair and sat across from Hayley. Trey sat between the two. His lips pinched together as he scrutinized his daughter.

Hayley closed the magazine and leaned back in the wrought-iron chair.

"Do you want to tell me what's going on?" Trey asked in a soft voice.

"I think you know."

His nod was nearly imperceptible. "I want to hear it directly from you."

"I'm leaving school."

"What do you hope to accomplish by that?" he asked in a quiet, calm voice.

"I hope to put my life in order."

"Your life is messed up?"

"Yes, sir."

"In what way?" He stroked his chin.

"I'm not committed to my course work. I need to find a new focus. Something I truly believe in. And whatever that is, it's not at college."

Trey reached across the glass-topped table and touched Hayley's hand. "Honey, it's not in your best interests to leave college. Trust me, if you do something like this you'll regret it for the rest of your life."

"Why?"

"You said it. You'll find a new focus. Then years from now, when that focus burns out, you'll wonder why you didn't complete college."

"I can go to school anytime."

"But how many years are you going to waste until you realize how important a college education is."

Hayley clenched her free hand. She set her jaw and looked Trey directly in the eyes. "Does what I *want* to do mean anything to you?"

"Sure. That's why we're talking about this."

She pulled her hand from his and placed it in her lap. "It's my life. It's my track. I'm the engineer of this train. I'm leaving college. End of discussion."

Trey scoffed. "So at eighteen you know everything and you have no need for advice on an important matter like this?"

"If you have something to say other than 'no,' go ahead."

Trey stood and walked to the window where he surveyed the backyard. Hayley walked to his side and looked out.

"We had a lot of fun out there," he said with a rasp. "Maybe one day I'll be out there with grandchildren."

She gave him a hug. "Not so soon, Daddy. I have other things I want to do first."

"That's why we're talking. I thought you wanted a career."

"I do."

He took her hand. "Honey, there will be times in your life when a close friend or someone you love unconditionally will ask for a favor. Their appeal to you might not be based on logic or fact or inside knowledge. Their request will rest solely on their relationship with you. And your response to their appeal will be strongly conditioned on your relationship with them. This is one of those times." He took a deep breath and let it out slowly. "I'm asking you for a favor. I'm asking you to delay leaving college until the end of the semester. I'm asking for six weeks. Just six weeks. Can you give me that?"

Hayley stiffened and pulled her hand from his. "Daddy, I love you, and I don't mean to disrespect you, but I need to think about my answer. Would you mind if I give you my decision tomorrow morning?"

"Of course."

"So do you mind if I spend the night at the beach house?"

"That's probably a good idea. But just one night. There's a storm coming up the coast."

CHAPTER 9

*H*ayley popped another aspirin against her hangover, adjusted the strap of her sports bra, and stepped out on the back porch. The ocean shimmered in the blinding morning sun.

She inhaled the tangy air. Palm fronds rustled in the offshore breeze as she stepped from the porch and walked toward the ocean. At the end of the path, she turned right and headed south down the empty beach—wide, open space of soft, warm sand where her bare feet and foggy mind could awaken. Paradise.

College or not? She wasn't sure. She had a responsibility to develop whatever skills she had, no doubt about that. But which abilities and how? She hadn't a clue. Confusion about something as important as this wasn't good. She wanted it sorted out. She took a breath and started a slow jog to loosen up.

Was she really leaving college because of a lack of direction? She didn't have to declare a major for another year. Emerald was a fine school. Why not shelve her indecision and stay in college? If nothing else, staying in school would abate the family drama for a while. She angled down toward the wet, firm part of the sand. Once there, she punched the button on her sports watch and sped up.

Was her rush to leave college something else? Could she be running away from the workload? Not really. The collegiate challenge invigorated her. Her grades evidenced that she excelled when pressed.

It was Atlanta she was running from. Month after month of miserable winter weather. Gray. Depressing. Brash people who seemed hardened by the weather. Entire days spent indoors. The dry air. Brown lawns. Barren tree limbs.

She was miserable in Atlanta, and Savannah seemed so beautiful and personal and, most of the time, so very happy. Happiness or misery? Not much of a choice there. Others had abandoned college and done well. Why not her? Still, should she make life-changing decisions based on Atlanta's misery index?

As she passed the rickety home that marked her first mile, she checked her watch. Seven minutes. Spot-on. Her heart rate and breathing seemed right. She sped up, challenging herself, striving for six and a half minutes for the second mile.

Staying in school made no sense. But did everything have to be sensible? Not necessarily. Though Atlanta was crummy in the winter, winter was over and spring was well on its way. Flowers. Grass. Robins. She supposed she ought to give Atlanta more time. Another six weeks wouldn't hurt.

Plus, she chuckled to herself, there was always Shawn.

* * *

THE NINETEENTH CENTURY CHATHAM COUNTY COURTHOUSE, no longer an active courthouse, stood proudly at Savannah's heart. Across the square in a converted historic home was the law office of Alton and Alton, founded in the late 1700s. Back then, as befitted a major port, the Alton practice focused on maritime law. Over the next 250 years, the practice grew into one of the top law firms in Georgia if not the Southeast.

Patricia sat in the elegant black marble and mahogany lobby, waiting patiently for her appointment with Isabel Alton, daughter of Lucius Alton and last family name bearer. Isabel, who had handled legal matters for Patricia's mother for years, had summoned Patricia to discuss probating her mother's considerable estate. Not a task Patricia was eager to do, but necessary nonetheless.

Isabel appeared precisely on time and greeted Patricia with an awkward hug. Unlike her diminutive father, she was a big-framed person, nearly six feet tall. Dark brows. Pronounced cheekbones framed a masculine face with no makeup. She wore a loose gray suit.

Radiating certitude, Isabel smiled. "Shall we?" She gestured down the hall.

Patricia followed Isabel into the corner office and sat in one of the two beige leather chairs positioned in front of the floor-to-ceiling bookcases. Isabel sat in the matching chair.

"So," Patricia said, anxious to get the business over.

Isabel's face tightened. "I'm afraid I have some disturbing news."

Patricia's breath caught. "Disturbing?"

Isabel nodded. "Your mother died destitute."

Patricia stiffened, then gripped the armrests. Heart thudding, she studied Isabel's features, questioning what had been said. "Impossible. Mama had several million in interest-bearing government bonds and owned a great deal of valuable port property."

Isabel nodded, her expression stern. "That she did, but it's all gone."

Patricia shook her head. "Gone? How do you know it's gone?"

"I was assembling an inventory of her assets for you to use in probating her estate. When I contacted her bank, I was told all her money, a little over three million, had been withdrawn."

"When?"

"Recently."

"That makes no sense. I have to ask Meredith."

"It was Meredith who told me the news."

"Meredith! My God, why didn't she say anything to me?"

"Maybe she didn't know until I asked her to look."

"The bonds? Her property?"

"I don't know about the bonds, but according to the County Assessor all her property has been sold."

"When?" She cocked her head to one side. "She never mentioned that."

"A number of transactions in the last three weeks. The property is no longer hers."

"What about the proceeds from the property sales? Those properties were worth millions."

"Gone."

"There must be some mistake." Patricia turned her palms up toward Isabel. "How could everything just disappear?"

"I'm her attorney, not her accountant. I don't know where it went."

Patricia wrung her hands. "Well, I guess I need to contact Mama's accountant, Sonny Carothers."

"Knowing how shocking this would be on top of your mother's unexpected demise, I stepped over my bounds and tried to contact him for you." Isabel shifted position in her chair and leaned forward. "For the last couple of days, I've tried. First thing this morning, I even went over there. His office is closed and his mailbox is full. Like your mama's money, he appears to be gone as well."

Patricia's head pounded. Mama trusted Sonny completely. Was Sonny behind all this? Did he murder Mama? "What the hell is going on, Isabel?"

Isabel raised her eyebrows. "With the missing assets and your mother's sudden death, we have to consider the two things are related. I have a fiduciary responsibility to your mother and her estate, so I've contacted the police. I had no choice. And the faster the police get on it, the better chance they have to figure it out."

"My God. But it was a heart attack. Or so I thought. Are you saying she could have been murdered?"

"I'm just letting you know the direction the police are likely to go in an instance like this."

Patricia massaged her forehead. "And what do you suggest I do?"

"I told the police that all contact with you has to go through me. So you do nothing."

"I bet they were happy about that."

Isabel shrugged. "It's routine. They understand."

Patricia began to tremble. Unable to calm herself, she bolted up. Paced. "I'm having a lot of trouble getting my head around this."

"It's just a possibility." Isabel walked to Patricia and reassuringly took her hand.

Patricia's head compressed. She sucked in air. Couldn't get enough. A red veil tinted her vision. Only red. No shapes. Her ears rang. A piercing, mind-shattering screech. She shivered. She was so cold. So hollow. So numb. Her legs gave away and she dropped. Fell endlessly. No bottom. Only darkness.

PATRICIA'S DARKNESS DISSOLVED INTO A GHOSTLY GRAY FOG. As the mist lifted from her unconsciousness, she slowly breathed in and opened her eyes. Too bright. She snapped her lids shut. The musky smell of old leather registered. She was lying on a couch. Her head pounded with a migraine.

Urges to make sense of this, to regain control, and to protect herself skittered about like crabs on the beach. Seeking answers, she forced her eyes open again just a tad. A wavering shape hovered.

"Patricia, are you back?" Isabel asked. "An ambulance is on the way."

With Isabel's kind face moving in and out of focus, Patricia took a deep breath and nodded, only to stir up the headache. "No, please cancel that. I'm fine. All I need is do … you have any Excedrin?"

"I'm not certain I can cancel a 911 call."

"Excedrin?"

"I think so," Isabel said. "Just relax while I fetch it."

Moments later, Isabel returned with a glass of water and a familiar white pill.

Still in the searing grip of the migraine, Patricia downed the medicine with a gulp of chilled water. "What happened?"

"You fainted. Are you feeling better?"

The terrible news that precipitated the blackout surged back. Unfinished business. Nasty business that required a clear, focused mind. "I've got a monster headache, but I'll live." Patricia took another sip of water, then put the crystal glass on a coaster on the end table. "I think we were talking about next steps."

"Are you sure you want to discuss this right now?" Isabel asked, concern etched in her face.

Patricia nodded. "Absolutely."

"Let's see what the police can do, but if they can't or won't move quickly to get to the bottom of what happened my father knows people who have tremendous resources," Isabel said. "They could help get to the bottom of this. I'd be happy to discuss what I know with my father."

"I hate to involve the Cotton Coalition in this." Patricia went to stand and teetered as shifting dizziness forced her back down. "If you could hand me my purse, I need to contact Trey about this."

* * *

TREY PULLED THE VIBRATING PHONE FROM ITS HIP-MOUNTED case and glanced at the screen. Patricia. She seldom called at work. Concern simmering, he accepted the call and put the phone to his ear.

"Trey, honey, I'm sorry for interrupting you, but something *bad* has happened. Can you talk?"

A shudder ripped through him and his senses sharpened. His right foot pressed the floor button that closed the door to his office, ensuring utmost privacy. "Certainly."

"It seems Mama's assets have disappeared. What with her sudden, unexpected death and—"

"Let's take this one step at a time." Suppressing his alarm, Trey grabbed a pen and pulled a pad of paper closer. "Mama's assets have disappeared?"

"Yes. Isabel, bless her heart, was preparing an inventory for me to use in probate and, well, Mama's bank accounts are empty. And Isabel said that according to the County Assessor, all of Mama's properties have been sold."

Trey's grip on the pen tightened as he jotted notes. "What about her bonds?"

"Isabel is checking with her broker, but he hasn't returned her call yet."

Trey took a deep breath. "Okay. She banked with Meredith, right?"

"Right."

"And Sonny Carothers is her accountant?"

"Right."

Trey jotted Sonny's name below Meredith's. "What does Sonny have to say about all of this?"

"Sonny's missing and his mail is piling up at his office."

Trey swore, then cleared his throat. "Have the police been notified?"

"Isabel contacted them, but—"

"I'll get on it right away."

"Mama's death was so unexpected."

The tremble in her voice worried Trey. Jaw clenched, he glanced at the silver frame with her photo. He desperately wanted to protect her from mayhem and wanted to shield her from maliciousness. Struggling to keep his concerns from overwhelming him, he chose his next words carefully. "I'm going to have the Coalition look into this."

"I didn't want to have you do that."

"Your mother was a prominent philanthropist. It's entirely appropriate for the Coalition to look into it."

"Okay."

"Leave everything to me. But just to be on the safe side, keep your pistol handy."

CHAPTER 10

The Married Women's Bridge Club was coming for cards and lunch in a few hours. The caterers were in the kitchen setting up and the valets had just arrived. The timing wasn't ideal, what with Mama's death, Hayley's college desertion, and the investigation into Mama's missing assets and questionable death. But commitments were commitments. A lesson Hayley needed to learn.

Sheila, a petite widow who owned the corner floral shop, showed up shortly afterward and pulled Patricia into a hug. "How are you holding up?"

"Thank God for this luncheon. It's keeping my mind off Mama's death."

Sheila gave her another hug, then set about arranging bouquets throughout the house.

Patricia's cell phone rang. She checked the display. Alisa.

"Hi, Patricia," Alisa said. "Sorry to bother you this morning. I'm sure you have your hands full with the luncheon. I just wanted to let you know that my brother called and told me someone has been searching your husband's name in the county records."

Alisa's brother was the clerk of court, so Patricia knew the information was legit. "Did he say who?"

"Someone using the public computers at the main library. There were several searches, the first about a week ago."

Why wouldn't someone search from their home or office? To hide their identity? And multiple searches? What on earth? "What were they looking for?"

"Everything in the online records related to Trey."

"Is there much there?"

"Apparently so."

Public information is public for a reason. Trey's a good man. If someone wants to research him, so be it. "Thanks for the heads up, Alisa."

"No problem."

A change of clothes and a splash of lavender cologne later, Patricia glanced out the window. The ladies, including her three closest friends, decked out in elegant tea dresses, hats and gloves so different from the somber black they all wore to the memorial, gathered in the formal courtyard outside her front door. They always waited outside until all had arrived. Normally, Patricia looked forward to entertaining the women, but not today. Her mind was elsewhere. They'd known each other for ages and got along famously. She knew they would understand if she wasn't quite herself. At precisely eleven, she opened the door and greeted them all with, "Welcome, everyone, to our home."

Like fillies going to the starting gate, the thirteen other members and their guests entered the double doors and swarmed down the wide hall to the rear parlor, their designer heels clicking on the black Italian marble floor.

Established in the 1890's, the bridge club was an umbilical cord to the past. But the fourteen carefully vetted members lived very much in the present. And, as a group, they wielded immense political and economic power in Savannah. Power measured by social action rather than social standing. Power measured by cunning rather than coyness. Each woman possessed more confidence than an alligator stalking lunch, and just as much patience.

An hour of duplicate bridge followed. Patricia's game suffered because her mind continued to run in circles. There was no focus to her thoughts and no end to the recycling.

Precisely at noon all playing ceased, champagne was served and the ladies conversed while the bridge tables were transformed with linen, china, crystal, and her heirloom vermeil flatware.

Patricia joined a clutch of three women who stood like entwined vines at the back of the room. They exchanged cheek kisses. What a special team they were. A fortress against life's abuses. The four had accomplished so much together. Having her three friends with her seemed to ease her sadness somewhat.

"I'm so sorry your mother passed," Judy said. "Such a lovely lady." She was decked out in white chiffon with a white on white print. Her red hair was coiffed in a simple pageboy cut. She was the newest member of the club. Tenderhearted, outspoken and stunningly beautiful.

Filled with sadness and unable to reply, Patricia nodded.

"If there is anything, anything at all, you need please call me," Judy said.

"Thank you."

Judy threw her arms around her and gave her a warm hug, an understandably complex maneuver in the wide-brimmed crimson hat she wore.

As soon as Judy retreated, Meredith surged forward. She had selected a pink floral number for the luncheon. Her dark hair hung in waves down her back, a sultry look Meredith frequently cultivated. She swept Patricia into a bear hug that seemed entirely appropriate coming from Meredith. "Don't hesitate to call me if you need to talk. Maybe we could do lunch later in the week."

"Thank you," was all Patricia could squeak out.

Meredith stepped back and took Patricia's hand. "Your mother will be missed, but her fine work will go on and be a vivid memorial to her."

Alisa was next to embrace Patricia. "Your lovely mother and your family are in my prayers," Alisa whispered. When she stepped away, Patricia saw tears in her eyes. Not much of a surprise. Of the three, Alisa was the most emotional. She wore a gauzy dress in powder blue that accentuated her big blue eyes and blond hair. She had a marvelous body and an off-the-charts IQ.

"God, my husband's a jerk." Judy's green eyes narrowed. Judy and Alisa were partners in the same boutique law firm in central Savannah. Though Judy was still searching for her social role, Alisa had gained a reputation for impressive fund raising for charities.

Alisa shifted her tall, willowy frame as her Botoxed eyebrows arched as high as possible. "What has Beau done now, besides cheat on you?"

"He's being a chauvinist, as usual." Judy flashed her laser-whitened teeth. "He doesn't think Alton's daughter, or any women for that matter, should be permitted to serve in the Cotton Coalition."

"It's the twenty-first century." Patricia shuddered at the thought of Hayley ever being invited to join that brutal bunch, but Trey had assured her over and over the Coalition was a males-only organization.

"That's what I told him." Judy's porcelain cheeks reddened. "He told me I didn't know what I was talkin' about. Can you imagine?"

Meredith, CEO of her own bank, looked incredulous. "Doesn't he think women are capable of killing?" She patted her purse.

Meredith's marksmanship was well respected among the four women. Patricia had no doubt that Meredith wouldn't hesitate to use her concealed gun to protect herself. Of the four, Meredith would be the only likely candidate for the Cotton Coalition. But Meredith as an assassin? Nah.

"Apparently, Beau underestimates us." Judy let out a puff of disgust as she ran her hand over her designer purse. "Why does he think we tote these things?"

Alisa tossed her nose into the air. "You gonna give your man a good old-fashioned comeuppance for his discourteous remark?"

Thank God for Alisa and common sense.

"He's not getting into my garden until he's done a whole bunch of weedin' and feedin' and growin'." She turned to Patricia. "Has Trey mentioned Lucius Alton's proposal to have Isabel replace him on the Cotton Coalition?"

"No, he hasn't." The things Trey had done for the Coalition played in her head. How he'd broken the law and the commandments. How he'd ordered the killing of those who had chosen wrong. The guilt he carried. The mountainous stress. The sleepless nights. Did she really want to see Hayley subjected to that?

Yes, Patricia carried a gun. Yes, she occasionally broke the law to rescue abused women, and, yes, she occasionally threatened to hurt people who tried to prevent her from transporting the women. But, no, she really didn't want Hayley to be like her ... or her three friends.

Judy raised her eyebrows. "How do you feel about the idea of women in the Coalition?"

"As I said before, it's the twenty-first century," Patricia said, her tone flat and devoid of emotion.

"I'd say we need to remind the boys of that," Meredith said.

"I'm up for that," Alisa chimed in.

Judy smiled. "Ladies, are we in agreement on this?"

Meredith, Alisa and Patricia nodded.

The ladies raised their champagne flutes and clinked them.

* * *

SHORTLY BEFORE FIVE, PATRICIA HEADED DOWN THE SIDEWALK to the corner florist to thank Sheila for the lovely bouquets she made for the luncheon, and to drop off some leftovers.

Patricia loved Falcon Square. Its historic homes and their residents were antique charms on the bracelet of love that lined the square. Clouds, born and raised over the Atlantic Ocean, bejeweled the dazzling blue sky.

Halfway down the block, a sensation that someone was watching her pestered like a mosquito. She glanced around and saw no one staring, other than a bushy-tailed gray squirrel, so she forced her focus back to the entrance of Sheila's small shop.

Patricia opened the door and went in. The store always smelled fresh and fragrant. Sheila sat in a worn armchair. She put aside her paperwork, stood, and greeted Patricia with a smile.

"Leftovers from the luncheon," Patricia said as she handed the box to Sheila.

"You shouldn't have."

"They'd only go to waste."

Sheila took the box and put it in the fridge. "I was about to have tea. Would you care for a cup?"

Tea being just the thing she needed, Patricia nodded.

"How was the luncheon?" Sheila poured tea into china cups and handed one to Patricia.

"Your bouquets were a hit with the ladies." Patricia took a sip of tea. "Just the right touch."

Sheila looked down into her cup. "Why thank you, Patsy. Thank you very much."

Calm silence followed.

Sheila raised her head and gave Patricia a searching look. "Are you okay?"

Torn between the desire to be comforted and the urge to be private, Patricia bit her lip. "Just thinking about Mama."

Sheila put her teacup down and touched Patricia's hand. "Sure enough, she took a piece of your heart with her."

Patricia nodded. Though her eyes burned, she held back the tears and took a calming breath. "I know. I miss her so much."

"Everyone leaves us sooner or later. We never fill that void, but we still go on with life."

"She didn't leave, she was taken from me. Someone killed her."

Sheila's hand darted over her gasping mouth. "Oh my God."

"It's the only logical explanation," Patricia said.

"Any idea who or why?"

"Might be her accountant, Sonny Carothers. He's missing and so is her money."

"Oh my. Don't rightly know the man. I'm sure the police will take care of everything. Meanwhile," she touched Patricia's shoulder, "you should do your best to get on with your life."

Patricia sighed. "It's hard."

"It's necessary." Sheila patted Patricia's hand.

"I know." Patricia took a deep breath and let it out slowly.

She took a long sip of tea and put her cup on the table. Sheila's wisdom and kindness helped. Helped a lot. Feeling a bit better for Sheila's understanding and words of comfort, Patricia stood. "I should be going. Thank you for your kindness."

"Will you be okay?"

Patricia nodded and walked to the door with Sheila by her side.

"Can you come for tea tomorrow?" Patricia asked. "Say two o'clock?"

"I'd like that. And if you get to fretting again today, you hurry back, Patsy."

"Thank you so much. You're a wonderful friend." Patricia gave Sheila a hug, opened the door and stepped out.

As the door swung closed, she looked up and down the street. The feeling of being watched returned with the force of a lightning bolt. She swiveled her head, checking the street both ways as her fingers touched the hard lump in her bag, the Kimber 45. She saw nothing suspicious on the street, but the goose bumps remained. She had learned to trust her instincts—not a pain-free education. She compressed her lips and scurried down the block straight toward her home.

Though no one seemed to be out, she couldn't shake the feeling she was being observed ... or stalked. Thank God she had the presence of mind to carry her purse this time. But could she use her gun so soon after her failure at Faith's house? She quickened her pace up the stairs and across the shaded porch to the front entrance. She keyed the lock, stepped inside, and bolted the door.

A glance in the foyer mirror revealed eyes deep with concern and a stern face framed by wild strands of blond hair. A vein on the side of her temple pulsed. She rolled her shoulders to ease the tension, armed the security system, and went to the kitchen. Leftovers were stacked in insulated containers on the counter.

She wished Trey were home. Hoped Hayley's time at the beach was helping her make her mind up. Suddenly, she felt so very alone. Alone and scared.

CHAPTER 11

"Good morning. Sorry I'm late," Judy said from the doorway of the bank conference room. She walked to Patricia and gave her a hug. "I'm so sorry for your loss. I still can't believe it. I just played tennis with her."

Judy hugged the remaining women, stopping at Meredith. "I'm so glad you gathered us to support Patricia."

Meredith, dressed in red, pushed her chair back and stood. "OK, ladies. Now that Judy is finally here, let's get down to business. The possible murder of Mrs. Snyder and the embezzlement of her estate," Meredith said without emotion. "Let's start listing names of people with a motive."

"Don't you think we should let the police do this?" Judy asked.

"Of course," Meredith said. "But it doesn't hurt for us to look into it too. Now, who has a motive?"

Patricia took out a notepad. "Well, there's Jamie Gilcrest. He never forgave Mama for the foreclosure."

"And there's Willie Maye," Alisa said, "the reporter who hated Henrietta."

Though Patricia's mind was swamped with revenge, she was proud she could keep herself externally composed while they added four more names to the list.

"Any more people with a motive?" Meredith asked.

Patricia shook her head, amazed that her mother had made so many enemies.

"Okay. Let's move on," Meredith said. "A week ago, all your mother's funds at my bank were transferred to an account at the main branch of the Hong Kong and Shanghai Bank. I'm sorry I didn't detect the transfer earlier, but we have so many accounts and unless I'm—"

"I understand," Patricia said.

Meredith's face was red, which was common when she was agitated. She took a deep breath. "The Hong Kong and Shanghai Bank is a major institution my clients deal with regularly, and one where I have excellent relationships. I called in some favors and was advised that once the funds were received the money was immediately transferred back to an account at a private bank on Hilton Head Island." She twisted her hands up. "A facility I've never heard of and can find no record of. So far."

"What's the name on the Hilton Head Island account?" Patricia asked.

"I only have an account number," Meredith said. "And if I don't know someone important at the institution, that's all I'll have. But don't go fretting, Patricia. Private banking is tight-knit and chances are I'll know one or more of the directors, or someone who knows them. I just have to track down who owns the institution."

Maybe Mama's money was safe and sound. Maybe they were overreacting. "It's a relief her money is so close."

Meredith shrugged. "We don't know if it's her money anymore or even that it's still at the Hilton Head Island bank.

That's why I need to determine if I have any contacts there who could help."

"And if you don't have a friend or a friend of a friend?" Patricia couldn't help the disappointment in her voice.

"Then we go to our Treasury sources. They closely monitor all major fund transfers."

Patricia stiffened and forced a smile. "Another friend?"

"Like I said, we're a tight-knit group." Meredith nodded. "Okay, Alisa, what do you have on Henrietta's bonds?"

"Henrietta requested bearer bond certificates from her broker six weeks ago. The certificates were issued and delivered to her shortly afterward."

"Delivered to her home address?" Patricia asked.

"Yes," Alisa said.

"I've inventoried her safety deposit box and there are no bonds there," Patricia said, impatience building.

"Did she have a safe at home?" Alisa asked.

"She never mentioned one."

Alisa's pale eyes flinched. "What did she do with her jewelry?"

"Safety deposit box."

"How inconvenient." Alisa scrunched her nose.

"That was Mama," Patricia said. "She was very careful with all her assets. That's why I know something is terribly wrong here."

"I'll have her credit card records printed out for you," Meredith said. "When you have time, go through them and see if she had transactions with home security firms in the past five or ten years. They'd do the install of a home safe, if there is one."

"If there's no safe?" Patricia's jaw tensed at the thought.

"Then, as far as the bonds go, we're out of luck," Meredith said. "Bearer bonds are virtually impossible to trace."

Judy lifted an eyebrow. "Do you suppose this has anything to do with some sort of get-rich-quick scheme?"

Patricia glared at Judy. Where was she going with a question like that?

Meredith's eyes widened. "Oh, I hope not."

"Let's not speculate," Patricia said. "Let's concentrate on getting facts before the trail goes cold. What do we know about her accountant's whereabouts? Sonny Carothers." She pronounced the accountant's name with distain, like it was Lee Harvey Oswald.

"I've looked everywhere. Planes, trains, rental car, buses and boats. I can't find any trace of Sonny anywhere," Alisa said, returning her coffee cup to the saucer. It settled with a loud clunk, courtesy of the missing little finger she had lost as a little girl on a go-cart. Her normally sparkling sapphire eyes seemed troubled. "His disappearance doesn't make sense at all. Unless he's done something wrong and he's hiding."

They were silent for a few seconds.

"Or if he's dead," Judy said.

"I searched his personal and professional credit reports," Alisa said. "Nothing unusual."

"That's okay, Alisa," Judy said. "We can only do our best. And sometimes our best isn't enough."

Alisa glared at Judy.

Seeing the elevated emotions, Patricia clenched her teeth and ran fingers through her hair. "Let's go back to before the beginning on Sonny. Parents. Grandparents. Siblings. Let's dig into his formative years. Education. Early career. No assumptions. All facts. Let's know him better than his own mother. Let's pick through his background like vultures on road kill. Focus on finding motive, as well as a possible hiding place. Who wants to do the background on Sonny?"

Both Alisa and Judy put their hands up.

"Y'all want to flip for it?"

"So far, I haven't come up with much on him," Alisa said. "Let Judy do it."

"Okay, you've got it, Judy. If this guy has gone over the edge, I want to know when and why. And check his clients, the deceased ones. See if any of them died in unexpected poverty."

Judy's eyebrows shot up.

"Also, I'll check Falcon Memorial to get his medical records, if he ever used the hospital," Patricia said. "And I'll get an Insurance Institute report on him."

"We're going to have to track down your mother's real estate transactions," Meredith said.

"I'll take that," Alisa said.

"Okay then," Patricia said. Nervous sweat pasted her hair to her neck. "I think we can wrap it up until tomorrow at the same time when we'll see what y'all come up with. Hopefully we'll be able to begin to make some sense out of this nasty situation."

* * *

THE PAPAL NUNCIO, A HEARTY SOUL WHO HADN'T INTRODUCED himself, squared his narrow Italian shoulders and handed Father John the encyclical, a large brown envelope, and an airline ticket back to Savannah.

All old news to Father John. Though the messenger was always different, every one of his papal covert assignments commenced the same way. A phone call. A meal in a calm restaurant in a distant city. The papers. And always ended with a blessing.

A light cough startled John. He put the materials in his worn leather satchel and, as he stroked his square chin, looked up into the dark eyes of the weathered nuncio.

"Shall we pray?" the old man whispered.

Father John bowed his head and closed his eyes. He didn't like the covert work, but it was his vocation as ordained by the church and the Holy See. Redemptive, blessed work, however illegal it might be. He worked within his limits and that seemed to satisfy his superiors.

In his twenty years of service, he'd concluded the devil had to be working double duty and weekends to instill the evil he'd encountered. He missed the naïve, clean world most people foolishly believed they lived in, a belief he'd held as well in his youth.

Father John blessed himself as the nuncio finished his prayer.

* * *

TREY HAD THE TAXI PULL OVER ON THE SOUTH END OF FALCON Square. After leaving the cab, he crossed through the square to the alley, then hesitated until a shadowy figure in the second-floor window signaled the all clear. He strode into the alley past the first guard, a balding man sitting on a bench, and went to the end of the alley where he exchanged a wordless greeting with the second guard. The man opened an antique wrought-iron gate that swung silently on well-oiled hinges while activating an alarm inside the fortified dwelling.

Trey entered a brick courtyard and crossed to the back door of the historic home. After palming the sweat from his forehead, he ran a passcard through the security device, entered, and descended the stone staircase.

Bright lights illuminated the Cotton Coalition's meeting room. The directors, Alton, Simpson, Potter and Hempfield, were seated in their usual positions around the walnut table. Behind Potter and Hempfield stood their eldest sons. An empty chair remained at the table. Trey's. Trey approached the weathered table, sat in the high-backed chair and activated his computer with the token he carried.

"Thank you for coming on such short notice," Trey said. "You've read the briefing report?"

The others nodded.

"Good. Let's get started. Simpson, what do you have as a likely cause of Henrietta's death?"

"The immediate cause of death was a heart attack," Simpson said. His clipped words seemed forced. "Since we now suspect murder, the heart attack could have been induced by any number of drugs. She was my patient and was on normal meds for a person her age. I had the containers with her meds tested to see if the contents matched the label. Every drug checked out. I also had her kitchen, bedroom and bathroom searched for any meds that were prescribed by someone other than me. None were found. If she consumed a fatal drug on the day of her death, it was likely done outside her home."

"Potter, have your boys compile a log of her activities on the day of her death," Trey said.

Potter nodded.

"Okay. We need to look at Sonny Carothers also. The missing accountant. Hempfield, I want a copy of the security tapes for Sonny's office building and those in the immediate area. Have your friends at Fort Stewart run them through facial recognition. If Sonny is cavorting with known criminals, I want to know who they are. Potter, I also want a minute-by-minute log of Sonny's activities the day Patricia's mother died. I want his telephone records, client list and—"

"I know the man" Simpson said. "He doesn't seem the murdering sort."

"Agreed," Trey said. "A good old boy like him would have to have help."

"The authorities have started their investigation of him," Alton said. "Chief Patrick assures me that we'll get everything they document. By the way, I have to leave in fifteen minutes."

* * *

"DAMN IT!" RHETT SWALLOWED HARD AND SQUATTED TO examine the dead cat, one of the strays he fed daily. A fellow traveler. The cat's once-gleaming dark eyes were glazed gray. Sorrow over the loss of an innocent life tore at him. He looked closer, afraid to give into tears, as if focusing his eyes would quell the emotion.

No blood. No flies. An intact corpse. Probably a natural cause of death, but a death nonetheless. Loneliness and bewilderment descended. Relinquishing a friend to the hereafter, if there was such a place, did that to him.

He lifted the stray, cradled it in his arms and carried it to a newly tilled flowerbed in a quiet corner of the square. After assuring no one was watching, Rhett lay the cat down on the grass and dug a deep, wide hole with his hands at the back of the bed. The rich loam brought remembrance of freshly plowed tobacco fields. They called it the *good earth* up there. Not so good for him. As he dug he wondered who, if anyone, would bury him when his time came. He came up empty.

After gently positioning the cat in the bottom of the dark hole, he patted the stray's head, took a deep breath and said a tearful prayer.

Songbirds chirped in the tree above. He quickly filled the hole. With a groan, he rose and stomped down the loose dirt, then turned and left. He didn't want to stay in the sad place any longer than necessary.

The breeze in the old oaks picked up as Rhett left the square and headed to the public library to wash his hands and continue his pain-driven search for his irresponsible father.

Suddenly, he knew where to search for his birth father—the church that the Falcons attended.

ary of being videotaped, Rhett scanned the sanctuary stairwell for a security camera. It was true that he had a perfectly good reason to be at the church archives, and he wasn't on anyone's watch list. It was just that he preferred his privacy.

Seeing no cameras, he descended. He made his way through the dimly lit hallway in the church basement, checking the signs on the doors. The damp air was cool and sour like a sewer.

As instructed by the parish secretary, he entered the Archives Office door without knocking. A quick scan assured there were no security cameras there either.

A wiry stick of a man in clerical clothing came around the littered desk, pale hand extended and a faint smile on his thin lips. The fluorescent light seemed to accent his age-wrinkled face. He looked more like one of Savannah's infamous ghosts than a man of the cloth. A fly perched on the old man's shoulder, cleaning its legs. "How may I help you, my son?"

"Is this where the baptismal records are stored?"

"Yes."

"I'd like to examine one of them."

"What time frame?" The cleric raised his arm and scratched an armpit.

"Twenty-five years ago or so."

"I'm afraid those records are unavailable to the public."

"Why?"

"Rules." The old man sighed and brushed the fly off his shoulder. "The church has a lot of rules. Some rules have outlived their purpose. Some don't make sense. That's why I'm down here. Trapped by a senseless church rule. Ah. The sin of pride. Forgive me, Lord." He blessed himself. "Enough of me. Though you can't examine those records, *I* can. What specific information do you seek?"

"The name of my father."

The priest touched his fingertips to his forehead. "Are you trying to unravel a tangled past?"

Rhett nodded.

The old man searched Rhett's face. "What do you know about this man?"

"He might be a Falcon?"

"Oh my." The priest glanced at Rhett from head to toe. "The Falcons have been beloved members of this church for generations. Let's see." The cleric sat down at his computer and gestured Rhett to sit in a wooden guest chair that had clearly outlived its usefulness. The priest squinted at the computer screen. "Oh yes. There were only two male Falcons alive twenty-five years ago. Trey and his father, Joseph Arian Falcon the Second." The cleric jotted some notes on a scrap of paper, then stood. "Give me a moment, son, while I check the actual records. Twenty-five years or so you say?"

"Yes."

The cleric left the office through a dark doorway behind the desk.

Rhett had intended to keep his quest absolutely secret, so that when he killed his father no one would associate the death with him. Now this sequestered priest knew and there was no guaranteed way to keep him quiet other than—

"What did you say your name was?" the priest asked from the doorway. The fly had returned to his shoulder.

"Trevor," Rhett quickly replied.

"Well, Trevor, this could take some time. Would you like to come back later?"

"How much time?"

"It might be an hour or so."

"I'll wait."

"Suit yourself. There's a pot of coffee in the kitchen." The old man gestured to a side door off the cluttered office. "Help yourself."

As the priest hobbled into the darkness beyond his office, Rhett wondered what the cleric had done that resulted in his exile to the archives. It was a question without a ready answer. One of many.

Rhett stood, walked behind the desk, and examined the computer screen. On display was an alphabetical list of parishioners with birth and death dates, as well as membership information. Rhett right clicked the mouse and selected the print command, careful to print only the current page. The printer sprung to life and spit out the copy. Rhett put the printout into his back pocket and headed for the kitchen.

A small metal table with two padded folding chairs was positioned at one side of the kitchen. A stained coffee maker with a mostly full pot of coffee sat on the beige Formica countertop. Rhett found a ceramic mug in the overhead cabinet, poured himself coffee and took a seat at the table. He brought the mug to his mouth and sipped. The coffee was strong and bitter. Just the way he liked it. He glanced down at the newspaper, curious to find out what was going on. He hadn't read a newspaper since leaving Virginia, not that he read them that much up there.

Rhett froze. The paper was open to the obituaries. Henrietta Snyder's obituary filled the first column. The photo that accompanied the obit closely resembled Mrs. Falcon. A quick read revealed that Mrs. Falcon was Henrietta's daughter and only survivor. Rhett found it interesting that Henrietta, a member of St. Gregory's, had been born in his home state, Virginia, and moved to Savannah rather late in life. There was a copier in the kitchen, so Rhett made a copy of the article and put it in his pocket with the computer printout.

Rhett spent the next hour reading the rest of the newspaper and drinking two more cups of the coffee.

The cleric returned somber-faced. He went to the coffee maker and wordlessly poured a cup.

Was somber the man's normal face or had he found something that upset him? Rhett figured he'd know soon enough.

The demoted priest sat across from him and blew on the top of his coffee. He probably didn't get many visitors, so there was no point in rushing things. That was fine with Rhett, as long as he found his father.

"What do you think of my coffee?" the priest asked.

"I like it. Where's it from?"

The old man smiled. "One of our missions in Guatemala."

"Do they sell it in stores?"

"Not in the United States, but they do a good trade in Guatemala. I got hooked on it when I was down there. They ship me beans whenever I need more. A thoughtful member of our parish roasts them for me."

Rhett nodded toward the back. "You find anything 'bout my baptism?"

"There were no Falcon infants baptized between Trey,

forty-five years ago, and his daughter Hayley, eighteen years ago."

Damn. He should have known just asking was too easy. But he couldn't ignore that he was somehow connected to the Falcons. "Do you have any suggestions?"

The priest cupped his pointed chin. "Where did you say you were born?"

"Virginia."

"I'd say your answer could be up there, Trevor."

Yeah. He'd wasted too much time in Savannah. But he kinda liked it here. Hell. He'd lived twenty-five years without knowing who his father was. Another week or two wouldn't matter. Maybe he'd speak with Trey Falcon. Maybe Trey would fill in the blanks on why the Falcon Law Group was sending money to his mother.

* * *

Judy's breaths came in quaking gulps as yet another massive climax ripped through her, simultaneously filling her and depleting her. She wanted more, but wondered if she could survive another. An utterly delightful situation. There was only one way to find out. She squirmed, urging Preston Somerset on. When he responded with vigor, climaxes came to her in waves until she finally submitted with, "Okay. Enough. My God, enough."

After Preston rolled off, air from the ceiling fan chilled her. She yanked the sheet over Preston and herself, squeezed his hand, and said, "That was the best ever."

"You say that every time."

She cuddled further into his body and hugged him. "Preston, honey, I sincerely mean it each time I say it. I swear, not only are you incredibly sexy, you also keep getting better."

"As long as you're happy." He gave a knowing grin.

So thoughtful. So perfect. Well, not quite perfect. To be perfect he'd have to have lots of money and he didn't. Not cash, anyway.

Although he was from old money and had become a law firm partner before reaching thirty, he claimed he never had any cash. He attributed his plight to his father's mountainous debt and the costs to maintain the rambling old mansion and hundreds of oceanfront acres of overgrown property he'd inherited. He was obsessed with both keeping his assets and improving them.

But what Preston lacked in money, he made up for with his power. He knew everyone in the Savannah establishment and knew things about most of them that forced respect to the point of servitude.

Judy didn't need his money, at least not now, but she would gladly use and abuse his power.

He rolled to his side and smoothed a thumb over her cheek.

She loved how he touched her after sex, never rushing her, letting her bask in the afterglow. He was the best, he was single, and he was hers. Hers alone. She'd made sure of that.

"Why haven't you married?"

"Too busy."

"Too busy chasing women?" she asked.

"Too busy chasing justice."

"You're a lawyer. Do you actually call what you do justice?"

"My clients do."

"I've always wanted to have children."

"So what happened?" he asked.

"Medical issues." She touched her stomach. Unresolved medical issues.

"What about adoption?"

"I wanted to adopt, but Beau refused." She let out a long

breath. "He said he'd rather have his side of the Simpsons terminate than contaminate his family name."

"Uptight, pompous jerk."

The years were passing too quickly. Years she'd never get back. Beau was a loser. It was past time to dump him. Time to move on. "Yeah. He is uptight, but maybe you and I can loosen him up a bit."

"Did you get the pictures?" His words were slow and deliberate, his face somber.

The abrupt change of topic startled her. She stared at him.

"Judy, did you get those damn pictures?"

Her sexy mood spoiled, she pulled away from him. "Not yet."

His eyes widened. "You *have* to find them. Destroy them."

She tucked the sheet under her chin. "You don't *have* to lecture me, Preston."

His eyebrows arched. "Just tell me where the pictures are."

"I don't know."

He grabbed her arm and clenched down. "Find them and destroy them."

She tossed the sheet off, stood and scooted to his bathroom. At the door, she turned and said, "I've had enough of your nagging about those damned pictures. I told you I'd take care of it, and I will."

"You're not going to do something stupid?"

"Not unless you do." She stepped into the bathroom and turned on the shower. She pulled her hair up and glanced in the mirror. Under her flushed skin, she looked tense and tired. Sleeping around was fun, but it was never easy. Complications abounded.

Preston came up behind her and nuzzled into her neck. "Come back to bed," he whispered.

"I need to dress." She cocked her head to one side, away from his, and forced a smile at his reflection in the mirror.

"Why?"

"I have a meeting." Keep it vague. They all thrived on mystery.

"Oh." He pulled away.

She stepped into the shower, the hot water washing his telltale scent from her.

* * *

THAT NIGHT, JUDY WAS BACK IN BEAU'S OFFICE TO FIND THOSE photos he claimed to have. She booted up his computer and methodically searched his picture files, finding nothing incriminating.

She tried the original images file. The folder was empty. She tried the trash bin. It had been cleaned out. Sensing Beau had recently purged his computer of anything that might compromise him, she checked the electronic calendar she had copied earlier. It too had been wiped clean.

She knew Beau was meticulous and kept files on everything. Flying blind was not in his nature. He hadn't erased anything. He'd just moved it somewhere else. But where?

Judy checked the web browser's favorites. Nothing unusual there. Then she clicked the browser's history file to see where Beau had visited in the past couple of days. She sighed. It had been cleared out.

Perhaps he had copied the photos to a DVD or a flash drive. She rummaged his desk looking for one and found nothing. But she did stumble on a short, alphabetic list of websites, usernames, and passwords on a three-by-five card in his pencil drawer.

A half hour later she'd found and deleted all copies of the seven incriminating photos. And she'd printed out the calendar, address files and financial information he'd removed from his computer and tried to hide on the web.

Satisfied, she returned the password card to the drawer and stood to leave.

Oh no. Thank God she remembered. The computer's history log would show the browser had been to all the file locations tonight. That wouldn't do. She deleted the history files, shut down his computer, wiped her fingerprints from the keyboard, and left.

Now Beau would have nothing on her, and she could sue him for a divorce and support. Preston would be happy and, with his legal expertise, helpful.

With just a few keystrokes, she'd screwed them both. One financially, the other passionately.

CHAPTER 13

*T*uesday morning, the morning Patricia usually had
breakfast with her mom, seemed bittersweet. For
the first time in several nights, she'd slept soundly. Though
still filled with grief, she'd awakened rested and eager to
learn what her friends had unearthed about Sonny and her
mother.

Trey had been bright and cheerful over breakfast. He left
home seemingly looking forward to his day.

Hayley was back in school for the semester, and had
called to let Patricia know she'd made it back to Atlanta
without incident. That disaster had been averted, if only
temporarily. Trey, her rock, had worked his magic once
again. Sure, he could use lethal force when necessary, but he
could also charm with equal effectiveness.

Shortly after Trey had left, Rhett had shown up to prune
the foundation shrubs. A couple of hours later, Patricia took
him some water. As he drank from the bottle, she gestured to
one of the trimmed shrubs. "You seem to have a talent for
shaping the bushes naturally."

"Thank you." He took another large gulp of water then

screwed the cap on and put the bottle on a patio table. "Could you do me a favor, Mrs. Falcon?"

"Depends on what it is."

"Your husband is a lawyer, isn't he?"

"Yes."

"Could you set up a meeting for me and him?"

"He's a busy man."

"Wouldn't take but five minutes."

"Do you need a lawyer, Rhett?"

"Actually, I need some advice."

"About what? As I said, my husband is a busy man. Maybe someone else could better advise you."

"It's really personal, Mrs. Falcon."

"Five minutes?"

Rhett nodded.

"I'll see what I can do." Patricia went inside and called Trey, who accepted the five-minute appointment for later in the day. Patricia went back outside and found Rhett. "Meeting with my husband at three this afternoon."

"Thank you, Mrs. Falcon." Rhett wiped sweat from his brow. "By the way, last night just after two there was a black pickup truck parked at your curb. Someone was sitting in the cab. When I went over to ask what they were doing they drove off."

"Did you get a license number?"

Rhett looked down. "No ma'am."

"If you see the truck again, get the number. There's no telling—"

The ringing of her cell phone startled her. It was Judy.

"I have to take this," Patricia said as she headed back inside.

"Bad news," Judy said. "The paper trail on Sonny is surprisingly monotonous."

Patricia sighed. "Bring every shred you have to our lunch

meeting. When we get everything together, some of the dull, insignificant bits might take on greater significance."

"I sure hope so 'cause what I found doesn't add up to much."

Alisa called Patricia shortly after citing car trouble that had interfered with a couple of key meetings.

Patricia encouraged her to continue checking people right up to the lunch meeting.

It was the call from Meredith that put Patricia over the edge. Because of an unscheduled bank audit, Meredith had gotten nothing done on the case. It was as if God had decreed that Mama's murderer would have a get out of jail free card for the past eighteen hours. *That* just wouldn't do.

She called everyone and postponed the lunch meeting until the next day. Once done, she ran her fingers through her hair. What had she overlooked? Twisting a strand in her fingertips, a thought gelled. Mama was gone, but her hair remained. Hair in her hairbrush. Hair that would hold traces of her medicines and possibly of a foreign substance.

* * *

TREY'S OFFICE INTERCOM BEEPED.

He acknowledged the call.

"Mr. Rhett Putnam is here to see you."

"Show him in." Trey stood and buttoned his jacket.

The office door opened. Rhett, dressed in clean jeans and a fresh blue work shirt, filled the doorway.

Trey couldn't help but notice the strange and yet almost endearing look on the man's face as he approached him. And when Trey took Rhett's hand, he thought it odd Rhett cupped Trey's hand with both of his. Trey gestured to the set of high-back leather chairs arranged around the glass coffee table. Rhett took one, Trey the other. The receptionist hovered.

"Would you care for some coffee?" Trey asked.

Rhett nodded as his fingers traced the brass rivets clamping the leather to the oak frame of the chair.

As soon as the receptionist left for the coffee, Trey said, "Patsy and I are quite impressed with your work around the yard."

"Thank you, sir."

"Please call me Trey."

Rhett smiled. "Thank you, Trey."

"Are you new to the city?"

Rhett, apparently a man a few words, nodded.

"Planning to stay?"

"Don't rightly know. Might. Might not."

"We'd be pleased if you'd tend the yard for as long as you're here."

"My pleasure, sir. Ah, Trey."

The receptionist returned with the coffee and left.

"You asked for this meeting, Rhett. Patricia said you were very insistent, and yet you wouldn't give her a subject. Normally I require a subject, but you had a great ambassador in Patricia. What is it you wanted to talk about?"

Rhett sat like a mannequin for a long second, staring at Trey. Then he squirmed in his chair, leaning forward. "This." Rhett pulled a folded plastic sleeve from his rear pocket and eyed it for a second, as if the object had great worth, before extending the mystery item toward Trey.

The folder contained a letter on old Falcon Law stationary. The letter was dated ten years previous and was addressed to Kira Putnam at an address in Virginia. It was signed by Trey and appeared to be one of the standard cover letters he used for sending money to the foster parents of the children Henrietta had supported. All seemed to be in order. "What do you want to know about this letter?"

Rhett pushed back his long black hair. "Kira is ... was my mother. Why were you sending her money?"

"Give me a moment," Trey said. He stood, went to his computer, and brought up the master file on Henrietta's wards. All twenty of them. As he had suspected, Rhett was one of the twenty, and Kira Putnam was his foster mother. Trey returned to the chair and sat. He sipped coffee as he studied Rhett, then said, "Henrietta Snyder, my mother-in-law, was a kind and generous woman. One of her many acts of kindness was to provide financial aid for a number of orphans from the rural areas of Virginia. When Henrietta moved to Savannah, she asked me to handle the monthly distributions, which kept her participation anonymous. You are one of the children she provided for."

Rhett nodded. He looked like he was about to ask a question, but he remained silent.

"Is this letter why you came to Savannah?"

"Yes."

"Are you satisfied?"

"I had hoped to find out who my father was."

"Ah." Trey glanced away. "I think I understand. Did you think I was your father? Is that why you're here? Because I was sending your mother money?"

"Yes, sir." Rhett rubbed his hands together.

Trey reached out and clutched Rhett's hands. "I'm very sorry, Rhett, but I was just providing a service for a lovely and generous Southern lady. I'd guess you'd have to go back to Virginia to get more information about your dad."

* * *

"PRESTON, HONEY, I FOUND AND DELETED ALL THE DIGITAL

copies of seven compromising photos of us in your bed."
Judy shifted the phone to her other ear. "All the photos are
from the same angle and were taken the same day, though
with considerable time between the shots." As she talked she
scanned the kitchen for a hidden camera. Anyone who would
sneak a camera into Preston's bedroom could just as easily
have put one in her kitchen. Paranoid? Sure. A normal
reaction.

"What angle were the photos from?" he asked. "I'll look
for the camera tonight."

Was her phone or computer bugged? Just to be safe she
should buy a new phone. One identical to her current phone
so Beau wouldn't notice the switch. Probably buy a new
computer too. And she'd change her passwords as soon as
she got off the phone. There was no telling how far Beau's
investigation of her had gone.

"Judy, what angle?" Preston's clipped words signaled
agitation.

"If the camera is still there, it's probably hidden in something on top of your dresser."

"Thanks. I'll check. Can't have any more pictures turn up.
Any idea what day the photos were taken?"

"According to the photo properties data, they were taken
a week ago. Friday afternoon."

"Interesting."

"How?"

"I had a party Thursday night."

A chill ripped through her. "That narrows the list of
suspects."

"I'll say. Beau wasn't there, but several of my guests that
night are chums with Beau."

She debated how to reply. She'd slept with many of Beau's
chums and, given the secrets she knew about each, she questioned if any would risk alienating her. But the camera

planter might reasonably assume his participation would remain a secret. "So what do we do next?"

"If the camera isn't there, we'll know someone removed it, presumably the person who put it there in the first place. I can't imagine Beau involving two people in this. He'd want to keep the number of conspirators to as few as possible. So, if there's no camera I'll draw up a list of who's been in my home since the party and run that against the party list. *Voila.* Our culprit."

"What then?"

"I'll confront the informant, turn him to our side, and unleash him on Beau."

She laughed at the thought of Beau being badgered by his own helper.

Preston didn't.

* * *

TREY CLOSED THE BACK DOOR OF THE COALITION meetinghouse, waited for the electronic deadbolt to engage and, steadying himself with the rail, descended the stone stairs to the secure basement meeting room.

How many times had he gone down the stairs to find solutions to insurmountable problems? At the foot of the stairs, murmurs replaced the silence. He stepped into the room, crossed to the table, and shook hands with each man. Each revealed his present state of mind in his response. Touch. Tone. Expression. Each seemed eager. That pleased Trey.

"Shall we start?" he asked, then sat in his designated chair. "Beau, what do you have on the medical situation?"

"I've spoken with our pharmacist contact. He can find no record of any pharmaceuticals being sold to Henrietta Snyder other than those I've prescribed."

"Potter, how are you coming at reconstructing her activities that day?"

"She seems to have been at home alone all morning until she left to visit her Patricia, then went to her club to play tennis with Judy Simpson, whom she played with each week at the same time. Henrietta spoke with the pro shop professional before the match and had a late lunch with Judy after the match. She had no other contacts that I could determine. Club security cameras fix the timing of her arrival and departure."

"Do we have copies of those videos?"

Potter nodded.

"Have Beau look at them to see if he can notice anything unusual about her behavior."

"Will do." Potter consulted his computer. "Our TSA contact says Sonny's name isn't on any recent commercial flight manifests and Immigration has no record of him recently passing out or into the country. Buses and trains equally negative. Though, with the amount of money available to him, he could easily travel undetected anywhere."

"What do you have, Alton?"

"Chief Patrick says Sonny's car is in his garage and his bank accounts were emptied shortly before Henrietta's death. Police investigators found Sonny's passport in his safety deposit box, and there has been no activity on his credit cards or cell phone since early the day of Henrietta's death. Chief Patrick suspects Sonny is no longer with us."

"I'll believe that when I see his corpse," Trey said. "Relatives?"

"None living."

"Hempfield, what do you have on Sonny's activities at work?"

"Facial recognition of security footage indicates Sonny has recently associated with Russian organized crime figures.

Analysis of his books indicates three are clients. All three clients visited during the week before Henrietta's death."

"Do we have any relationship with those Russians?" Trey asked.

"We're in negotiations with one of them over using a warehouse on the wharf, though the negotiations are bogged down."

"See if our negotiator can shed any light on Sonny."

"Right."

"Okay. Good work. Keep digging," Trey said. "Same time tomorrow."

CHAPTER 14

The rising sun shimmered on the calm ocean. Standing at the back of the boat with Trey, Patricia twisted the urn's lid. She placed the top on the starboard bench and, with a slight catch in her voice, prayed. "Dear Lord, bless these final remnants of Mama."

Once the ashes in the urn were merged with the salt water, Mama would only exist in spirit. Not gone. How could she ever be gone when she lived so vividly in memory?

An old conversation with her mother came to mind. "I want to die on a tennis court, not in some God-awful hospital bed."

Well, Mama, you almost got that wish.

Then there was the time last month when they'd walked on the beach and watched sea worm castings being erased by the waves. Her mother had pondered how transient life was that day. A premonition?

Patricia's wedding came to mind. Mama had doted on her and had been so happy. Now her mother wouldn't be able to dote at Hayley's wedding, whenever that occurred. *How could Mama be gone?*

A recent conversation with her mother surfaced. Mama had pushed her to give more back to Savannah, to provide more plentifully for the unfortunate. A tear rolled down Patricia's cheek as she thought of her mother's generosity. Her eagerness to help, to serve. Mama was as giving as they came. She was always helping others, always giving time, money and love. She'd changed so many lives with her generosity.

With her back to the wind, Patricia shook the gray powder into the breeze and watched the dust dissolve into the ocean's surface.

"Goodbye, Mama." Not really goodbye. It was goodbye to remnants, not to memory. Mama would live in memory for all eternity.

Patricia stooped at the transom and washed out the last flakes from the urn. Cleansed of Mama's dust, the container no longer had any significance. Now it was just a cheap plastic urn destined for the garbage bin. The urn had been precious with Mama's ashes. Emptied, it was useless.

She put the container into her backpack, nodded to Trey, and sat on the bench, her face turned to the rising sun. The inboard engine started up, heralding her return to reality, to normalcy. If there was such a thing.

Trey popped the cork on a bottle of Henrietta's favorite champagne and they toasted her dear Mama.

* * *

FATHER JOHN SAT IN SILENCE AS BISHOP REILLY, PRELATE OF St. Gregory's, read the papal encyclical. The bishop's empty alabaster face gave no hint of his reaction, even as he finished reading and removed his glasses. He glanced down at the reading glasses, idly turning them from side to side, then let out a breath and looked up. "Mrs. Snyder's untimely death troubles us all." His voice resonated from deep in his chest. "Naturally we will cooperate fully with your investigation."

"Thank you, your Excellency. I'd like to speak with her confessor."

"I'm her confessor."

"Do you know if anyone in particular would want her dead?"

The bishop folded his hands. His eyes never left Father John's face. "I know of no one who would want her dead."

"Did she have any enemies?"

"I wouldn't say she had enemies, though there are some who concerned her."

"Concern, or fear."

"Closer to troubled her, though she feared a few."

"I'll need a list."

His brow furrowed. "Now?"

The papal encyclical was clear on the matter. Everything was to be made available. "If you don't mind, your Excellency."

The bishop made the list and handed it to Father John. There were five names.

"What can you tell me about these people?"

"Trey Falcon, the first person on the list, is her son-in-law. Henrietta moved here from Virginia relatively late in life. Trey and Henrietta seemed to have a cordial relationship until recently when she acquired the notion Trey was after her local property. I can't fathom how she ever came to that conclusion."

"Do you know this Trey Falcon?"

"Oh yes. His family has been members of this parish since our founding. He's a fine, upstanding man."

"Capable of murder?"

The bishop massaged his forehead with his fingertips and mumbled, "Most certainly."

"Is he likely to have murdered Mrs. Snyder?"

"Not at all." He folded his hands once again.

Father John rearranged himself in the office chair. "Beau Simpson, the second name. Why is he on the list?"

"Beau is ... was Henrietta's cardiologist. They argued frequently over her medications."

"Why didn't she change physicians?"

"I wouldn't know."

"Is he a murderer?"

The bishop took in a breath and released it slowly. "Some of his patients have died."

"That's not murder."

"Under the right conditions, it might be."

"Were the circumstances surrounding Henrietta's death the right conditions?"

"I'm not a doctor, but from Dr. Simpson's perspective they could have been."

"His perspective being?"

"She had money. He didn't."

"He's a cardiologist."

"And an unsuccessful investor."

"What kind of failed investments?"

"Land."

"That he bought from Mrs. Snyder?"

"Precisely."

Father John looked down at the next name on the list. "Willie Maye?"

"He's an investigative reporter for the *Savannah Post*. He wrote a scandalous article some time ago that sullied Henrietta's reputation. Though she claimed the information was false, the newspaper never printed a retraction."

Father John nodded. There was at least one sharp investigative reporter in every major city. After a few years, they had few friends.

"A parishioner?"

"Yes. Knights of Columbus."

"Tell me about Preston Somerset."

The bishop shook his head. "A lawyer without scruples."

"A murderer?"

"Potentially."

"Any motive to kill Henrietta?

"Are money and power motives?"

Father John nodded and then tapped his finger on the last name on the list. "And Vladimir Olneki?"

The bishop stood.

Father John stood as the bishop rounded the desk.

"I'm not certain about the last name, but Henrietta was quite concerned about him."

"Why?"

"He was insistent about buying her port property, but she didn't want to sell. He implied repercussions if she didn't change her mind."

"What kind of repercussions?"

"Vague enough to avoid legal proceedings, but serious." The bishop's eyelids drooped; he was the picture of fatigue.

"I'm sure it's been a long day for you. Just one more question. Is this Vladimir fellow a member of your parish?"

"No."

"Have you ever met him?"

Bishop Reilly shook his head and extended his hand. Father John knelt, kissed his ring and left. It had been an exceptionally productive meeting.

* * *

FATHER JOHN STOOD, CANE IN HAND, OUTSIDE A SEAFOOD restaurant on River Street waiting for Willie Maye, the reporter. Willie said he'd be wearing a tan seersucker suit.

John spotted him half a block away. Ginger hair, a bit too long. A thin cigar. Darker pigmentation than healthy. White buck shoes. Shorter than Father John's six foot two, and stouter.

Willie tossed his unlit Tiparillo in the cigarette depository, opened the door, and ushered Father John straight to the bar.

"Faster service," he explained.

They ordered draft beer and fried shrimp platters.

Once the beer arrived and the obligatory small talk subsided, Father John asked, "I understand you wrote a controversial article on Henrietta Snyder a couple of years ago."

Willie waggled his hand. "Controversial, yes. About Mrs. Snyder, not really. She was a secondary player in the scheme."

"Scheme?" Father John had already read the article.

"Real estate fraud."

"Local?"

Willie nodded.

"You built a file on Mrs. Snyder?"

"Is this about her death?" Willie sipped his beer.

"I'll need to see Mrs. Snyder's file."

"Why?"

"A church matter of the greatest importance."

Willie raised his bushy eyebrows. "A church matter, huh?"

When Father John didn't answer, Willie's shoulders slumped. "The file is big."

"I want everything you have."

"Okay. Stop by my office around four. I'll have it copied by then."

Father John nodded his approval as their shrimp platters arrived.

"You know," Willie gestured with a shrimp, "I could be of

big help to you. I know this city and its secrets like the back of my hand."

"I'll think about it."

Willie took a bite of shrimp, obviously pleased with his meal if not with the outcome of his lame proposal.

* * *

WHEN THE DRIVER OPENED THE LIMO DOOR, TREY TOOK Patricia's arm and guided her to the familiar entrance. Honeysuckle-scented, air-conditioned air enveloped her as she stepped into her favorite restaurant. Though the main dining room was full, the hushed atmosphere invited relaxation.

The maître d' led them to a secluded corner, their table, and took their wine order. Seated with Trey, she felt safe, optimistic, and eager. Pleasant memories of special occasions celebrated at this table swelled her heart.

Trey smiled from across the table. Care. Consideration. Love. It was all here. An exceptional life with an exceptional man. She was so fortunate. How great it was to have Trey to lean on during this difficult time.

"Did you know Judy had lunch with your mother the day she died?" Trey asked.

"They had lunch after tennis every week."

The sommelier poured Trey a taste of the Pommard wine. On Trey's approval, the wine steward completed the service.

"Do you know if Judy noticed anything unusual that day?"

Patricia thought back to her conversation with Judy. "She said Mama was completely on her game."

Trey swirled his glass, studied the wine, and then looked up. "Chief Patrick thinks that if Mama's accountant isn't dead, he's still in town. Sonny's car is in his garage and they found his passport in his safety deposit box."

"That doesn't add up to much."

Trey nodded. "There's been no activity on his credit cards or cell phone since the morning of Mama's death, and from security video they can tell Sonny saw three Russian organized crime figures in the week before he disappeared."

Her pulse sped. She leaned back in her chair. "Do you think they embezzled Mama's money and killed Sonny?"

"It's possible." Trey took a sip of wine. "Too bad Henrietta requested cremation. Not knowing the exact cause of her death complicates the investigation."

Patricia removed a small paper bag from her purse and handed the crinkled sack to Trey.

"What's this?"

"Mama's hairbrush."

He blew her an air kiss. "Good thinking."

CHAPTER 15

*S*eated at the bar, Willie touched the digital recorder in his pocket, certain he'd captured every word of his just completed conversation with Father John. His instinct told him there was a story there, a big one. Pulitzer Prize big. But where? He took a long sip of beer. Father John had made it clear he represented the Pope. Why would the Vatican be interested in Henrietta Snyder after her death, in particular his article and his full file about the alleged fraud?

Henrietta had tons of money. Was she a big contributor? She owned prime land. Could the Catholic Church be involved in Henrietta's land schemes?

Why was the Holy See interested? Willie rubbed his chin. Why?

He'd heard rumors about the church's tentacles in Savannah. They probably had unrivaled resources for investigating anything in the city.

But destiny had brought this dark, intriguing person named Father John to *him*, turning his day upside down. Running his fingers through his tangled ginger hair, Willie stewed over how to play the opportunity. A time-sensitive story like this required decisive action. Indecision could kill a reporter's career. Should he follow the enigmatic Father John or jump right into further researching Henrietta's death?

Like a spider on a web, Willie wondered which path was best. If Henrietta Snyder had been murdered, someone knew the secret of her death. The motive. The means. Right now, Father John knew more than Willie. The priest seemed extremely focused. He didn't seem like he'd waste time. Each step he took would be measured and relevant. Who the cleric visited mattered. Research could wait.

Willie downed the last of his beer and left. The red brick sidewalk stretched out before him. He glanced right and left down cobbled-stoned street, finally spotting the black-robed cleric two blocks away. He hastened after him, maintaining a good distance.

Dodging the tourists, he savored the thought of another front-page story. A juicy murder mystery. Sensationalism. That's what drove him to investigate and write. That's what paid the bills and provided whatever success he'd had since graduation from Ohio University's School of Journalism.

The hobbling cleric was surprisingly fast. Then the priest slowed, weaseled into a tangle of pedestrians exiting a tour bus, and ... disappeared.

Damn.

Willie stopped, wiped sweat from his forehead, and jammed a fresh Tiparillo into his mouth. He never smoked them. He just liked the hard image he projected with one hanging out of his mouth. He crossed his arms. The pounding in his chest ebbed.

"Why?" he asked, drawing out the word. "Why would the church be so interested in Henrietta Snyder?"

* * *

PATRICIA'S THROAT CLENCHED AS SHE READ THE HEADLINE. *Savannah Port Official Murdered*. After reading the first paragraph, her suspicions were confirmed. She knew the man. Her mother had done business with him

A bizarre thought made her shudder and blink. What if this man's death was somehow related to her mother's? She leaned back in the kitchen chair and said a silent prayer for the man. Then she dug her fingernails into her palms and continued reading. The poor man was found dead in his car after being shot once in the head. Mob style. There was no mob in Savannah. The Cotton Coalition had made sure of that. What the heck was going on? Still, two deaths so close?

Sure, she was grasping at straws. What else could she do? They hadn't been able to come up with a logical hypothesis for Mama's death and her missing money. Patricia's stomach knotted.

A mob connection wasn't entirely farfetched. That nasty land scheme Mama was accused of by the *Post* was said to have involved the Mafia. Mama's money and property provided a motive.

Patricia poured a fresh cup of coffee. Could Mama have been able to identify the thief? Fingering a criminal would be reason enough to kill her. And if she could identify the thief, she would have had contact with the crook. Thank God the team was working on sorting out whom Mama had seen or spoken with in her final days.

* * *

A CHILLED SIX-PACK OF BEER IN HAND, WILLIE CLIMBED THE rickety wooden steps of the old Craftsman home, rapped on the wooden door, and stepped back. When no one answered, he pounded on the door with the heel of his fist. Eventually the deadbolt clicked and the door cracked open to reveal

Burt Goodwin's scowling, craggy face. His broken nose supported wire-rimmed glasses. Salt and pepper hair framed his face.

"What do you want, Willie?"

For as long as Willie had known Burt, a retired police sergeant, he'd greeted everyone the same gruff way. Willie elevated the six-pack. "Would you believe I was in the neighborhood and decided to visit an old friend?"

Burt shook his head. "You got no legitimate business in this neighborhood. And watch out who you be callin' a friend."

The door swung open and the two men embraced. Despite his age, Burt had kept himself fit, and his vigorous hug took the breath from Willie.

Willie followed Burt to the tidy kitchen and plopped down at the rustic maple table. Though old, the table was spotless. Not a surprise. Burt obviously did more dusting than most home plate umpires.

Burt pulled two beers from the six-pack, sat across from Willie, and shoved a bottle to the center of the table.

"Thank you kindly," Willie said.

"How you been?" Burt asked, then chugged half his beer.

Willie took a long pull on his brew, then said, "Been fine. You?"

"Can't complain. You still at the paper? Haven't seen your name on a story for a coon's age."

"Still there. Working on a story." Willie dug at the wet label on the bottle. "I need some help."

Burt leaned forward and squinted. "What kinda help?"

"Same as always."

Burt smiled. "Who's the lucky duck this time?"

"Don't rightly know yet." Willie stroked his chin. "I was hoping you might help me sort it out."

Burt finished off his bottle and went to the fridge. "Another beer?"

"One's plenty. I'm driving."

Burt returned to the table with a fresh brew cradled in his massive hand. "So, what do you be needin' from me?"

"You ever hear of Henrietta Snyder?"

Burt's eyes widened. "That ole society broad that died a few days ago?"

"That's the one." Willie lifted his bottle and drained the rest of it. "If your buddies downtown happen to be looking into her death, I could use whatever they dig up."

Burt nodded. "No problem, man."

"I knew I could count on you. How's your daughter doin'? She finish college yet?"

"She graduated with honors last May. Workin' at the coroner's office."

"At the coroner's office?" Willie scooted forward on his chair. "Ah, you think she might know something about Mrs. Snyder's passing?"

Burt flexed his shoulders in the middle of a swig.

"Mind asking her?" Willie asked.

Burt nodded through a belch.

"I knew your daughter would do well." Willie stood. "As much as I enjoy spending time with you, I gotta go. Tell your daughter I said hello."

"Sure 'nuf, Willie." Burt walked Willie to the door. "Don't worry none, man. I'll get that information right quick."

"I 'preciate that."

* * *

WILLIE'S NEXT STOP WAS HIS OFFICE. HE STILL HAD TO COPY Henrietta's full file for Father John.

Twenty minutes later, Willie took the worn granite steps

of the *Savannah Post* building two at a time. He didn't want to give Father John the research file on Henrietta Snyder, but the priest had been clear that cooperation was required.

Willie smiled at the familiar guard, bounded through the security arch in the black marble lobby, and dashed for the open elevator. After a quick ride to the third floor, he exited the elevator and went to the central records department, where he asked the clerk to retrieve the file.

Back at his desk, one of many shoved together in the center of the reporter's pool, he took off his jacket, jammed a fresh Tiparillo in his mouth and pawed through the thick file, removing some sensitive documents. He had no idea what the penalty was for failing to give the priest everything, but information was his only power.

After making some quick notes for his own research, he dropped the file off at the reproduction room, getting a snarl from the clerk when he asked for the job to be completed immediately. Willie knew everyone asked for the same priority and took no offense at the snarl. He also knew the copies would be done promptly, well before the four o'clock deadline.

On returning to his desk, Willie keyed in Henrietta's original surname, Duff, to the news network search engine. Her obit came up as the most recent item. He printed that off. He also printed out a slew of articles about her father, Richard Duff, who was reported to have CIA connections. He'd unravel Richard's story later.

What intrigued Willie most was a short article about Henrietta joining the Peace Corps right out of college and being sent to a remote village in Italy, the birthplace of the present pope. Could that be the connection?

A bit later, Willie found an article about Richard Duff contributing a substantial sum to a parish orphanage in Italy. Shockingly, the priest overseeing the orphanage was the man who was now the pope. The link was established. But why would the pope be interested in Henrietta's death? There had to be more than money.

The copies of Henrietta's file were delivered shortly before Willie received a call that Father John had arrived. Clamping down on his anxiety, Willie went to the first-floor lobby.

Father John gave him a firm handshake. Too firm. With Willie's hand still in Father John's vise-like grip, the priest said, "Mister Maye, you made a big mistake following me earlier. You do not want to provoke me. When I leave you this time, don't even think about following me. *Capisce?*"

Willie looked into Father John's eyes. Willie had seen piercing eyes like that only once before. He shivered. Fear tightened his throat. Willie reached for his Tums and nodded.

Father John released his grip. "Where are my copies?"

"Upstairs."

Willie, heart racing, led the priest to the third floor and into a small conference room. "Coffee?" he asked, trying to sound relaxed.

"If you don't mind."

Still disconcerted from Father John's threat, Willie returned with the copies and a carafe of coffee. He poured two mugs, shoved one across the table, and sat opposite him. "I found something interesting."

"What's that?" Father John asked.

"Henrietta worked in the Peace Corps in the same village where the present pope was born. Sometime later, her parents took an interest in the Holy Father's work."

Father John shrugged as if it was old news.

"But that alone wouldn't explain why you're investigating her death. So, what gives?"

"I'm investigating the circumstances of her death, not her relationship with the Sovereign Pontiff. Anything else?"

"I'd really like to work with you on this."

"I work alone." Father John's eyes again bore into Willie's. "And I will not tolerate any interference from you. Find something else to work on."

Willie waggled his hand. "Just trying to do my job."

"At this point, Willie, *your* job has absolutely nothing more to do with Henrietta Snyder."

Yeah, right. Willie slid the file copies across the table to Father John.

"Not a word of this to anyone," Father John said as he took the file and stood.

"I understand." Willie's skin tingled. You bet he understood. He understood there was a huge story here. That's what he understood. And nobody, not even the Pope, was going to stop him from getting it.

CHAPTER 16

$\mathcal{T}$rey's four Cotton Coalition colleagues and their aides had all arrived at the secure bunker within ten minutes of the two o'clock start time. Not an easy thing for any of them to do on short notice, but none groused. The murder of the port official had to be addressed promptly since he was a friend of Henrietta's. Trey didn't believe in coincidences.

"Let's get started." Trey scanned the faces of his peers and, seeing no objection, continued. "Chief Patrick has concluded the port official shooting was a professional hit. One shot. Large caliber rifle bullet. From elevation. Middle of the day. No witnesses. No evidence at the presumed shooting site."

"Other than our Russian visitors, no one in town has this level of expertise," Alton said, his voice weak having just returned from radiation treatments.

"Plus, Vladimir has made it clear his organization would like to control at least a portion of the port," Beau added. "That's certainly motive."

"Before we jump to conclusions, we need to be sure it's the Russians," Hempfield said in a booming baritone. "After all, our dialogue with Vladimir has been cordial if not decisive. We're making progress in our discussions with him. Why would he risk offending us with an assassination? He's well aware of our position on felony criminal activity in Savannah."

Trey could always count on Hempfield, a former state senator, to prioritize logic over emotion. "At this stage, we don't know Vladimir well enough to fully understand his methods," Trey said. "But if he's behind this, we have to quickly shut down this kind of activity."

"Confront him?" Hempfield asked.

"Not until we're certain he's behind it," Trey replied. "Beau, let's bring his associates into the operating room, one at a time, and see if we can get a reliable confession."

Beau smiled. "I'll get on it as soon as the meeting is concluded. Hempfield, I'll need to know where his three thugs are today and their pub preferences. Potter, I'll need your magic for half an hour at five."

Potter, an amateur magician as well as a noted architect, nodded.

Hempfield texted. Moments later his mobile phone chirped. He read the text and then said, "Vladimir's boys live in separate rooms at the same hotel. Each drinks and eats alone. Apparently, they feel they're harder to track individually. They do more drinking than eating. Same bars each night. All in the historic district within walking distance from their hotel." Hempfield keyed his laptop. A photograph of a man came up on Trey's laptop. "Based on our psychological profiles of the men, this one, Boris, seems the one most likely to break."

"Why?" Trey asked.

"Lack of commitment. He's in with these thugs for the easy money. If things get hard for him, we believe he'll turn."

"We'll take him tonight at happy hour," Beau said. "If he doesn't cooperate, we'll take the other two after dinner."

"Sounds good," Trey said. "Any new leads on Henrietta's murder?"

"We've dug into everyone who saw Henrietta on the day of her death," Potter said. "Everything fits. There's nothing suspicious."

Trey's back stiffened. He'd been hoping for a breakthrough. "What do you have, Hempfield?"

"As you know, Sonny had considerable contact with the Russians the week before Henrietta's death. Other than them, Sonny's contacts were normal. I spoke with Vladimir this morning. He said they use Sonny to handle large sums of their money. I've confirmed the money is still in their escrow account. They also used Sonny as a front for some large land acquisitions near the port facilities. Vladimir said he didn't realize Sonny was missing, but wasn't surprised. He wouldn't go into specifics."

"You may be onto something there. Keep digging," Trey said.

"Sonny's activities on the day of Henrietta's death were normal," Potter said. "Until he disappeared."

"What time is the last documented record of activity for Sonny?" Trey asked.

Potter consulted his laptop. "A five-minute cell phone call at ten a.m. from Preston Somerset, a long-established client. Preston has no known connection to Henrietta or to organized crime. Sonny took the call at home. After that, nothing."

Trey straightened. He didn't much like Preston. The man was always scheming. Not as bad as Preston's father, but scheming nevertheless. "I'll look into Preston's relationship with Sonny."

"Chief Patrick says his homicide investigator is baffled by

Henrietta's case." Alton cleared his throat. "He asked if we'd found anything yet. I told him no. Apparently, the church is looking into her death as well. A priest from out of town contacted Chief Patrick and asked for information."

"Why would the church be interested?" Trey asked.

"Chief Patrick asked the same question and was stonewalled by the priest."

"Is he cooperating with the priest?"

Alton nodded. "When the priest showed Patrick a papal letter of authority, Patrick, as a loyal Catholic, offered full cooperation."

"See if you can get the priest's name, photo, anything from Chief Patrick we can use to identify him."

"My daughter's working on it as we speak," Alton replied.

"Beau, did you have an opportunity to look at the country club security tapes from the day of Henrietta's death?" Trey asked.

"I did. She appeared somewhat unstable when she left the club after lunch. She was stable going in."

"Indicating?"

"Possible intoxication of some sort."

"Did you check her lunch receipt?"

Beau nodded. "She consumed no alcohol at lunch."

Trey bolted from his seat. "She entered stable and came out wobbly. Something had to have happened to her at lunch."

"Hold on, Trey," Beau said. "Ruling out intoxication, there are possible medical causes of wobbliness."

"You're her doctor." Trey locked eyes with Beau. "Did she suffer a medical condition that would explain her sudden unsteadiness?"

"No."

Trey raised his hands, palm up. "So, she had or developed a condition you were unaware of?"

"Possibly."

Trey narrowed his eyes. "Doesn't sound like murder."

"It wouldn't be, unless someone induced the condition."

Trey cocked his head. "We have the hair sample. Could that reveal a chemical that would affect her motor functions like balance?"

"It might, if she used or abused the chemical over an extended period of time."

"When will we receive the lab results?"

"A couple of weeks for the detailed analysis we requested."

"Too slow."

Beau sighed. "It's been expedited, but because hair grows so slowly the analysis won't help if the inducement occurred the day of her death."

Trey took a deep breath. "So, someone who works at the club could have put something in her food that would cause her death, and it wouldn't show in her hair?"

"Yes. That's a possible scenario."

"Potter, check everyone at the club who had access to her food or beverage on the day of her death."

Potter nodded.

"Anyone have any other business?" Trey asked. "If not, we'll adjourn."

* * *

BEAU WATCHED THE RUSSIAN KNOWN AS BORIS TRAVERSE THE shaded square and lumber into the corner pub, a well-known local hangout frequented by lawyers and business people. All the historic woodwork had been salvaged from a reclamation project in Ireland. A touch of home for those who could pay the price of a drink. Beau checked the time on his smartphone. Happy hour. The place would be busy.

A minute later, Potter, dressed in black slacks and a gray short-sleeved shirt, followed the Russian in.

With an eye on the pub, Beau sat on a park bench and stretched his legs. His muscles were cramped with tension. He didn't like exposing himself to the possibility of criminal charges if he made a mistake and got caught. But, tension or not, this nasty business required his expertise.

He rose from the bench. As he walked toward the bar, touched the vial of doctored vodka in the front pocket of his slacks. Tasteless. Colorless. Odorless. Just enough to produce the right symptoms.

He glanced down the adjacent side street. The ambulance that would respond was in place. Soon the Russian would be stretched out on Beau's operating table.

Beau's heart hammered as he followed a young couple into the bar. Happy hour chaotic. Perfect cover.

He wiped his sweaty palm on his pants, moved to the entrance wall, and waited for his eyes to adjust. He scanned for security cameras and saw one focused on the cash register. No others were apparent.

Beau loosened his tie and adjusted the scratchy collar of his starched oxford shirt. His anxiety was too close to the surface and would draw attention to him. He was known; his picture was often splashed on television and in the papers. He had to calm down and blend in with the crowd, until needed. He took a deep breath.

Someone tapped Beau on the shoulder. Beau turned to face a severely inebriated redhead he didn't recognize.

"Thank you, Doctor Simpson, for saving my husband's life."

So much for being inconspicuous. "My pleasure."

"Can I buy you a drink?"

"I'm on call."

"Coffee? Tea?"

"I'll take a pass."

"Well, thank you again for saving his life," she said, then turned and headed deeper into the pub.

Potter sat at the bar next to the Russian, keeping to himself. The Russian was chatting up a young blonde half his age.

Beau came up behind Potter, their eyes briefly meeting in the mirror, then leaned his elbows on the bar between the Russian and Potter to yell a drink order at the bartender. Beau's hand lingered over Potter's drink and emptied the drugged alcohol into Potter's glass. Beau retreated when the bartender filled his order.

Potter, an amateur magician, stretched his arm in front of the Russian to grab a menu from a vertical stack clipped to the bar. As his shoulder blocked the Russian's forward view, he deftly exchanged drinks with the Russian.

Beau headed for the men's room to clean and dispose of the vial.

Potter paid his bill and, when Beau emerged from the men's room, went to the front of the pub.

Beau moved closer to the bar and kept an eye on the Russian.

One minute after the Russian took a hefty gulp of his vodka, he slumped to the floor. Patrons around him backed away.

Beau rushed in. "I'm a doctor," Beau shouted as he knelt by the man. "Someone call 911."

Potter noticed the bartender reaching for his phone. "I've already got it," shouted Potter, elevating his phone. Potter called the driver of the complicit ambulance, then left.

Beau gave CPR to no avail until the fake EMS crew arrived.

"We'll take it from here," a paramedic said.

Beau, shoulders bunched from the CPR, left.

* * *

THE RUSSIAN WAS ALREADY PREPPED AND STRAPPED TO AN operating table when Beau, dressed in surgical scrubs and mask, entered the mock surgery room. The Russian, Beau and Trey were the only ones in the room. Beau, his hands still unsteady from being recognized at the pub, glanced at Trey standing in the shadows above the head of the bed so he couldn't be seen. The Russian was in the twilight of conscious sedation under the influence of a common truth serum. Aware, but relatively immobile.

Beau looked at the Russian's scowling face. Glaring eyes. Flushed cheeks. No fear there, just raw anger. The thug was partially drugged and fully restrained. He could hear and speak. He might pee himself, and he'd certainly spew all his secrets.

After checking the Russian's vitals and finding them in order, Beau turned on the overhead light.

The Russian's eyes snapped shut.

Beau settled on a stool next to the operating table and brought his masked mouth to the Russian's cauliflower ear. "Can you hear me, Boris?"

"*Da,*" the Russian said in a husky voice.

"English, please."

Boris remained silent.

Beau quelled his impatience. Bedside manner was critical at this stage. Boris was a professional criminal. He certainly knew the drill, as well as the likely consequences for resistance. He just needed some encouragement. "This can be short or long, Boris. If you cooperate you'll be back in your hotel room within the hour. *Vy ponimayete maniya?* Do you understand?"

Boris remained silent.

"*Zhdu vashego otveta.* I'm waiting for your response."

"*Da.*"

Beau sighed his displeasure. "English, please."

The Russian's blunt features softened. "Yes."

Beau sat back on the stool. "Good. Now that we understand each other, let's get down to business and get you right back to your hotel."

Boris nodded.

"A port official was killed yesterday. I'm interested in knowing if Vladimir was involved. If you or Vladimir were involved, I'm not here to punish. I only seek information."

"I understand," Boris mumbled. "No one will know of this?"

"No one." *Not even you, thanks to the amnesia effect of the conscious sedation.* "So, tell me, was Vladimir involved?"

"Vladimir ordered assassination so certain others would know how serious he is about success here."

"Others?"

"A secret local organization we know as Cotton Coalition. Bad people. Very dangerous."

"Thank you. Just two more questions and then we'll return you to your hotel. Was Vladimir involved in the killing of Henrietta Snyder?"

"No. But he *vas* interested in purchasing all her property near the port."

"Did he actually purchase her land?"

"No. But the negotiations were ongoing."

"Thank you. Last question. Was Vladimir involved in the killing of Sonny Carothers?"

"Killing? Mr. Carothers is dead? Where? How?"

"Thank you." Beau reached a gloved hand up to the drip line and added more sedative.

Moments later Boris was fully sedated. He'd awaken hours later in his hotel bed with a headache and no memory of the interrogation.

CHAPTER 17

*T*he front door bell pealed. Patricia went to the foyer and checked the security monitor. She froze. It was the reporter who had slandered her mother. The bell pealed again. She doubted he'd leave of his own accord, so she released the deadbolt and opened the door.

"Hello, Mrs. Falcon. I'm Willie Maye." He extended his hand.

"I know who you are," she said, not accepting his offered hand. "And I don't have anything to say to you."

"Was your mother on any medications?"

"No comment." Patricia began to ease the door closed.

He stepped forward. "Was your mother murdered?"

She wasn't about to get into any discussion with him. "No!"

"Then why is the church looking into her death?"

She opened the door and stepped up to the man. "Who told you that?"

"A source."

"And your so-called source thinks she was murdered?"

He stepped back and nodded.

"And *you* think she was murdered?"

"It would make a good story if she had been."

"And you're looking to tell it?"

"I am."

"Look, you can't report on that right now. There are things going on that you don't understand."

"What things?"

"I'm not at liberty to say."

"OK. I have a fair amount of details. I'll print what I know."

"You know you don't have enough to go to press. That's why you're here talking with me. Hold off and I'll give you everything when I get the full facts. An exclusive."

"Are you directly involved in the investigation?"

She nodded.

"Are you working with the police?"

She nodded.

"Then I can talk to them."

"You know better than that, Willie." She locked eyes with him. "Their spokesman will say they can't comment on an active case."

He let out a long sigh. "But you will? Exclusively?"

"Of course. Provided you hold off."

"Okay. I'll hold off publication for a week. After that, I'm going with what I have."

He extended his hand.

This time she took it.

Back in the great room after Willie left, she saw Mama's photo and recalled their last Easter together. Patricia wasn't looking forward to Easter without her fun-loving, effervescent mother. All Patricia had now were memories. Good memories. And gratitude for all Mama had done.

She hated the idea Mama's good name might be sullied again by another so-called news story. But there was little

Patricia could do. The reporter would write his story with or without her. A story no doubt carefully constructed with libel-proof innuendo. Like any family, her family had enough scars to guarantee a sensational story.

It was his timing for the story that troubled her most. Did he know something substantial about Mama's death that would make his story news? Something Trey may not already know?

She tapped Trey's phone icon on her phone display.

"Trey, honey, a *Savannah Post* reporter was just here asking questions about Mama. I—"

"What kind of questions?"

"Her medications. The possibility she was murdered. He said he had sources. The church. I refused to answer and sent him on his way. I'm concerned he might know something about the circumstances of her death, otherwise why would he be interested in writing an article about her death right now?"

"Did you get his name?"

"Willie Maye. The one who did that horrible story a couple of years ago. He said the church is looking into her death. That he's going to publish a story. Trey, you have to do something."

"I'll get on it," Trey said. "And don't worry, I doubt whatever he thinks he has will be published."

* * *

JUDY STRODE INTO THE OSTENTATIOUS LOBBY OF BEAU'S medical practice and asked to see her husband about something important.

"He's with a patient," the young receptionist said with a smirk.

Without hesitation, Judy went to the mahogany door of

his office and turned the knob. It was locked. No surprise there. Behind her, she heard the receptionist say, "I'm sorry, Doctor. I tried to stop her but she's on her way in."

Judy spun to the right and scooted down the hall toward the secondary door, just as an attractive, buxom, middle-aged woman slinked out of Beau's office buttoning her blouse. The woman's blond hair needed a brush.

Judy went in the back entrance and found Beau seated on the sofa, sipping what was probably scotch. Dressed in wrinkled khakis and a navy polo shirt, he didn't look very professional. Far from it. Heck, he didn't even have his shoes on. He opened his mouth to greet her.

"I want a divorce," she said without preamble.

Beau stood and ambled over to her. He took a drink, gave her a cold smile. "Sure."

Her stomach churned. There was a time when his confidence inspired her. Not anymore. Now it seemed curiously misplaced. "I want half of everything you acquired during our marriage."

"No problem. My practice has been losing money for several years. Everything is mortgaged to the hilt. It would be nice if you took over the payments."

She gritted her teeth. "You know what I mean."

"No, I don't know what you mean. Enlighten me."

"I need money to live."

He shrugged. "Not my problem once you divorce me."

"It will most certainly be your problem once I get done suing you for adultery."

"Go ahead," he said as he closed the secondary door. "I'll countersue just to keep the record straight."

"What is that supposed to mean?"

"Look, Judy, I know about your affairs, just as you, apparently, know about mine. Neither of us has any business being married, especially to each other. I have no problem giving you a divorce. But you're not getting a dime."

With blood thundering in her ears, she moved closer and tilted her chin up. Their eyes locked. His glared. "You have no idea what you're up against. I have the best divorce attorney in the state," she said. "And detailed records of your indiscretions."

"Doesn't matter." His face blazed red. "We're broke. Get it through your thick skull. There. Is. No. Money!"

Her mind whirled. No. She knew better. She'd seen the deeds for his Caribbean hideaways. And Sonny, bless his heart, had found several well-financed holding companies that Beau had established. Beau had money. Plenty of it.

"That ain't gonna work on me." She stalked to the door. "See you in court."

* * *

A THUNDERCLAP BROUGHT HAYLEY'S WANDERING MIND BACK to the grim reality of her chemistry textbook. She reread another paragraph then stared out the third-floor dorm window just above her desk. Rain pounded the glass and the courtyard below appeared flooded. The weather didn't matter. She wasn't going anywhere. With studying her top priority, she never went anywhere. The incessant demands of college had broken her, stolen her spirit, and drained her strength.

In high school, she'd been fun-loving and full of energy and expectation. Back then she couldn't get enough of her four buddies. They'd been friends since first grade. Now they were spread all over the country and all they did was text each other. It wasn't the same.

She glanced down at her book, looking without seeing.

Weary, she slammed the book closed. Five more weeks and she'd be free of the insanity.

From the far side of the courtyard a lone figure in a yellow slicker came into view, running toward her dorm. She perked up. Curiosity surged. She couldn't see his face, but she'd recognize Shawn's yellow slicker and athletic gait anywhere. He hadn't called. Was there a problem?

Moments later, there was a knock at her door. Opening the door revealed a bedraggled Shawn. His smile pierced her concern. Rain pooled at his feet. He removed his slicker. His clothing was soaked from the waist down. Why had he gone through all this trouble?

As if reading her mind, he said, "I thought you might like help studying for tomorrow's chemistry exam."

"Fantastic. But look at you. You're in no condition to study. You need to dry off first. I can put your clothes and shoes in the dryer downstairs."

Shawn went into the bathroom and came out with a lavender bath towel wrapped around his waist. He handed her the wet clothes.

"I'll be right back," she said.

Five minutes later, she returned with two mugs of hot chocolate from the dorm snack bar. She handed one to Shawn. "This should warm you up a bit."

"Perfect," he said, cradling the hot mug between his large hands. Shawn sat on her bed. "Do you have any plans for summer vacation? Work? Travel?"

She sat at her desk, across from him, and admired his sleek, muscled chest. "Just hanging out at my parents' beach house a lot. You?"

"I got the approval for that summer job at the American embassy in Paris."

Hayley reached out and adjusted the towel to cover his thigh.

He chuckled.

"Clerking in the non-immigrant visa section?"

"Yeah."

Shawn seemed so focused. School. Summer job. Career. She wished she were focused. But she wasn't. She couldn't seem to find a direction that interested her. Maybe she needed a summer job other than lifeguarding at the club. She wouldn't know where to start.

"I wish I could do something interesting like that." She envied him. His bright world was expanding. Hers was uncertain.

"Come visit."

Images of the Eiffel Tower and Notre Dame Cathedral flashed into her mind. "You think?"

"Sure. You could stay with me."

"You already have a place to live in Paris?"

"Dad completed the paperwork a month ago. It's an apartment not far from the embassy. There's an extra bedroom for visitors."

She chuckled. "Your dad thinks of everything."

"Not really. He just wanted me to be close to the embassy, and the two-bedroom unit was the closest one."

"I'll talk to my parents about it," she said.

"Good. Now, about this chemistry stuff."

Her stomach tightened. "I suppose so."

CHAPTER 18

*P*atricia had been awake since two a.m. with an active mind flooded with unanswered questions.

Every time she felt like she was getting used to the fact her mother was gone, she'd see or hear something that made her think of picking up the phone to call her mother, only for it all to come crashing back.

Now at nine a.m., she slumped at the kitchen table with her third cup of coffee and the unread newspaper. The exuberant newscasters on the countertop television provided background noise that failed to distract her from her preoccupation with those unanswered questions.

When her phone pealed Meredith's ringtone, Patricia perked up. Perhaps Meredith had good news. However, not wanting to risk being further disappointed, she braced for bad news and picked up her phone.

"I found Henrietta's money," Meredith said. "What the—"

An abrupt crash sounded from the phone, followed by a sharp pop. Then hollow silence.

An electrifying bolt zapped Patricia. She shuddered. "Meredith, Meredith?"

Silence.

"Are you okay?" Patricia squeezed the phone to her ear and paced through excruciating silence. Then car sounds briefly. An accident? Adrenaline spiked. Her heart raced. "Meredith, are you there?"

Faint groaning. Muffled. Far away.

Patricia stopped. "Meredith. Meredith, talk to me! What's going on?"

"Pa ... Patricia. It's— Oh my God, no!"

A deafening boom exploded from the phone, blasting Patricia's inner ear. She gasped and dropped into a crouch. A cold sweat beaded her forehead as her mind concluded the explosion had sounded like a gunshot. "Oh God, no. No! Meredith. Talk to me. Say something." Patricia wheezed as panic grabbed her throat. "Anything."

Solitary, ear-droning nothingness.

Meredith had been there, had just spoken. Then what sounded like a gunshot, explosively close to the phone. What had happened? Fear bubbled. *Gotta call the police. Now.* Her ear ringing, she lunged for the house phone and punched 911 then moved the handset to her good ear.

"911. How may I help you?" a gravely male voice asked.

"My friend just called. I think she was in her car. And then it sounded like there was a collision, an accident. She might be hurt."

"Do you know where she was?"

"No. But then she tried to talk to me and it sounded like there was a gunshot very near the phone. Oh my God, I think Meredith has been shot. Maybe killed. You've got to do something."

Pressing her bad ear failed to ease the persistent pain. She looked at her fingers as if she expected blood, but she saw none.

"What is your friend's full name and cell phone—"

"She has OnStar, my friend has OnStar."

"What's her name?"

"Meredith Stanwick."

"Did she tell you anything about the accident?"

Patricia took a long, slow breath. "No. We had just started talking. There was a crash, then a pop. Then some moaning followed by an ear-splitting boom. Please help her."

"I have OnStar on the line. They have her location. We're dispatching someone to investigate."

"Where is she?"

"I'm sorry, I can't provide details, but I need your contact information for possible follow-up."

Patricia answered all the questions then hung up. Her mind whirled. Weak-kneed, she sat down. But she couldn't stay still. She stood and paced. Thanks to the ringing in her ears, the horrible explosion played over and over in her mind. *Oh my God, what had happened to Meredith?* Trey. Trey would be able to find out. He had the contacts. If information was available, he could get it. She pressed Trey's icon.

"I'm unavailable. Please—"

Patricia pressed the end icon. Alton and Chief Patrick were best friends. She found Alton's number in her contact list and pushed the call icon.

"Hello, Patricia," he said in weak voice. "It's been a long time. How've you been?"

"Meredith Stanwick had an accident. Her car may have exploded." Tears poured down Patricia's cheek. She brushed them aside.

"Is she okay?"

"I don't know. She was on the phone with me when it happened. I just called 911. OnStar located her car. 911 said they dispatched someone to check, but they wouldn't tell me what happened. I thought Chief Patrick—"

"Of course. Give me ten minutes and I'll get right back to you."

Patricia disconnected. Her gaze locked on the now silent phone in her trembling hand, willing the phone to ring with good news but fearing the worst. She debated the alternatives and decided that regardless of what had happened she needed to be with Meredith. Patricia messaged Trey to call her, grabbed her Bible, and headed for the car.

She sat in the quiet car in her driveway waiting for Alton's call, not knowing whether to go back into the house or to drive to the hospital. Problem was, she had no idea which hospital to go to. Her stomach churned. Stroking the smooth phone case, she thought of poor Meredith. What if Meredith was hurt? What if—

The ring of her phone broke her thought. Patricia straightened, sucked in a ragged breath, and brought the phone to her ear.

"Meredith is alive," Alton said.

"Thank God."

"She was shot in the head."

"Head? Oh my—"

"She's being rushed to Falcon Memorial. If she makes it there, she'll go straight into surgery."

"Since she was targeted in her car, is she safe in the hospital?"

"There will be protection for her there. Where are you, Patricia?"

"In front of my house." Patricia wiped her eyes, started her car and backed out the driveway, pausing for at the end. Falcon Memorial was just fifteen minutes away. "I'm heading to the hospital."

"Do you have your gun with you?"

She patted her handbag. "Yes I do."

Patricia ended the call, then scanned the streets and sidewalks. Not a car or person in sight. She backed the Escalade out into the main street and drove two blocks before slowing to a stop for a red light. Impatience mounted. She so wanted to be at Meredith's bedside when she came out of—

Suddenly the rear-collision warning system alarmed.

She shot a glance at the monitor.

A truck with a huge grill barreled in on her. It wasn't going to stop.

A quick glance ahead confirmed cars crossing the inter-section. Waiting cars blocked her right and left.

Trapped. Rear collision imminent.

Putting the steering wheel in a death grip, she floored the accelerator and shot into the gap between two slow moving cars. Horns blared. The side collision alarm sounded. Brakes screeched. She was almost through the intersection when a decelerating car scrapped the right rear bumper of her Escalade, jerking her steering wheel. But she held fast, keeping her vehicle straight until she cleared the intersection.

Shaking violently, she pulled over and called 911, then Trey. He was still unavailable.

The police and EMS arrived quickly. A female officer took her statement. Fortunately, no one was injured. Unfor-tunately, there was no trace of the truck that had tried to ram her car. The police said they were sure the intersection cameras recorded the whole incident.

Because her SUV was only slightly damaged, she was permitted to continue to the hospital.

As she neared Falcon Memorial, Patricia called Alisa.

"Meredith's been shot and someone's after me," Patricia blurted. "I'm heading to the hospital."

"What?"

"Alisa, whatever you're doing stop, go get your gun, and go to the safest place you have."

"Where are you?"

"Approaching Falcon Memorial."

"Why?"

"That's where they took Meredith."

"Oh my God. I'll meet you there."

"It's not safe. Stay home."

"I'm coming."

Patricia ended the call, then called Judy, but the call went into voicemail.

Her phone chimed. It was Trey.

"I heard about Meredith," he said. "Where are you?"

"In front of Falcon Memorial. I was almost killed."

"What do you mean?"

"A truck tried to ram me."

Trey swore. "Do you have your gun?"

"Round is chambered and the safety's off."

"Get inside the hospital. Beau is there. I'll be right over."

Patricia called Beau as she drove through the hospital entrance gate and up the shaded, live oak lined drive. "Hi, Beau. Meredith is—"

"I know, Patricia," he said. "I'm at the hospital. It doesn't look good."

"I'm in the parking lot. Did you let Judy know? I tried to call her and couldn't reach her."

"Yes. She's on the way over."

"Thanks, Beau. I'm parking my car right now."

"I'll meet you in the lobby."

As soon as she got out of her car, Patricia saw Beau, dressed in a white lab coat, standing at the entrance. He gave her a brief hug, then they hurried into the hospital together.

"Do you know what happened, Beau?" Patricia asked.

"A single gunshot to her head. She's in emergency surgery. I'm in contact with the trauma surgeon. She's in the best hands."

A uniformed officer seated outside the waiting room stood as they approached and blocked the entrance. *What was going on?*

"Who are you?" he asked.

"Her cardiologist and friend," Beau said.

"Name?"

"Dr. Beau Simpson." Beau offered the man his hospital photo identification.

The officer turned to Patricia. "How about you?"

"She's with me," Beau said.

"Sorry, doctor, I'll need her name," the officer said, a scowl on his boyish face.

"Patricia Falcon." Patricia put her Bible down and dug in her purse for her ID.

The officer consulted his iPad. "You're not on my list. Sorry."

"I can vouch for her," Beau said, impatience creeping into his tone.

"Doesn't matter. It would take the chief himself to add a name to this list."

Patricia grabbed her phone.

Moments later, after speaking with Alton, the officer told them her name and two others had been added to his list.

"What was that about?" Patricia asked Beau as they entered the secure waiting room.

"Protective custody."

Shortly after they arrived at the waiting room, Alisa surged in. "What happened?"

"Someone shot Meredith," Patricia replied as she embraced Alisa.

Alisa brought her hand to her mouth just as Judy bounded into the room and asked, "What happened?"

"Someone shot Meredith," Alisa said, wiping tears from her eyes.

"Why?" Judy muttered.

"Probably because she was getting too close to identifying Mama's killer," Patricia said through a fog of guilt and fear.

Alisa flinched. "You think?"

Patricia nodded. "And we're probably next. Someone tried to ram me on the way over."

Alisa's jaw dropped.

Trey arrived and wrapped Patricia in his arms. She sobbed. "Meredith's in surgery. Beau says it's going to be hours before we know anything."

"She's got the best available care."

"I know." She sniffled. "It's the waiting. The uncertainty. Oh, Trey, this is terrible."

"We'll take care of it, Patsy."

She stepped back and wiped her face. "You always do."

He gave her a smile. "Can you talk about your accident on the way to the hospital?"

She nodded.

They sat and she filled him in on the details.

When his questions were answered, he called Alton and gave him details about the car incident.

INTERMINABLE HOURS LATER, BEAU GOT A PAGE AND LEFT. TEN minutes later he returned.

"Well?" Patricia asked.

"She's in recovery. At the moment it looks promising," Beau said. "However, with an injury like this anything can happen in the next twenty-four hours."

"I want a private nurse to be with her twenty-four seven," Patricia said. "Can you arrange that, Beau?"

He nodded.

"The best," she said.

"Of course," he replied. "And I'll be monitoring her care as well. The staff in this unit is exceptional. She'll get the quality care this hospital is noted for, Patricia."

She knew that, but it was calming to be reassured. Patricia let out a long breath. "Who wants to be the first to sit with Meredith?"

After agreeing Patricia would be first, the others left. Beau took Patricia and Trey to the Intensive Care Unit.

They paused outside Meredith's cubicle. Beau's eyes met hers. "She's in a medically induced coma."

Suddenly unable to breathe, Patricia bit her lip. *Dear Lord, please give me the strength to bear this.* "Why would they induce a coma?"

"The coma is necessary for her recovery."

Patricia surged into the room. Meredith lay on the bed with a sheet pulled up to her chin. The top of her head was fully bandaged.

Patricia's stomach cramped. Guilt rose.

A beeping machine with row after row of pulsing displays sat next to Meredith's bed. A drip line hung on the other side. A cannula fed oxygen to her nose.

Patricia pulled a chair closer to the head of the bed and sat. She took Meredith's limp hand. "Dear Lord, please heal Meredith. Please make her whole again." Tears flowed. Was her pleading prayer presumptuous? What else could she have prayed for?

Well, it would be nice to know who did this, but she knew the Lord wasn't in that business. That would be up to the Coalition and her team. "Dear Lord, Meredith's recovery is in your hands. Please treat her kindly. As for us, Dear Lord, guide us in our search for the person responsible. This I pray in the name of the Father, the Son, and the Holy Spirit. Amen."

* * *

FATHER JOHN WATCHED PATRICIA LEAVE FALCON MEMORIAL, noting some new damage to her Escalade.

The attack on Meredith Stanwick had to be related somehow to Henrietta's murder. The security videos from the bank parking lot were sharp and might shed some light on who attacked her. And Patricia, as a close friend, might know why. How to convince Patricia to be forthcoming remained an issue. He knew she was a Catholic and wondered if she still practiced confession. Who would she confide in that he could influence beyond the bishop? No one came to mind.

Father John called the bishop and instructed him on what to do. Together they would protect the church.

CHAPTER 19

*T*rey drove Patricia home from the hospital and escorted her into the house. She paused in the kitchen.

"It's been a horrible day," she said, tilting her head up to him. "I'm so relieved to be home."

He eased her closer.

Absorbing his warmth, she melted into him and sighed.

"Do you want to talk?" he asked.

She swallowed hard and nodded. "Meredith might ... die because of me."

He stepped back. "Why would you say that?"

Patricia crossed her arms. "I asked her to follow the transfer trail of Mama's missing money."

His jaw dropped. "Why would you do that? You should have come to me."

"We asked her to use her connections."

He squinted. "We?"

"Alisa, Judy, Meredith and I are trying to figure out who killed Mama."

"Why on earth would y'all do something like that? That's

why we have police. They have the training, the manpower, and the experience to investigate murders."

"They're my friends, and …" She skimmed his cheek with her fingertips. "Trey, honey, Meredith called me just seconds before her car wreck. She'd found Mama's money."

His dark eyes widened. "Really?"

"Those were her last words, then the gunshot." Her chest hitched. "Oh, Trey, it's like I pulled the trigger." Her hand covered her mouth.

"Okay. Give me a moment." He pulled away, ran fingers through his graying hair, and paced. "This isn't good. We have a few things to figure out here. First, who else have you told about Meredith locating Henrietta's money?"

"Just you."

He hesitated at the window and turned. A ray of sunlight struck his face, making it glow. "The rest of your girl-friends, have you told them Meredith found Mama's money?"

"Of course, I had to tell them. We're working on it together."

He grimaced. "Have they told anyone?"

"I honestly don't know," she said. "Why?"

He returned and draped an arm around her shoulders. "The person who tried to plow into your Escalade could be the same person who tried to kill Meredith or someone related to him. The assassin could have checked Meredith's phone to see who she was talking to when he shot her. Meredith tipped her hand by tracing the money, then she inadvertently led him to you. He killed Mama for her money. He tried to kill Meredith because she got too close. And he tried to kill you because he doesn't know how much you know. He's likely to know about Alisa and Judy as well, since the four of you spend so much time together. Damn. This isn't good." He shook his head. "You all need to go into hiding until he's apprehended. It's best y'all leave town immediately. The farther away the better."

"How would someone link Meredith to us?"

"You four are inseparable. Assuming the person was watching Meredith for any length of time, he'd know who her friends are. Did y'all get together recently?"

A shiver went down her spine. "Yes."

"There you go. We can't take a chance. Call everyone, let them know about the danger, and advise them to disappear for a few weeks. The police and the Coalition will take care of the attempted murder investigation from here."

"Call them now?" She had the feeling he had more to say.

Not looking at her, he nodded.

Though he seemed preoccupied, she called Alisa. "Trey thinks we're in danger because of our association with Meredith. He thinks we should leave Savannah until Meredith's assailant is caught."

"Leave?" Alisa asked. "The last thing I want to do is leave. The guy who shot Meredith has no idea who he's messin' with."

"We can't afford to be wrong," Patricia said in a softer voice. "Trey assures me the shooter will be caught."

"I suppose Trey is right. But it's so sudden. So much to arrange, so little time. I'll have to rearrange hearings and find someone to handle my clients. And how does one select an appropriate destination on such short notice? Oh my. Where are you going, Patricia?"

Patricia's mind whirled. "I haven't gotten that far yet. It's probably best we don't all go to the same place, and that we keep our destinations secret."

"I'm not sure what I'll do without y'all around."

Patricia shifted the phone to her bad ear, then realizing what she'd done, shifted it back to her good ear. "You'll have to manage, Alisa. Dump your phone and credit card and go somewhere you've always wanted to go. Do stuff there you'd never do in Savannah. Good stuff. Take a class. Join a local book club. Then, when this mess is over, we can compare notes."

"I always wanted to go to Rio. I could learn the Argentine Tango. I could—"

"Now you're talking. Okay, hun, I have to call Judy."

"Patricia?"

"Yes."

"Can we communicate while we're gone?"

"I'll ask Trey to set up a secure way for us to text and Skype. I'll call you back with details as soon as it's set up."

"Thanks, sweetie. Bye."

Patricia speed-dialed Judy.

"Because of what just happened to Meredith and me, Trey thinks our lives are in danger. He suggests we leave Savannah until the criminal is jailed."

"Honey, I feel safest right here," Judy said. "Beau's way ahead of y'all. He's already arranged for round-the-clock security personnel to move in with us. If I went somewhere else, I'd have to have a bodyguard there as well. Plus, I'm sleeping with my gun."

"If you disappeared, why would you need a bodyguard?"

"Get real, Patricia. Whoever is behind this money business knows what he's doing. Do you honestly think you and I could actually disappear when a pro is after us?"

"Sonny's doing a good job of it."

"Sonny's at the bottom of the ocean," Judy said. "With enough weight attached to him to assure his body will never surface."

"You don't know that."

"Okay, Patricia, I don't. But I'm staying put. If someone is foolish enough to take me on, they'll find my protection more than adequate." Being bullheaded was in Judy's nature. "I understand. Be safe."

"You too."

Patricia put her phone away and went over to Trey. "Alisa is leaving. Judy isn't."

"What's wrong with Judy?"

"Beau has arranged live-in security for her."

He rubbed his chin then nodded. "That's workable."

"Why don't we do that too? Judy pointed out that if I go somewhere else, I'd need a bodyguard there also."

Trey ran fingers through his hair again. "She has a point."

"So, what do we do?"

"Give me your keys and phone." Trey extended his hand.

"Why?"

"We'll get a guard in here round-the-clock and a chauffeur/bodyguard for when you go out. I'll have biometric locks installed this afternoon. You won't need your keys. As for your phone, it's traceable. I'll get you a secure device this afternoon."

Trey touched an icon on his phone. When someone came on the line, Trey said, "I need protective service at my home. Immediately. Live in. A few weeks. I'll wait. Code word is Chatham."

Listening to Trey take command was like a double shot of espresso to Patricia.

Trey put the phone down. "Someone will be right over. While we wait for them, why don't you fill me in on exactly what Meredith was doing?"

"Since all of Mama's money was in Meredith's bank, she had no problem determining that it was transferred shortly before Mama's death to an established bank in Hong Kong. Meredith knew someone at the Hong Kong bank who was able to provide her with the next transfer destination, a private bank on Hilton Head Island that was new to Meredith. Meredith was having trouble getting details on the principals of that bank, but was determined to find an insider who would furnish information on whether the money was still there."

"Do you know the name of the bank in Hong Kong?"

"I don't remember, but Meredith said she'd done a lot of business with them. It shouldn't be hard to check her international phone records or her financial transactions with Hong Kong banks."

"We'll get on that. I see no reason why we can't follow Meredith's lead. Did Meredith tell you the name of the Hilton Head Island bank?"

"No, just that it was unfamiliar to her, so that should rule out most of the banks up there."

"Do you remember anything else Meredith said about the money?"

Patricia shook her head.

"After security arrives, I'll be leaving for a meeting. I'll make arrangements for your new phone and for a chauffeur service on the way. Meanwhile, I want you to keep your gun within arm's reach."

Patricia removed the gun from her purse.

"Do you still have the clip-on holster? It might make it easier to keep your gun handy."

She nodded and went to the safe to retrieve the holster. A couple of minutes later, she returned with the holstered gun clipped to the waistband of her khakis.

"Your code word is Chatham," Trey said from the bar. "From this point on, if a stranger approaches you and doesn't give you the code word, pull your gun and take cover. You won't be out much, so the situation shouldn't happen. But if it does, don't hesitate to pull your weapon. If it's the killer you won't get a second chance. If it's not the killer, the stranger will back off. Get it?"

"Got it," she said, not trying to sound as bold as she felt with the gun strapped to her.

"And wear your shirts tucked in so you can get to your weapon easier. Remember, if the killer comes after you, seconds count."

* * *

A HALF HOUR LATER, A KNOCK ON THE DOOR INTERRUPTED THE silence.

Trey went to the door and asked, "Code word?"

"Chatham."

When Trey opened the door, Simon, Trey's go-to man for personal security, filled the entrance. He was dressed in a white polo shirt and gray slacks. A large black duffle sat at his feet.

Trey waved him in. "Hello, Simon. Glad you could make it."

"Mrs. Falcon. Mr. Falcon," he said in a low, rumbling voice as he entered. His eyes darted. "Where would you like me to put my bag?"

"Follow me," Trey said.

Five minutes later, Simon and Trey returned.

Patricia's stomach seized.

Simon now wore a black flack vest and a side arm. He also carried a stubby automatic weapon. "Okay," Simon said, "here's the deal. We have a man out front and one in the back. I'm inside. Even though the guys outside will assure only approved visitors get to your porches, I'll always answer the door. A locksmith will be here at 6:30 a.m. tomorrow to install new locks. Y'all stay away from the windows as much as possible, otherwise go about household business as usual. Mr. Falcon, I understand you'll be leaving frequently. I suggest you and the Mrs. always travel with a chauffeur."

"I'll be arranging for one this afternoon."

"Trey, are you sure you should be leaving? Wouldn't it be safer if you worked from home? And with everything going on, I'd certainly appreciate the company."

"I have some papers at the office I have to pick up and a critical meeting I have to attend, then I'll be home. I don't believe anyone will tie me into Meredith's inquiry, so I should be safe. You may be isolated here until I get home, but with three pros on the premises you'll be protected."

She sighed.

"Please give it a try," Trey said.

She nodded, wishing he would stay, but knowing that was hopeless.

"I'll be home in a couple of hours max."

She gave him a brief kiss and a long, lingering hug. "Be careful."

"You too."

Shortly after Trey left, Simon came into the great room with a black box in his huge hand and earphones on his ears. "Checking for bugs," he said by way of explanation.

She nodded.

As he passed her, he pushed back the earphones and pointed to her gun. "Do you know how to use that?"

"Yes."

"Have you been trained?"

"Ranger course in small arms."

His chin went up. "You went through Ranger School?"

"No. Just small arms training. My husband has connections."

"I'm very familiar with his connections. He's a mighty fine man and a great asset to this community."

Her pride welled.

Patricia followed Simon into the kitchen where he put the black box on the table, pulled out a notebook, and sat.

"I'll need the names and schedules of your current house-keeper and gardener."

Patricia gave him the information.

"Why do you do this kind of work, Simon?" Patricia asked.

"I like to kill people," Simon said in a voice as smooth as a combat knife sliding into its sheath. His face showed no trace of emotion.

"Seriously, Simon?"

He leaned forward and folded his strong, calloused hands on the table. "I'm being serious. There are bad people who create havoc and mayhem, and who contribute nothing of value to our community. People like that annoy me. When my superior tells me a bad person should die, I'm happy to make sure that happens. Quickly. I'm proud that what I do improves life for so many."

"And you trust your superior to always know the bad guys from the good guys?"

"Like I said, your husband is a mighty fine man."

Patricia swallowed.

"Are you concerned about your own safety?"

"I don't fear it, if that's what you mean. Fear inhibits. To do what I do, I can't afford to be inhibited."

"Ruthless or just a dedicated patriot?"

"I reckon a bunch of both, ma'am."

* * *

Trey met Vladimir Olneki outside The French Bakery. Trey recognized him from the photos in the case file Hempfield had assembled on the man. Vladimir's suit was as black as his hair and looked to be expensive. As did the Rolex watch and diamond ring he sported.

After ordering coffee and sandwiches, they went to the

back of the shop and sat at a small, isolated glass-topped table that Trey usually used for meetings like this. Being able to see both above and below the table was imperative. Both were seated with their backs to the wall so they could observe the room.

Their coffees arrived promptly.

"Good to finally meet you, Mr. Falcon," Vladimir said in flawless English.

"I wish I could say the same, Vladimir." Trey looked around to make sure they were not being observed. "I'd like to remind you that my primary mission is to protect this city."

"Ah yes, you and your friends, the protectors of the city."

Trey locked eyes with Vladimir, whose unsteady eyes were buried in sockets made deeper by his high cheekbones and bushy eyebrows. "There is a matter that troubles me. Murder and attempted murder are suddenly on the rise in Savannah. Why do you suppose that is?"

"Perhaps you are not protecting your city as well as you think you are. In fact, I myself had a man go missing for several hours yesterday. Why do you suppose that is?"

"Vladimir, if you plan to do business with me, you must be honest. I assume you're aware of the power I represent."

"I'm aware you are quite influential in Savannah and have a considerable reputation for getting things done."

"That's not the awareness I'm talking about." Trey cleared his throat. "I was hoping you were aware your life as you know it would be in jeopardy if you disturbed the peace in Savannah."

"Are you threatening me?"

"It's only a threat if you misbehave. Otherwise this is just a straightforward conversation between two people who *could* have a long and mutually beneficial relationship ... under the right conditions."

"And what conditions are you proposing?"

"I'm not proposing anything. This is not a negotiation. I'm demanding you operate peacefully in my city. Which you have not."

Vladimir's head jerked backward.

"Vladimir, if you insist on not being truthful with me, then I must ask you to take your operation elsewhere. Immediately. I want you and your cohorts out of Savannah by midnight. If not, you'll all find yourselves immediately on a one-way trip to the operating room."

"Operating room?"

"A place where we extract the truth one way or the other."

Vladimir clenched his teeth and straightened. "You want war, you get war. You see four of us today. In twenty-four hours there will be four hundred more. I give orders, not you."

With his eyes fixed on Vladimir's, Trey slowly shook his head. "Not in this city."

"You want four hundred assassins in your town?"

This tiresome man is an idiot. "What you're suggesting is illogical and suicidal. Let me spell it out. I assume you'll send in your top twenty or so troublemakers. My retired Rangers and retired Special Ops contractors will kill your people before they do much damage. And then what? Twenty more? The second, less competent squad will go down quicker than the first echelon. At some point, you'll realize your strong-arm tactics don't work against the best-trained, best-equipped paramilitary force in the world. Why go through all the trouble?"

"You're bluffing. Nobody but the US government has a force like that."

Trey leaned forward. "And where do you think those elite combat veterans prefer to live after their active duty is completed? Certainly not in a crime-infested city. They want to live where they were based for active duty and where their families were raised. Savannah. And they have an exceptionally low tolerance for anyone who disturbs the peace in their community."

Vladimir pushed back in his chair. "You expect me to believe that?"

"Your skepticism would prove fatal. Check around. See how many criminals have disappeared in Savannah. Ask yourself why. Before you bring another person to Savannah, do your homework. Quickly. And when you're ready to talk, and talk honestly, contact me."

Vladimir stirred his coffee, staring into Trey's eyes.

Trey counted the seconds, preparing to leave. When enough time had passed, Trey pushed back his chair.

Vladimir let out a long sigh. "I'm ready."

Trey's neck hairs bristled. "Okay. My next questions are critical. I want you to be absolutely honest with me. First, are you responsible for the murder of the port official?"

"Yes."

Steady eye contact from Vladimir affirmed his answer. Or was he a well-schooled liar? The rapid-fire questions would make it hard for Vladimir to simultaneously create lies and tightly control his physical reactions. "Are you responsible for the murder of Henrietta Snyder?"

"No."

Good so far. "How about the murder of Sonny Carothers."

"I didn't realize he was dead. I've had important business dealings with him. He seemed like a nice guy."

"He's missing without a trace. Did you arrange for his death?"

"No."

"His disappearance?"

"No."

"Did you have anything to do with the shooting of Meredith Stanwick?"

"Who's that? No. I know no such person."

Trey would have an expert go through the high definition video of the interrogation later, but on the surface Trey was satisfied with Vladimir's candor. "Okay, Vladimir. I believe you."

Vladimir seemed to relax a tad on that news.

Trey took a sip of latte. "I need you to do something for me."

"What would that be?"

"I need you to make sure a certain *Savannah Post* reporter doesn't write another word about Henrietta Snyder."

"Does this reporter have a name?"

"Willie Maye." Trey shoved an eight-by-ten photo of Willie and a dossier of background information across the table.

Vladimir scanned the photo. "I assume he must survive."

"Most certainly."

"Do you have any suggestions on how I might accomplish the task?"

"I suppose Willie could be taken on a trip to Russia for a couple of months."

Vladimir smiled for the first time. "Consider it done. Now about the Port of Savannah, we have ships we would like to dock here with no interference. Could you arrange that?"

Trey leaned back in his chair. "What cargo would they discharge?"

"Nothing. They would be here solely to take on cargo."

"I can arrange that, provided the export cargo has no military use."

"Not to worry. Only American-made civilian items not readily available in Russia will be loaded."

"How many loadings?"

"Initially, one a month. Once my supply channel is well established, as many as one per week."

"Why be so secretive?"

Vladimir took a large gulp of espresso. "The import of such items would be frowned upon by the Russian authorities, and my funding source to purchase the goods in America wouldn't make your financial regulators happy."

"Anything else?"

"I want a docking facility and some warehouses."

"Not possible. They're in private hands beyond my control."

"I know. I propose to build new facilities for my exclusive use. I just need permits."

"You have land?"

Vladimir nodded. "But no permits."

"Recently acquired land?" Trey though of Henrietta's property.

Vladimir nodded.

"I can arrange permits."

They shook hands.

"No more killings," Trey said, still grasping Vladimir's hand. "Ever."

Vladimir glanced to the left and nodded.

The lie didn't surprise Trey. Vladimir would have a tail until he left Savannah.

CHAPTER 20

*P*atricia watched the locksmith, a short, plump man, install a biometric deadbolt on the front door. "Not many historic homes have heavy-duty steel doors and doorframes like y'all," he said. "From the looks of it, they've been in place for quite some time. When did you have them installed?"

"That steel door has been there as long as I've been here. At least twenty-five years."

"Well someone spent a lot of money to make this home secure." He hitched up his wrinkled khakis. "Unfortunately, your old lockset was the point of greatest vulnerability. Not anymore." He patted the new lock. "No one's getting through those doors unless this armor-clad baby lets them in."

"The lock is armored?" Patricia asked.

He gave a wide smile. "It's made to absorb the full force of a battering ram and to deflect .45 mm armor-piercing bullets. As strong as your steel doors are, they can't deflect steel-tipped bullets. These locks cost plenty, but they're worth every penny. Yes indeed."

Before starting on the entrance doors, he had installed

the same kind of deadbolt on the steel door to their safe room, Trey's walk-in closet. She'd always thought of the closet as a sturdy place to go in case of bad weather. Now, safe room had taken on a more ominous meaning.

A chauffer/bodyguard arrived with a new car similar to hers and a new, secure phone for her. Eager for contact with her friends, she went to the kitchen and sat at the table, going through the phone instruction manual.

Someone close cleared their throat.

Startled, Patricia looked up.

It was Simon.

"Do you know someone named Rhett?" Simon asked flatly. He held a cell phone identical to her new one.

"Yes. Why?"

"One of our outside men has him detained until you authorize his entry. Your friend, Rhett, says he has something important to tell you. Do you want to speak with him?"

She closed the instruction manual. "Yes."

"In person?"

She nodded, wondering what could possibly be on Rhett's mind.

"Send him in," Simon said into his phone.

Moments later, the entrance chimes sounded. Simon left the kitchen, presumably to let Rhett in. When Simon didn't return, Patricia went to the foyer, arriving just as Simon finished scanning Rhett with a black wand. "What can I do for you, Rhett?" she asked.

Rhett's eyes darted. "What's going on with all the security?"

"Don't answer that question, Mrs. Falcon," Simon said.

Patricia shrugged. She supposed the extreme caution was justified. "You said you had something important to talk about?"

"Yes, ma'am. That black truck I saw before was back last

night after midnight for about two hours. You told me to let you know if it returned. It had an out-of-state license. I wrote down the number."

When Rhett reached into his pocket, Simon stepped between them, blocking her view. Simon's hand rested on his sidearm.

She went rigid. Unlike her, this man had instincts, reflexes. And he liked to kill people.

"Take your hand out of your pocket slowly," Simon said to Rhett.

"Hey, man, I don't want no trouble. I was just getting the paper with the license number."

"I'll get it," Simon said. He retrieved the paper and turned toward her, note in his hand.

"Will you trace the license number?" she asked him.

"Sure," he said, offering her the note.

"Won't you be needing the number?"

He pointed to his head. "I've got it."

"Thank you kindly, Rhett," she said, taking the note from Simon.

Rhett smiled and nodded.

She tucked the note into her shirt pocket. "By the way, do you have time to trim some bushes today?"

"Yes, ma'am."

Patricia gestured to Simon. "This gentleman wants the shrubs trimmed away from the house and windows to make the grounds more secure. He'll instruct you on what needs to be done."

After Simon left with Rhett, Patricia returned to the kitchen table to put phone numbers into the new phone. When she was done, she took Rhett's note from her pocket and studied it. The out-of-state truck had been outside twice, maybe more. The license number might be the breakthrough they were looking for.

* * *

"Do you have a hedge trimmer?" Simon asked as they descended the stairs to the front yard.

"It's in the garage," Rhett said. On rounding the side of the house, he noticed a large, smartly dressed man get into Patricia's car and back it out to the curb. "Who's that?" he asked.

"He's with us," Simon said flatly.

"Why's he in Mrs. Falcon's car?" Rhett asked, following as Simon entered the garage.

Simon stopped and turned to face him directly. "You ask too many questions."

Simon's unquestioned authority grated Rhett. He expelled air and grabbed the battery-powered hedge trimmer. "I'm just trying to stay on top of things," he said, hoping to keep irritation out of his voice. "Okay, what do you need removed?"

Simon led Rhett to the front of the house and explained.

Rhett started up the trimmer and brought it down the backside of the first bush, removing eighteen inches of growth. "Like that?" he asked.

"Exactly," Simon said. "And keep the height below the window sills."

Rhett passed the trimmer through the top of the shrub, removing six inches of height, then shaped the shrub.

"How do you know Mrs. Falcon?" Simon asked.

"We met over there." Rhett pointed toward the square. "She asked if I'd like to do some yard work."

"You're pretty handy with that trimmer."

"Thank you."

"Why were you watching the Falcon house last night?"

Rhett looked up from the bush. "After the first night the truck was here, Mrs. Falcon asked me to get the license number if the truck returned."

"How long ago was the first time?"

"Three nights ago."

"And last night was the second time?"

"Right." Rhett went back to trimming the next shrub.

"There could be a pattern developing here. The next time you see anything suspicious, you come to me immediately, not to Mrs. Falcon. Understand?"

"Yes, sir." He didn't like the idea of bypassing Mrs. Falcon. She'd done so much for him. But Simon seemed like the kind of person who could make a lot of trouble for him if he didn't cooperate. Trouble he didn't need.

"Very well. When you're done with the trimming, let that man over there know." Simon gestured toward an old man sitting on a park bench at the edge of the square, then headed back toward the front of the house.

Though the old overseer wore shabby clothes, he hadn't fooled Rhett. He knew all the street people in this area, and this person wasn't one of them.

* * *

PATRICIA ACTIVATED THE PHONE AND CALLED ALISA.

"Thank you for the new phone," Alisa said. "I just activated it."

"I told Trey that if I had a new phone we all should have secure phones. I called your old number. You must have your calls forwarded to the new phone just like I have."

"My husband doesn't think I should leave," Alisa said.

"I'm staying too," Patricia said. "Trey arranged live-in security, a chauffeur/bodyguard, and secure phone service."

"Yeah, that's what my husband is suggesting we do."

"How are you coming on ferreting out Sonny's relationships?"

"He's had plenty," Alisa said. "But he seems to break up

with the women peacefully. I can't find anyone who speaks poorly of the man."

"That's odd."

"Yeah, I thought so too. He's too perfect."

"Okay. Keep at it. You're bound to find someone who hates the man enough to spill the beans on him."

Patricia was about to call Trey when Simon returned.

"About the truck parked outside last night," he said. "Do you have any ideas about why it was out there or who it might be? Theories? Guesses?"

"No. Not a clue."

"We'll keep an eye out. If they come back, we'll let them know to park elsewhere."

"The truck was there before," she said, opening her laptop.

"That's what Rhett said. We're taking a more thorough look outside to make sure we didn't overlook anything, and we're bringing in a bomb sniffing dog to check—"

"Bomb?" Her hands froze over the keyboard.

"That truck was out there for some reason. Given the circumstances, we can't rule out any possibilities."

"Oh my heavens."

Simon came over and sat across from her. "We're here to assure your safety."

She certainly hoped so. She returned her attention to the laptop and opened her email in-box.

"That's it!" Simon said, standing. "Are you using a home-based wireless network?"

"I wouldn't know," Patricia replied. "You'd have to ask Trey."

"Let me take a look at your computer."

She pushed the laptop toward him.

A few clicks later, he said, "You're on a home network. What's the network password?"

"I have no idea."

"I'll call Mr. Falcon," he said. "Meanwhile, do you mind if I check what was accessed on your computer last night after midnight?"

She sat up straight. "Why?"

"I suspect the people in the black truck were looking at your computer files or, worse yet, copying them."

Patricia's jaw dropped. All her notes on the case were in those files. Facts. Speculation. Assignments. Suspects.

Everything.

CHAPTER 21

ather John took the elevator down to the hotel parking garage, hobbled to a dark corner, and got in the cargo compartment of his van. He switched on a dim light at the desk, inserted one of the copied security DVDs from Meredith's bank parking lot into the player and, after hooking his cane over the side of the desk, sat.

He reviewed the discs for a couple of hours before taking a break. Studying DVDs was tedious work he normally farmed out, but being under time pressure he was doing this particular review work himself.

Slouched at the desk in the back of his van, he massaged the back of his neck. Though an impressive array of classified electronics filled the wall, he focused on nothing more than the monitor while he toggled yet another security DVD forward and backward.

Suddenly he straightened. His heart sped as he froze the video on a black truck that had entered the right side of the view and stopped in the shadows of the shaded parking lot. He zoomed in on the vehicle's front end. A heavy-duty grill was mounted on the bumper. Father John whistled. *This guy sure came prepared to do some serious damage.*

Curiosity battled excitement as Father John advanced the video frame by frame, but the truck remained stationary in the lot. Growing impatient, Father John upped the display speed to half motion. A moment later, Meredith's car entered the view from the other side. Father John stretched his stiff neck as his experienced mind devoured the scene. This clip had to be just moments before the head-on collision, but the two vehicles remained positioned on each edge of the screen like boxers awaiting the bell.

Save for the two vehicles, the portion of the parking lot in view was desolate. He scratched his head as Meredith's car backed up and went off the monitor. The black truck slowly followed. As it passed in front of the camera, Father John froze the frame and zoomed in on the driver's open window, noting the driver, a man, and the silhouette of a passenger.

Father John slid channeled levers on the console back and forth until the picture sharpened to reveal a useable profile of a man in his twenties. Father John captured the image, sent it to his printer, then emailed it to the Vatican Security Bureau for facial recognition.

Next, he repositioned the view on the passenger, but even with enhancement could only obtain a heavily shadowed image of a woman of indeterminate age. He saved that image and sent it to the printer. The image was too vague for facial recognition.

The truck exited the view to the left, affording Father John no chance to get the license number. He ejected the disc and inserted the last security DVD, one that covered an exit, hoping the new viewing angle would record the actual event, or at least the truck's plate number.

No such luck. Ten minutes later, Father John gave a frustrated sigh and removed the last DVD. Hopefully the driver's photo would get a match on the church's facial recognition program.

* * *

PATRICIA SAT AT THE KITCHEN TABLE, HER HEAD RESTING between her hands and her eyes closed. The criminal was free and well ahead of her. Simon had verified someone had accessed her files last night. How Simon had accomplished that was a mystery to her.

No one, to her knowledge, had ever invaded her computer before. She had her laptop security checked by a tech who visited her home monthly. The tech, like Simon, would have known.

There could be only one reason someone would open her files now—to see what she was up to. The only person who would need that kind of information would be the one who had killed Mama and attacked Meredith and her. Someone who had deduced that Meredith had colleagues. Smart of them to figure that out. Equally smart to get into her computer.

The killer would not only have her knowledge, he'd have her plans. He could block her progress by compromising sources or setting traps for her and her colleagues, and eliminating them.

So it was time to change the plan. But how?

She stood and paced. Meredith had been following the money and damn near got killed. Following the money was out.

What approach would the killer be unaware of?

The truck's license. She hadn't put that information into her laptop database. The license was the one path the killer didn't know about. So far.

Her phone sounded. She unlocked the screen and glanced

at the display. Bishop Thomas Reilly. "Could you come around later today?" he said. "Perhaps three or so? I have a matter to discuss with you."

Simon walked into the kitchen with his phone to his ear. "Have him come here," he whispered in her bad ear. "It's safer."

"Thomas, with Meredith's shooting I'm reluctant to go out," she told the bishop.

"I understand. Might I stop by at three?"

"Yes indeed."

After she completed the call, she turned to Simon. "Do you get all my calls?"

"Afraid so."

"Inbound and outbound?"

"Yep." He set his lips.

"Hmmm. No privacy?"

He shook his head. "None from me."

"By the way, did you track down the truck license plate yet?"

He smiled. "Can't say."

"Can't or won't?"

"I know it's hard being isolated like this, but a surprisingly large number of murders are committed by someone who knows the victim. We're working on the assumption that if the murderer knew your mother, it's likely they know you as well. So, we're being very careful about who gets close to you."

She nodded. It made sense, but it didn't please her at all. She went to the window and looked out at the backyard, her black thoughts blocking her full appreciation of the pink azaleas in bloom.

She needed freedom and privacy to pursue leads. She wasn't going to get that at home or on her phone. She turned and faced Simon. "Trey arranged a chauffeur/bodyguard. Am I free to visit friends?"

"Sure, just not as many friends nor as often as in the past. And only if the people you visit pass our security standards." He took out a sterling cable bracelet remarkably similar to the John Hardy designs she preferred and handed it to her. "This is a tracking bracelet just in case your bodyguard is compromised."

She shivered. "Killed?"

Simon, grim-faced, nodded. "Not likely. But we have contingency plans for everything we can imagine."

She looked the bracelet over. "It's a nice piece of jewelry."

"We don't want to advertise that you're wearing a tracking device."

She slipped it on. "Y'all think of everything."

"Anticipation is an important part of our job. Now, who do you want to visit?"

"To start with, Meredith, Alisa and Judy. Add Sheila down at the corner florist, Nancy at The French Bakery, and Bishop Reilly."

"I'm working on Bishop Reilly right now so you can meet him at three. I can probably clear the others within an hour."

"Did you clear Rhett?"

"You bet. He came back as clean as a whistle."

That was good. She kind of liked the man. "Where's he from?"

"Can't say."

From the sealed-off look on Simon's face, she could see that there was no point in trying to go any further. Rhett's mystery would remain for her to solve later.

* * *

WILLIE ENTERED THE CAFÉ AND IMMEDIATELY SPOTTED A

person matching the photo he had received with the email invitation. Creepy white skin. Combed-back black hair. Thick black brows. A huge angular chin that looked like a ship's prow. As Willie approached, the massive man rose. The giant's knuckles were thick with scar tissue. *Imagine the stories this guy could tell.* Willie prayed he wouldn't be one of them.

With as much nonchalance as he could muster, Willie looked up at the man towering over him and met the giant's stony gaze.

"My boss require you for matter of great importance," the man said in a strangely strangled voice.

Willie had heard that line before. It usually meant someone wanted to plant a story, which wasn't always bad, but required caution. After all, any story Willie released carried his by-line, and he didn't want to lose credibility with the public.

"What's in it for me?" Willie kept his voice level. There was no need to show eagerness.

"You get story," the man said with an odd accent Willie couldn't place. Perhaps Eastern European, but he wasn't sure.

"What's the story about?" Willie asked.

The big man smirked and shook his head.

"I'll need more details before I agree, and the facts have to check out."

The man gave a half-hearted smile and nodded. "My employer will answer all your questions. He is expecting us. We go?"

The question sounded more like a command than an invitation, but with an important story at hand Willie didn't hesitate to nod.

The giant pointed to the door. "Car outside."

Willie followed the massive man to where a silver stretch limo was parked. A uniformed chauffeur stood at the open door. As soon as Willie and his guide entered, the door slammed shut. Moments later, the limo eased into traffic and accelerated. The air conditioning in the limo was so cold his breath clouded in the glacial air.

The giant gestured to the bar and raised an eyebrow. "You want drink?"

Why did all the guy's questions sound like commands? Willie nodded.

"Vodka?"

Though this question also sounded like a command, Willie's stomach wasn't ready for vodka. "Just some soda water."

The man handed him a cut-crystal tumbler with ice and club soda.

Willie took a long sip, put the glass in the cup holder, and pulled out a Tiparillo.

The giant sneered.

"Just gonna chew on it."

The man gave a smirk. *Why did everything the guy do seem so intimidating?*

"If you don't mind me asking, where are we going?"

"Airport."

Willie straightened. He hadn't anticipated that.

"Not to worry, my little friend. Quick trip."

Willie settled back, rolled the Tiparillo to the other side of his mouth, and watched the city flicker by. An exclusive story of great importance was just what his career needed.

hen the front door chimes sounded at three, Patricia's nerves skittered like startled shrimp on the seabed. With Simon in the lead, she went to the foyer and stood to the side while Simon opened the door. She took the secluded moment to straighten her khaki shirtdress.

Bishop Thomas Reilly, dressed in black pants, black shirt and a Roman collar, stepped in. His bishop's cross hung from his neck on a simple chain.

Simon blocked Thomas from going further. "One final security check, your Excellency."

Once Simon had run the security wand over the bishop's torso, Thomas and Patricia retreated to the sitting room in the back of the house.

"Would you care for something to drink, Thomas?"

"A bit of iced tea, if it's no trouble."

In the kitchen, she filled two glasses with ice and the sweet tea she had brewed specifically for him, then placed the glasses on a sterling tray along with a plate of shortbread cookies. Back in the sitting room, she placed the tray on the coffee table and gestured for him to sit. When they were both seated, she passed him the tea and offered the cookies.

He took a bite of cookie, smiled so deeply his dimples creased, and asked, "Irish?"

She nodded.

"Aye. Ireland forever." He took another bite, then wiped his lips with a napkin. "You've been through so much, my dear. How are you holding up?"

Memories flooded her—Mama, Meredith and the truck trying to ram her SUV. Acid etched Patricia's stomach. She snapped her eyes closed, but the unwanted images persisted. She exhaled a long breath. "I'd be most grateful if you kept my family in your prayers."

"I'm sure the murder of your mother and disappearance of her assets is a lot to take."

"It's been difficult."

"That's why I came over. Henrietta was a wonderful woman, an angel. An unlikely candidate for murder. Henrietta loved the church, and we want justice for her. Because we look at situations through a different lens than Chief Patrick, we might find something critical to the case he hasn't seen."

"Does Chief Patrick know what you're doing?"

"Of course."

"You're here on his behalf?"

"No. Mine. The church's."

Apparently she hadn't realized the depth of Mama's relationship with the church. Mama was generous, no doubt about that. But for a bishop to take personal interest in identifying her killer? Who would have guessed? And Thomas, as intelligent as he was, was no murder investigator. Of course, what did she know of the resources available to him? Mind-boggling. Absolutely mind-boggling.

Intrigued, but unwilling to speak openly in the house, she gestured to the backyard. "Would you like to see my azaleas?"

Though he had a surprised look, he stood.

She led him to the back door, turned off the security alarm, and opened the door.

Patricia went to a concrete bench under a thick arbor in a secluded far corner and sat. The tangled jasmine arbor and brick walls gave a sense of privacy, which was why she and Trey had created the haven. Since Hayley had left for college, they hadn't used it at all. The brick walls kept the street noise and the gawking tourists out. The arbor provided shade. "There's more privacy out here," she told Thomas. "How can I help?"

"Where was Henrietta's money before it disappeared?" he said quietly as he settled on the bench.

"Meredith's bank."

"That's not surprising. She thought highly of Meredith. Henrietta found great comfort in doing business with her closest friends. Do you have any idea where Henrietta's money went?"

If Thomas followed the same path as Meredith, would he meet the same fate ... or worse? A chill went through her. If Thomas died pursuing Mama's killer, she'd never forgive herself. But, not telling him could mean walking away from major help in finding the killer.

"You know something, don't you?" His voice was soft, his tone understanding.

"I suppose."

"You can speak in confidence."

"It's not that, Thomas. I know I can trust you."

"Then what is it, Patricia?"

"This is a deadly situation. I'm concerned about your safety if you pursue the matter any further. Meredith was tracing Mama's money, and now she's in the hospital, lucky to be alive." She gestured around her. "Look at me. Because there's a killer out there, I'm imprisoned in my own home."

"I appreciate your concern, but I can assure you the resources at my disposal are perfectly capable of protecting me," he said firmly.

She leaned forward. "You live unencumbered. Anyone can visit your office. You walk and drive the streets alone. That's hardly a high level of security."

"I'm not going to discuss the details of my personal security with you, but I'm comfortable with them." He raised his eyebrows. "Surely that must mean something to you."

It did, but involving him still troubled her. She'd seen what the criminal had done to poor Meredith. She pushed away the anxiety the thought caused. On the other hand, nothing was going to change until the killer was apprehended. And the more resources on the case the better.

Suddenly, certainty came. She supposed it was intuition. There was no other way to explain it. She had to tell Thomas about Meredith's findings. After that, she'd close down like an oyster at low tide.

"How far did Meredith get in tracing the money?"

"Far enough to get shot."

"She found the money?" His voice had an edge to it.

"Those were Meredith's last words so, on the face of it, I suppose so."

"You were with her when she was shot?"

"No." The memory prickled her, inducing nausea. "I was on the phone with her."

"You've told the police?"

"Not yet, but Chief Patrick wants to talk with me."

"He's not going to be happy that Meredith took the law into her own hands. But I can understand why you asked her to. Did Meredith tell you where the money is?"

"She had traced the funds to a major bank in Hong Kong

and then back to a private bank on Hilton Head Island. A bank she'd never heard of."

"So, the money is on Hilton Head Island?"

"She wasn't sure. She said it could have been transferred elsewhere after arriving on Hilton Head Island. She was searching for an insider at the Hilton Head Island institution who might help her."

"I'm guessing she found one?"

She exchanged glances with him. "I suppose so since she told me she found the money."

"Do you have any suspicions about who's behind the theft?"

She shook her head.

"None at all?" he asked.

"Well, Sonny's disappearance is strangely coincidental."

"Sonny?"

"Sonny Carothers. Mama's accountant."

"Did she have trouble with Sonny?"

"Not that I know of. In fact, she was quite found of him."

"Did he handle most of her money?"

"All of it."

He rubbed his chin. "Was Henrietta satisfied with his financial management?"

"Thomas, you know Mama. She was always striving, never satisfied, but she'd never complain."

"What was the problem?"

"Earnings. Each quarter she always was positive regardless of what the markets did. And she had no clue why."

He raised his eyebrows. "Really?"

She arched her shoulders. "She was obsessed with him."

"Romantically?"

She chuckled. "Mama? Heavens no. She was obsessed with his financial techniques."

"In what way?"

"She questioned everything he did and spent a lot of time trying to get into his mind. It bothered him. He told her to find another accountant, but she stayed with him."

"Why?"

"Because he was so good, damned good. She was obsessed with finding out how he was so successful, plus I think she wanted to know his story."

"What story is that?"

"Sonny moved here from South Carolina twenty years ago. No one seems to know what he did before moving here, but once he set up business here he prospered. Word got around that he was an excellent money manager. Who doesn't want a guy like that on their team?"

"You said he disappeared?"

"Without a trace."

"When?"

"About the time of Mama's death."

His brow creased. "I see what you mean about the strange timing of his departure."

"What are you going to do with all this information?"

"The money path seems the best route to the killer. I'll have someone duplicate Meredith's work."

"I'm impressed. I didn't know the church has such resources."

"Nothing to be impressed with yet, Patricia."

A light breeze scented with the jasmine-like scent of tea olive picked up, cooling her skin. She gestured toward the house. "How about another cookie?"

He looked at his cell phone. "Thank you, but I really need to be on my way. I appreciate you being open with me."

Her mind settled. She'd done the right thing. The world around her brightened. Then, seeing Simon watching from a back window, she heaved a sigh. His endless spying on her seemed spooky. But she was vulnerable, and he was there to protect her. Though guilt surged at her not accepting and appreciating his oversight, she ached to be free of him.

Once in the house, she gave Thomas a bag of the Irish cookies and saw him to the door. He left smiling.

Patricia considered calling Chief Patrick to get that ordeal over with, then decided to put it off until he called. Instead, she sought out Simon, who had set up a command post in the formal dining room just as he had done on other occasions. Black-clad electronic gear nearly filled the over-sized table. Positioned in front of him was a large monitor tuned to the six exterior surveillance cameras he'd installed. One had a distant view of the arbor in the backyard. Propped against the wall next to Simon were several rifles with big scopes, a shotgun, and what was probably an auto-matic weapon. All black-clad. He looked up as she approached.

"Everything secure?" she asked.

"There's no such thing. We just try to tilt the odds more in our favor."

"I'd like to spend some time with Alisa this afternoon. Did you get the security clearance on her?"

He smiled. "Everyone came back spick-and-span, Mrs. Falcon."

"How do I do this?"

"Your driver, Mike, is outside right now. If you give me your phone, I'll put his number in as a speed dial. Would D, for driver, be okay?"

"Sure." She handed him the phone.

When he returned the phone, she asked, "Am I free to go?"

"Of course. Punch D and ask Mike to bring the car around. He'll let me know when he's at the curb. I'll escort you to the car. Mike will take you to anyone on our secure list. If you go to a public place, Mike will accompany you inside but will sit apart from you. In time, you won't even notice him."

She punched D.

Five minutes later, she settled into the backseat of the new Escalade. She smiled with joy. She was free from that damn prison. Free to go where she wished, when she wished. She'd never take her freedom for granted again.

"Where to, Mrs. Falcon?" Mike asked in a voice befitting his bulk.

"Just drive around for a moment while I make a call."

As the SUV merged with traffic, Patricia called Alisa. "How are you doing, Alisa?"

"Honey, I'm going stir-crazy. Too many restrictions. No privacy. How about you?"

"I broke out and thought we might have a chat and latte at The French Bakery."

"Oh my. I'd love that." Alisa's voice simmered with glee. "What time?"

Patricia noted her surroundings. "I could pick you up in five minutes."

"I'll be ready, and I'll be bringing my new bodyguard."

Patricia chuckled. "He can keep mine company."

When the call was complete, she gave Mike the address and settled back. It was nice not to drive. Under different circumstances, she could get used to that. Might even take time to appreciate the bountiful azaleas that graced each square they passed.

A block from Alisa's home, Mike's phone went to his ear. Patricia assumed he was calling ahead to let them know of his approach. At Alisa's house, the SUV swung to the curb and paused. Wrought-iron gates in the ivy-covered brick wall swung open. A tall, crew-cut guy dressed in black appeared and opened the side door. Alisa, in skinny black jeans, a white T-shirt and a topknot scurried across the slate sidewalk and into the Escalade. She gave Patricia a squeeze. She'd changed cologne again. This one smelled of oranges. Her bodyguard closed the door and went up front to sit with Mike.

"Where to, Mrs. Falcon?"

"The French Bakery on Sullivan."

As the SUV pulled from the curb, Alisa tucked a strand of blond hair into her messy topknot and turned to Patricia. "I'm so happy to be out of that infernal jail."

"Do they listen in on your calls?" Patricia asked.

Alisa grimaced. "Lordy, do they. They watch and listen to everything. I'm afraid to undress or shower. And poor Sterling had the nerve to try to get frisky with me last night. If they were listening to that conversation, they must think I'm a horrible wife. I'm so paranoid, I turn off the lights to pee."

"I know." Patricia looked around. "I wouldn't be surprised if they had everything bugged, including our cars."

"We do," Mike said from the front, then chuckled. "But don't worry, you'll get used to it."

Alisa raised an eyebrow. "Not the ladies room? Please tell me I can turn the lights back on."

"Nah," Patricia said. "They wouldn't."

Mike shook his head.

"Good," Alisa said. "Because I don't think I could do it with a guy in the same room."

Patricia folded her hands in her lap. Being guarded was a strange situation, and it was getting stranger by the hour. Like a rudderless ship, the only certainty for her was uncertainty.

The SUV pulled into a seedy alley. Mike cleared his throat. "Excuse me, Mrs. Falcon. We'll take you in the back entrance, if you don't mind."

"Sure." Who was she to object? She supposed alley entrances were standard security protocol when available and wondered what Nancy would think of Alisa and her traipsing through the bakery's prep area. Kindhearted Nancy would probably take it all in stride and not even say a word.

Just as the Escalade stopped, a metal door swung open to reveal Nancy, dressed in a red polo shirt and black slacks, beaming as always. Despite spending every day in a bakery, Nancy was eternally reed thin. Work didn't seem to faze her. Her short blond hair looked like she'd just left the beauty salon.

Alisa's bodyguard got out and went into the place. A couple of minutes later he returned for them. The garbage stench of the alley quickly gave way to the delicious aromas of fresh-baked bread and chocolate. The back of the bakery was spacious and tidy. A flour-dusted baker piped chocolate on a tray of Napoleons.

As Patricia and Alisa settled at a table in the back of the main shop, Nancy chin-nodded toward Alisa's bodyguard. "What's up with him?"

"After the attempt on Meredith's life, Sterling felt it advisable."

"Bless his heart. Y'all want something to drink?"

They both ordered latte.

Mike, a black tablet computer in hand, came in and sat, facing the front door, with Alisa's bodyguard, who continued to face them.

Patricia turned her back to the bodyguards, leaned toward Alisa, and whispered, "Bishop Reilly is going to see if he can duplicate Meredith's work tracing Mama's money."

Alisa's eyes widened. "Why?"

"Apparently, Mama had some special relationship with the church and they want to see her killer brought to justice as much as we do. With Meredith out of the picture, we don't have the ability to continue her work."

"And the bishop does?" Alisa asked.

"Apparently so. But wait, there's more. Our work has been compromised."

Alisa's lips parted. "What do you mean?"

"Someone got into my laptop last night." Patricia moved closer and, lowering her voice, filled Alisa in on the network security breach Simon had discovered.

"Who do you think it could be?"

"It's too coincidental not to be the person responsible for Mama's murder, the attack on Meredith and the attempt on me. Or someone at least connected with the killer."

"You're right."

"Anyway, I'm operating on that basis." Patricia slipped the note with the truck's license number from her purse. "The only lead not in my computer is the plate number of the hacker's truck."

"How did—"

"I'll tell you later. Right now I need to know if your cousin at the DMV can track down the owner of an out-of-state vehicle from the plate number."

"He's got all sorts of contacts. I don't see why not."

Patricia handed Alisa the note.

"I'll call as soon as I get the information."

Patricia gave a slight nod toward the bodyguards. "Don't call. I don't want the *boys* to know what we're doing."

"Everything face-to-face?"

"Exactly."

"What about Judy?"

"I'll call her later and set up something for the three of us for tomorrow. How's lunch sound?"

Alisa smiled. "That works."

After dropping Alisa off at her home, Patricia called Judy. "I'm just down the street. I don't mean to be a bother, but could I stop by for a moment?"

"Certainly," Judy said. "What's up?"

"I'll tell you when I get there."

She terminated the connection and gave Mike Judy's address.

Five minutes later, the Escalade pulled up to the gated entrance to Judy's drive. Two black-suited men patrolled the periphery stone wall. The ornate gate swung open, and Mike drove in.

"Please remain in the car until I come back, Mrs. Falcon." Mike said. "And after I return, don't get out until I open your door."

She straightened. "Is there a problem?"

"Though Mrs. Simpson is pre-cleared, I have to make sure there's no one else in there."

"She has live-in security."

"Good. That'll make everything quicker." Mike pulled a black automatic from inside his coat, opened the slide and checked for a chambered round. Then, gun in hand, he left the SUV and went to the entrance. A wiry man dressed in black jeans and T-shirt, also gun in hand, met him at the door. They talked and exchanged something, probably identification cards. Mike entered.

Patricia would have laughed at the absurdity of this security charade if her world wasn't unraveling.

Patricia caressed the grip of the pistol in her purse as she scanned Judy's manicured front lawn. This was not a good time or place to be alone.

The ornate solid wood front door of the home opened, and Mike, followed by a wide-eyed Judy, appeared. Judy, dressed in jeans shorts and a tank top, looked flushed and hastily thrown together.

Mike hastened to the SUV and opened the door. "I'll wait here," he said as Patricia got out.

"I won't be long," she said.

Judy stood in the doorway, talking on her phone. "Patricia's here. I've got to go. We're going to have a chat." She looked at Patricia and mouthed 'Beau.'

They cheek kissed. Judy seemed to have shrunk. Patricia looked down. Judy was barefoot.

"How're you handling the lockdown?" Patricia asked.

Judy shrugged, pulled Patricia inside, and dead bolted the front door. "It sure beats the alternative."

Patricia exhaled, attempting to mask her nerves.

Judy grinned. "Seriously, I'm enjoying the downtime."

"There's too much idleness for me," Patricia said. "By the way, does your security team monitor your phone calls?"

"Not that I'm aware of." Judy stuck her head into the dining room. "Hey, Joseph, do you listen in on my phone calls?"

"Yes, ma'am."

Judy, wide-eyed, turned to Patricia, arms extended. "I guess I'm wrong. Why?"

Patricia stepped closer to Judy and whispered, "Since they're listening to our calls, we can't discuss our investigation on the phone."

Patricia stepped back, meeting Judy's solemn gaze.

Judy nodded and gestured toward the back of her house. "Patricia, honey, would you like to take a stroll out back? The gardener put in some new annuals this morning," she said in a flat voice, her hand imploring. "They're simply gorgeous."

"Why yes." Patricia followed Judy outside to the fire pit on the other side of the garden. As she arrived, she studied the immediate area for a video camera but found nothing. They sat on a concrete bench facing away from the house.

"I've got some terrible news, Judy. Someone got into my computer last night and accessed my case notes."

Judy's jaw fell open.

"I think the hacker could be Mama's killer. If so, he knows who we are and what we've been up to. Luckily, while he was hacking my computer a friend of mine was jotting down his license plate number. Alisa's cousin is tracing the license number. For the time being, the killer doesn't know we're tracing his truck."

Judy just stared at her.

"Judy, say something."

"I don't know what to say."

"Since the killer knows who we are and what we've been doing, we have to be very careful from now on."

Judy scooted back and extended her hand, palm out. "Ah, wait a minute. Hold on. Are you sure we should take the risk to continue our investigation?"

Patricia clamped Judy's hand between hers. "I understand your concern, honey. You don't have to help if you don't want to, but Alisa is on board."

Judy's teeth bit her collagen-enhanced lower lip. Her eyes momentarily closed as she shook her head. A deep breath later, she opened her eyes and said, "So am I, Patricia."

"I'd like to meet with you and Alisa tomorrow at Cohen's at noon to discuss where we go from here. With any luck, Alisa should have the hacker's name by then. Are you game?"

Judy nodded.

"Remember, no phone calls about our business. Everything face-to-face."

"Got it."

A man's loud voice sounded from outside the rear wall of the yard. Both women jumped to their feet and looked in the direction the voice had come from.

An object hurled through the air toward the women.

Patricia grabbed Judy, threw her to the ground, and covered her with her body.

Tires screeched. More shouts.

Patricia eased her head up. Less than ten feet away lay a brick partially wrapped in paper. Gun in her trembling hand,

Patricia crawled over to the brick. The paper had writing on it.

"What is it?" Judy asked, as she pushed up into a seated position.

"A note."

"What does it say?"

Patricia eyed Judy for a second. "It says, 'You're next.'"

* * *

THE LIMO WITH WILLIE PULLED UP NEXT TO A SMALL JET ON the general aviation tarmac. "A private jet?" Willie asked.

"My boss likes freedom. Freedom from schedules. And he likes privacy."

"What kind of plane is this?"

The giant smiled. "You like?"

Willie nodded.

"It Cessna Citation X. Fastest civilian plane available."

Willie's eyes saw the luxurious plane, but his mind saw dollar signs piling up in his bank account.

Once inside the empty jet, he selected a seat with an unobstructed view of the cockpit. As he fastened his seatbelt, the hatch closed. Only then did it occur to him that the giant had not boarded the jet.

CHAPTER 23

Father John crossed his hotel room to the wall of photos, then wrote the name Herman Stockford beneath the enhanced photo of the driver of the black truck. The Vatican facial recognition service had matched the submitted photo to Herman's driver's license and had provided the name in record time. Below the picture, John taped a summary of the basic profile information he'd pilfered from the Joint Operations database. In the past hour, the profile of Meredith's attacker was slowly beginning to fill in, but it still had plenty of cavities.

Herman was ordinary enough. Out-of-state high school education. No criminal record. A Vatican researcher was working on locating any linkage between Herman and Henrietta. Another researcher was at work trying to locate the man through cell phone and credit card activity. With any luck, John would be speaking face-to-face with Herman Stockford in a matter of hours.

John pursed his lips. He'd have plenty of questions for the man. Was Herman Henrietta's murderer, or did he simply work for the killer? What did Herman know about the missing money? And why, just before crashing into Meredith's car, was Herman smiling? Just a coincidence or something sinister? Perhaps the man's primary motive wasn't money.

Yet, Henrietta's money had been transferred, probably on behalf of her killer. And if so, Bishop Reilly's interrogation of Patricia Falcon had been the key to reopening the financial path to Henrietta's killer. The Vatican's Financial Office had quickly duplicated Meredith's work and confirmed Henrietta's funds were still at the unregistered Hilton Head Island money transfer agency. Chinese specialists under contract to the Vatican Security Force were busy hacking the so-called bank's computer records. It was just a matter of time before they'd produce a name associated with the missing funds. And if the name wasn't Herman Stockford, there would be yet another person John would soon be interviewing face-to-face.

Staring at the photos on the wall of his hotel room, Father John shook his head. However well Herman Stockford had executed Henrietta's murder, his attack on Meredith was ill-conceived. Too many basic mistakes. The man was no professional, and that would be his undoing.

"You won't escape my justice," John said in a tired voice. "Good trumps evil." He swallowed his words. "Dear Lord, forgive me for being prideful," he prayed.

John reached for his cane and, walking reasonably well, went to the fridge for a bottle of beer. He took a long pull on the beer. He wasn't sure why the Lord had permitted his leg injury. Too much pride, he supposed. Pride was a cancer that eroded his redemption. He supposed the injury might be a kind of penance. Whatever the reason, he'd press on regardless of how long it took to fully recover.

He paused at the suspect wall and toasted Herman. "Just a matter of time, buddy. Just a matter of time."

John didn't have a lot of time. He was beginning to show his years. Gray hair and much less energy. He was scheduled for cataract surgery when he returned to the Vatican. Growing old sucked all the joy out of his work. But, compromised or not, with muscles like a competitive weight lifter and razor-sharp intuition, he was still a substantial weapon of justice.

* * *

THOUGH HERMAN STOCKFORD WASN'T WORKING, HE PARKED his battered truck in the restaurant employee parking area, keeping it well out of the line of sight of the uppity manager. Herman chuckled to himself. Soon enough he would be driving one of those fancy cars the manager liked to see parked out front. Not that Herman would frequent the dive after he made it big.

Herman, dressed in khakis and a navy polo shirt, swept in the restaurant's back entrance and through the noisy kitchen. The smell of grilled hamburger spiced the air. He left the busy kitchen and entered the main dining room. His sister sat at a corner table, far from the other patrons.

She looked terrible. Actually, he'd never seen her so unruly. Uncombed hair swirled around her face like a hurricane. Her rumpled shirt looked like she'd worn it for a couple of days. She wore no makeup. But what disturbed him most were her dull eyes. Normally they were ablaze with emotion, but in the past month she'd turned increasingly dark. He missed her sweetness and humor. Concerned, he met her gaze as he sat and said, "Hey. What's up?"

"Not much besides the outside temperature, bro," she said softly.

Sally, a server, arrived. Herman greeted her with a smile and ordered iced tea and a cheeseburger. Sally left, with a hint of jealousy in her over-the-shoulder expression.

Sally was the only employee at the restaurant who was nice to him. Maybe after he cashed in on all his sister's jobs he'd take Sally out on the town. From the waist up she was a knockout, but she had the butt and thighs of an offensive lineman. And the only thing heavier than her makeup was her lilac perfume. He'd reward her kindness and get laid at the same time.

"How are you managing?" his sister asked.

He was still rattled that the last target survived, but he wasn't going to admit it. "Fine."

She stared, slack-jawed, spearing him with a look of disbelief. "Are you sure there's no remorse?"

He looked around and shrugged. "No. There's no remorse. A job is a job. The first was for money, the second was for survival."

Sally returned with the iced tea. Herman grabbed her free hand and held it. Sally's brows arched, then she smiled. Herman gulped the tea down and motioned for a refill. Sally pulled her hand free, sighed, and refilled his tea with a look of being trapped in subservience, then stomped away.

"Do you have another job for me?" Herman asked.

"Are you up for more work?"

"I'm always up for work like that." He gulped down the iced tea. He loved the brain freeze he got from doing that.

"Then I might have another job for you."

"How much?"

"The same."

"Who?"

"We'll talk later."

"You and your mystery. When?"

She rolled her eyes. "Your next job is upstate in South

Carolina, and because timing is critical on this one I want you to leave immediately and get into position." She handed him a printout with the address of a motel. "Once you check-in, give me a call. Do you still have the prepaid cell phone I gave you?"

"Yeah."

She held out her hand. "Give it to me?"

"Why? It has minutes left on it."

Her eyes went flint hard. "Damn it. Give it to me, Herman."

A chill rippled his flesh. What the heck had he done to warrant that? He was just trying to economize.

She extended her arm farther.

He handed over the like-new phone.

She dropped it in her purse, then gave him a new throw-away phone still in the bubble pack.

He'd been through the routine before. Frequently switching phones assured no one could trace him while on a job. He removed the packing, slipped the phone into his pocket and returned the garbage to her.

She pushed a prepaid credit card across the table. "This one's got $1,000 on it."

"That's very generous. Thanks." His heart raced. Money like that was a powerful stimulant. Anticipating a lot more when the job was completed, he put the card into his wallet. "Any more business?"

"No, that's it. Get up there as fast as you can, and don't forget to call." She paid the bill, then walked with him to his truck.

As he stepped up into the truck, an alarm buzzed in his head. He was being sent a long way from Savannah, and he hadn't been paid for the last job. He started the engine and slid the window down. "When are you going to be able to pay me?"

"Soon. You'll get what's coming to you soon. Trust me." She gave him a hug through the window. A different hug. Longer. Tighter. More affectionate than usual. "I love you, bro."

"I love you, too," he said wearily, then backed the truck out. As he steered his truck onto I-95, stillness settled through him. Man and machine, fused.

Thirty minutes later, just inside South Carolina, Herman suddenly felt extremely tired. He pulled to the shoulder and collapsed onto the steering wheel.

* * *

A LIGHT TAP SOUNDED FROM THE DOOR OF FATHER JOHN'S hotel suite. Annoyed at the unscheduled interruption, he grabbed his cane, hobbled to the dining room, and switched the main computer monitor to the hallway security camera he'd installed on arrival.

A profile of Bishop Reilly appeared on the high-resolution screen. He wore jeans and a white polo shirt. John canvassed the hall. Reilly was alone.

What was the bishop doing here? More importantly, how had Reilly located him? No one but Connie, his daughter and understudy, knew about the place, and she was isolated at the secondary safe house. Absolutely no one else knew. He'd been careful to rent the suite and set up his elaborate data center totally off the grid yet, incomprehensibly, Reilly was out in the hall seeking entry.

Ignoring Reilly wouldn't undo the fact Father John's command center had been compromised. If Reilly knew the location, who else did? The only way to find out was to grill Reilly, right now, before the news spread.

Father John left the dining room, careful to shut the

double doors on the massive array of sophisticated electronic gear.

The tapping turned to pounding.

Father John swung the door open. "Good day, your Excellency. So nice to see you. To what do I owe this visit?"

"Good day, Father. I thought you'd like to know someone else is also investigating Henrietta's murder. He's a very good friend of mine and an excellent investigator. In fact, once I mentioned your interest in Henrietta's case, he had no problem locating you. He'd like to discuss the case with you."

"I'm afraid that's confidential. Didn't I make that clear at our first meeting?"

Reilly stood completely still. Clearly a person accustomed to exercising authority. "You were perfectly clear. Nevertheless, my friend insisted I extend the invitation."

"I'd rather not meet with your friend."

"That would be a mistake, Father. Please reconsider?"

Father John shook his head. "Tell your friend to keep his nose out of my business. As for you, don't contact me again. If I want to speak with you, I'll contact you. Understand?"

Reilly's cheeks flushed. "I understand, but I doubt my friend will. He's quite insistent."

"Tell your insistent friend to bug off."

Reilly's full face turned bright crimson. "I got that. Just saying—"

"Just say goodbye." Father John moved forward a step.

Reilly frowned then, as the frown faded, he backed off.

Father John inched the door closed as Reilly turned and strode purposefully to the elevator.

Father John scanned the room. His location was compromised and had to be abandoned.

Suddenly, deep cathedral bells pealed from Father John's computer, indicating an incoming instant message from his daughter.

CN: *I located Herman Stockford.*

FJ: *Where?*

CN: *Jasper County Morgue.*

He let out a frustrated breath.

FJ: *What happened?*

Before she could reply, a knock sounded at the door of Father John's suite. He typed, *Got to go* and switched the monitor view to his hallway security cameras. Two powerfully built men Father John didn't recognize stood to either side of his door. Obviously security types. Too bulky for hotel security. Not the kind of people he wanted in his room. Not with all the military-grade security electronics. Father John gritted his teeth. He had an urgent case to solve. He didn't need these two jerks slowing him down.

He made a shooting motion at the screen, then activated the stun mat he'd installed outside the door.

Both men dropped to the floor. They didn't stay down long before they clambered to their feet, backed away from the door muttering, and left.

Father John began methodically locking out his systems and shutting down his hardware in preparation for abandoning the compromised suite.

Suddenly the lights went off, leaving the heavily curtained room in darkness save for the battery-powered laptop and the independently powered hallway security cameras, which showed nothing more than a totally dark hall. Apparently, the two had left to switch off his power. *So you two want to play in my domain,* he thought expectantly as he activated the inner stun mats and slipped into his body armor and headgear.

Battering rams crashed into both doors to the suite. Father John depressed the anti-flashbang button on his helmet seconds before one of the doors swung open and two flashbangs went off. Sound and night vision restored in time to see the second door open and two three-man assault teams hurtle into the suite and onto the considerably more powerful inner stun mats. The assaulters dropped their weapons like hot coals and went down, stumbling over each other.

Father John grabbed his cane and hobbled out in the confusion. With regret, he triggered the magnesium incendiary devices that would destroy the sophisticated electronics in his room, and probably trigger the fire alarm and sprinklers. He hit the call buttons for both elevators, then took the left fire stairs to the roof where he crossed over three other buildings before stashing his escape gear in a rooftop box and going down the fire stairs to his alternate room, configured identical to the one he'd just torched.

As he entered the backup site, Connie looked up from her position at the desk. "Hello, Dad."

Though lots of people called him Father, no one but her called him dad.

"I was watching on the monitor. What did those guys want? Did you forget to pay your rent?"

He chuckled. "Much worse. Someone pierced the veil. They know I'm here and knew where to find me. They sent the bishop to arrange a meeting to discuss what we know about Henrietta's murder. I told them no. Did anyone follow me across the rooftops?"

"Not a soul."

"Unfortunately, if their command could find me once, they could locate me again, particularly since this location duplicates the first. Whatever they used to detect the first hideout, they could detect the backup site too. Not for long." He methodically switched off all his electronic devices, including his secure phone. "Time to go. Leave everything."

They took the stairs down, then, using standard counter-surveillance methods, walked the three blocks to the hotel garage where the van was parked. He settled down at the electronics console and powered it up. Facial recognition had identified the two men in the hallway. Both were ex-Rangers currently living in Pooler, just west of Savannah. Father John requested profiles on the two Rangers, then shifted to the front seat and left the garage.

CHAPTER 24

*P*atricia padded upstairs and took a quick shower after her workout in the home gym. Trey wouldn't be home for an hour. The house was empty without him and she felt vulnerable. Strange, because Falcon House was so fortified. But the protections that kept strangers out also kept her in. In the unlikely event she barricaded herself in the safe room, she couldn't escape.

She sat at her vanity and pinned back her hair. Sheila had once said these historic Savannah mansions were connected by tunnels. When Patricia had asked Trey, he claimed the stories were urban myths. He further explained that, in colonial times, Savannah's infamous tunnels connected popular taverns to the waterfront. Pirates used them to Shanghai drunks. Nothing more. She'd dropped the subject. Now, feeling trapped, she wished she hadn't. What if the tunnels beneath the city were more extensive? What if the tunnels were connected to her home? A secret entrance. A secret exit. "Oh my," Patricia whispered aloud, wondering why that hadn't occurred to her before.

Surrendering to her paranoia, Patricia decided to explore.

She went down to the neglected, unfinished basement, turned on the lights, and began to search methodically. First the ballast-stone walls, then the packed dirt floor. Nothing suggested a tunnel entrance.

Miffed at being so foolish, she stomped up the stairs, stopping midway. She stepped down hard on the next step. It sounded hollow. Of course. Empty space beneath the stairs. What a fool. She hadn't checked under the stairs. She went back down and examined the paneled wall that enclosed the stairs. No door there.

Still, there might be an entrance concealed behind the paneling. She was used to calling her own shots, but Trey would have a fit if he knew what she was contemplating. Nevertheless, she grabbed a claw hammer and flashlight from the tool bench and removed a panel. The air beneath the stairs tasted stale. She panned the light into the void.

"Goodness gracious," she said, covering her mouth. Goose bumps erupted. Spiders. A huge colony of spiders scurried back into the shadows. Her hand trembled, bouncing the flashlight beam over the thicket of spider webs. Time to call the exterminators. Then she saw something else. Well beyond the dense webs loomed a huge dark shape that could be an old cabinet or vault. She gulped. Go in?

No. She couldn't go in. Too dangerous. Killer spiders. Though the thought snatched her breath, she squared her shoulders. It would be better not to think about checking out the cabinet right now. She'd heard of deadly brown recluse spiders and knew they were present in Savannah, but she had no idea what they looked like. Unwilling to go farther without that knowledge, she went upstairs to search the Internet for a definitive photo of one.

At the top of the stairs, she recalled that Simon had shut down the home network and confiscated her laptop. She went into the dining room.

Simon sat at the table removing a black box from her laptop.

"Simon," she said.

He looked up, wariness in his look, as though he was trying to figure out what she wanted before she asked.

"What the hell are you doing to my laptop?"

"Removing your hard drive," he said in a cool tone.

"That's my life you're doing surgery on. You can't do that. No. No. No."

"Your network has been compromised. Someone may have already copied all your files. Chances are they have. But if they haven't, I want this hard drive detached from your computer. No one can see what's on this drive when it's removed."

"And my computer won't run without the hard drive. I *need* my computer." Patricia thought about all her documents, bridge club letters, Junior League membership files. She felt mildly ill, but then she thought of the alternative; a killer on the loose. "Fine. A new computer."

She left the room shaking her head. After all this was done, if they survived, and if she still cared, she could replace all of that information. In the living room she composed herself, then called Trey. "Hi, honey. Sorry to bother you. Are you still at the office?"

"Yeah."

"I need a secure laptop."

"What's going on?" Trey asked.

"Simon says our home network has been compromised so he's shut down my computer and our home network. And I just saw some spiders in the basement. I think they may be those deadly ones." Her skin crawled at the thought. "I need a secure computer to look up pictures of bad spiders."

"Call the exterminators."

"Trey!"

"Okay. I suppose I can locate a secure laptop with satellite access for you. I'll bring one home tonight. I'll be late. Don't hold dinner. Can it wait until then?"

"I wish you were here."

"I do too, Patsy, but I have a job to do tonight that could lead to who killed your mother."

"Be careful."

*   *   *

AFTER FATHER JOHN AND HIS DAUGHTER WALKED INTO THE city parking garage, Trey left his vantage point and climbed into the passenger side of Alton's Mercedes to await their exit.

When Father John's van emerged from the garage, Alton pulled his Mercedes into traffic behind it. Trey kept radio contact with Beau, who trailed in his own car. Their backup plan for abducting the priest was progressing as intended, but the woman in the priest's van complicated things.

Trey wasn't sure why the priest had shut down his second command center. His profile made him out to be tenacious as well as effective. Did he know the Cotton Coalition was onto him? Probably not. He went straight from his second hideout to his van, making no obvious effort at evasion. Now he was driving without regard for being followed. Was he intentionally baiting them?

"Time to switch," Trey radioed.

Wheels thumping on the cobblestone roadway, Alton slowed the Mercedes and dropped back. Beau pulled his Jaguar up into primary position. The car with Bishop Reilly and his bodyguard kept up with them on a parallel street.

Tires screeched. The Mercedes abruptly stopped, throwing Trey forward into his shoulder strap. Pain raced through his shoulder. He bit his tongue to keep from commenting on Alton's driving.

Alton drummed the steering wheel as a horse-drawn carriage with a half-dozen tourists clip-clopped through the intersection. Down the block, the priest's van turned right.

"He's headed your way, Reilly." Trey shifted in his seat and checked the GPS. "Going west on Bay. Pick him up if you can."

"Got him," Reilly responded.

"Go primary, Reilly. Beau, take up secondary. We'll go parallel."

They continued all the way to the western suburbs and the Interstate. Had the priest had enough? Was he leaving town? That wouldn't do until he'd shared all he knew about the killer with the Coalition.

Alton pulled out a white handkerchief and mopped his pale face. "My old body is decaying," he said softly. "I don't have much time left. Before I go, I want to bring Henrietta's killer to justice."

"According to Bishop Reilly, the priest's information might fill in a lot of voids. Don't worry, Alton, you'll be there when we get the killer."

The homes of the Coalition's mercenaries started to appear on the GPS. Father John's van slowed. Trey straightened. What business could the priest have in Pooler?

* * *

PATRICIA'S SECURE PHONE CHIRPED THE ARRIVAL OF AN incoming call. She glanced at the display. Hayley. Patricia prayed school was going well.

"Hey, Mama. How're you doing?"

Patricia, phone to her good ear, headed for the great

room, thinking about how she'd answer her daughter's question. "I'm doing fine, sweetheart, considering."

"Considering?"

There was no point in beating around the bush. Hayley would find out sooner or later, and Patricia would rather tell Hayley the story accurately than have her daughter get some distorted version. "Meredith got shot and is in a coma—"

"Oh my God."

"And someone tried to ram my car, and our wireless network and my computer have been hacked. So, Daddy got us live-in security."

"Why security? What's going on?"

"The police think your grandmother was murdered and suspect her killer might be the person who attempted to kill Meredith and me, and who broke into my computer. Then yesterday when I was visiting Judy, someone threw a brick at us with a note that said, 'You're next.'"

"Oh my God."

"Daddy had the locks changed and we have round the clock, armed security in the house until this is over."

"Why would anyone want to hurt you?"

"Who knows? We Falcons have many enemies. But we'll find out who it is, believe me." She glanced out the back window. The twilight sky had darkened to gray. "How's school going?"

"Mama, you just told me someone might be trying to kill you. Why would I want to talk about my stupid classes?"

"Oh, honey." Patricia sighed. "Thinking about my situation right now is something I'd like a break from. Talk to me."

"Well, I'm still not connecting with my classwork. Maybe it's because I'm more advanced."

"You might be. But for right now, and especially with what's going on here, you really should finish the semester."

"Well, I, uh, tested out of all my classes. Passed them all."

Patricia let out a surprised breath. "Oh."

"Oh?"

"I'm sorry. That's great, honey. I had no doubt you were as smart as can be. But home isn't a safe place for you. Don't come home." Patricia gritted her teeth. She missed Hayley terribly, and she was so very proud of her.

There was a long pause, then Hayley said, "If I went to Europe for a while this summer, would you come over?"

"Why Europe?"

"I have a friend who scored a summer job in Paris. He invited me to visit him after school is out."

A chill rippled up her arm. "He?"

"Mom! He's just a friend. So, would you come?"

There was no denying Hayley's ingenuity once she became focused on something. "Europe is probably safer for you right now than Savannah. Summer weather should be nice on the Greek Isles. But I'm needed in Savannah until this nasty business is resolved."

"So it's okay if I go to Europe for the summer?"

There was no telling how long it would be until things settled in Savannah. "Since you passed your courses, I suppose so. But let me talk with Daddy first."

"Thank you, Mama."

"So, tell me about this friend of yours." Patricia rearranged the sofa pillows.

"His name is Shawn."

"Shawn? Isn't that the boy you've been seeing since the beginning of school?"

"Yeah. That's the one. He's cute and charming. A couple years older than me. He wants to go to law school."

"That takes top grades."

"He's got them."

"Where's he from?" She picked up the morning paper from the coffee table and put it next to Trey's chair.

"Virginia. His father is a corporate attorney."

"His mother?"

"A Mayflower blueblood. Clubs, afternoon teas, and the usual volunteer work."

She'd fit into Savannah nicely. "Brothers? Sisters?"

"Only child."

"What's he going to do in Paris?"

"Work in the US embassy."

Wow. She didn't see that coming. "Family connections?"

"I suppose."

"Sounds like a nice guy."

Hayley giggled. "He is."

"Is this relationship going anywhere?"

"Not so far."

Another surprise. She wondered if Hayley was being forthright with her. "Do you want it to be more?"

"Yeah."

That was certainly forthright. "Is he reluctant?"

"I wouldn't say that."

"What's standing in the way?"

"School. He's totally focused on acing every class."

Good for him. "There's no school in the summer."

Hayley laughed.

The prospect of a marriage tiptoed through Patricia's mind. "Text me a picture of him."

"He's on Facebook. You can look him up. His name is Shawn Wright."

"Okay, I'll do that. And I'll call you back after I talk with Daddy."

"Thank you, Mama. I love you."

"I love you too."

* * *

Night had finally arrived. Sweet magnolia scented the air. Crickets chirped. The black-clad snatch team had extinguished the parking lot lights and waited in the shadows. All that remained was to lure the priest out of his motel room and into lot. Given his penchant for electronic security, that wouldn't be hard.

"Now," Trey radioed.

One team member thumped the priest's van triggering a screeching security alarm.

Fifteen seconds later the priest, dressed in jeans and a polo shirt, rushed out the exit door closest to the van. Two snatch team members slipped in behind him and cautiously moved forward.

Trey, filled with anticipation, watched from a safe distance as the priest entered the takedown zone in the center of a relatively empty parking lot, well away from his van. The two massive takedown men rushed the priest, knocking him off his feet. Before the priest could scramble up, one man shackled his feet, the other cuffed his hands behind him.

As soon as the priest was searched, bound, and gagged, the searchlight was extinguished. The two takedown men carried him, struggling, back into the motel to an isolated room for interrogation.

Trey and Beau followed and waited as the priest was strapped to a chair in the room. Their work done, the snatch team left.

Trey removed the priest's hood.

The man's eyes snapped shut in the bright light.

"You were invited to meet with me and refused," Trey said. "Do you recall that?"

The priest didn't respond.

"I know you can hear me, and I know you can nod," Trey said. "I'll take your silence to mean that you need encouragement to answer my questions. I'm prepared to provide you more than enough incentive to talk, but I'm sure you already know that. So, one more time. Do you recall refusing my invitation to meet?"

The priest nodded.

"I'm truly sorry for the way you're being treated, John," Trey said.

At the sound of his name, the priest straightened.

"I reached out to you for cooperation and you refused, forcing me to take these measures. Do you understand?"

The priest nodded.

"Since you're cooperating, I'll let you speak." Trey removed the gag, then ran a damp washcloth over Father John's sweaty face. "I represent a local organization that vets certain unwelcome visitors to our fine city. You, unfortunately, fall into that category. Would you please explain the purpose of your visit?"

"I'm here on papal authority."

Trey gave a slight grunt of acknowledgement. "Purpose?"

"Confidential."

"Here's a revelation for you, Father John." Trey lowered his voice. "I know why you're here."

"Then why ask?"

To ensure Father John's attention, Trey took his time to answer, then said, "To assess your willingness to cooperate."

"I've told your representative I won't cooperate."

"I know. So, my friend, have you—"

"You're not my friend."

"Wrong, Father John. At this moment, I'm the only friend you have in Savannah. You can spare us all a lot of trouble by cooperating."

Father John's eyes softened. "I'm not looking for trouble."

"I'm not asking you to betray your instructions, just alter your methods. We both have the same objective—the quick apprehension and successful trial of Henrietta's killer. Correct?"

Father John nodded.

"Of course, I can progress my investigation without you," Trey said. "The fact that I could find you, send my good friend Bishop Reilly to see you, track your escape, and put you in custody should give you an idea of the scope of my resources. Resources that could be useful to your investigation. Here's what I purpose. In partnership with you, we can accelerate our mutual investigations and get the killer into jail as soon as possible. What do you think?"

"I work alone."

Trey reached into his pocket and brought out a note. "This is a message to you from Bishop Reilly verifying who I am and confirming I do good things for the community." He handed the note to Father John. "Father, I need your help."

Father John eyed the note. "He said the same thing to me in person. It's just that—"

"I know, you work alone. Ah, you and the young lady that is."

"Where is she?" Father John glanced around the room.

"Your daughter's fine and in her room."

The priest rocked back ever so slightly. "How do you know she's my daughter?"

"I know many things, such as how a priest can still wear vestments and have a daughter. And I didn't learn that from Bishop Reilly. Now, will you help us, Father?"

Father John eyed Trey up and down, then sighed. "It might work."

"You won't be disappointed," Trey said warmly as he removed the straps from Father John's legs. "If I remove the rest of your restraints, can I trust you?"

"Of course."

"I believe you." Trey removed the strap from John's left arm. "Have you determined who killed Henrietta?"

"Nothing conclusive."

"Any suspicions?"

"Herman Stockford and Sonny Carothers are probably involved, though neither seems capable of orchestrating a crime of this complexity. One's a hired gun. The other's a CPA. The CPA has handled other people's money for years. Why would he take money now?"

"Conditions change," Trey said.

"How would a CPA find a reliable hired gun or a sophisticated poison?"

"Who's Herman Stockford?" Trey asked.

"The late Herman Stockford shot Meredith Stanwick."

"Her assailant is deceased?"

"Recently. In Jasper County. Autopsy will probably show he was poisoned. Likely the same poison that killed Henrietta, but we'll never know."

"You have conclusively linked Mr. Stockford to Meredith's shooting?"

"Herman was in his truck in the parking lot at the time she was shot. I'm sure a forensic exam of his front bumper will provide paint fragments from Meredith's car."

"But you're not certain."

"Correct."

"How does Herman relate to Henrietta?"

"I don't know, but my Vatican office is looking into it. They're quite thorough. If there's a connection, they'll find it. So, what do you know about Mr. Stockford?"

"Never heard of him."

Father John squared his shoulders. "You're kidding?"

"Not at all," Trey said. "What about Sonny Carothers?"

213

"I have nothing on his location or degree of involvement, if any."

"We've drawn a blank too," Trey said.

"Did you know Meredith Stanwick was working on what happened to Henrietta's money?" Father John asked.

"Yes."

When Father John flexed his fingers, Trey noticed one was arthritic. "I believe Ms. Stanwick got too close to finding out who the killer was, and the killer wanted her out of the way."

"Did she find where the money is kept?"

Father John locked eyes with Trey. "Probably."

"Have you?"

Father John nodded.

Beau stepped close. "Sorry to interrupt. There's been a new development."

CHAPTER 25

*P*atricia put the case file aside and keyed a text to Alisa.

PF: *Any update on Sonny's acquaintances?*

When Alisa didn't reply, Patricia phoned Alisa without success, left a voicemail and then glanced at her cell phone. Nine-thirty. Like the evening outside, the den was dark and still. She tapped her fingertips on the arm of the upholstered chair. The smooth rhythm of her life had turned to chaos. Unfamiliar had plunged like a knife into familiar.

She grabbed the mohair throw and tossed it over her legs.

The doorbell chimed, bringing her back to her senses.

Patricia shoved the throw aside, turned on a lamp and waited for Simon to summon her.

He promptly appeared in the wide doorway with a glum-looking Chief Patrick. Simon left as Chief Patrick, dressed in a dark suit, entered.

Patricia stood, taut, sensing something was amiss, hoping Trey and Hayley were okay. Thoroughly worried, she struggled to maintain her composure.

As was their custom, they greeted each other with a polite

hug. When Chief Patrick stepped back, she noticed his brown eyes were bloodshot.

Seeing hesitancy on his round face, she asked, "Long day?"

He nodded. "And a sad one as well. Alisa had a heart attack earlier this evening—"

"What?" Her knees failed her and she plopped down in a chair. "Oh no, not ..." The lump of despair in her throat made it difficult for her to talk, to swallow, to breathe.

"I'm sorry to have to tell you this, but she passed away before her husband could get her to the hospital."

"Oh my God." She shook her head as a pain-induced moan pushed past her clinched lips. This was too much. The last straw. She clutched her arms and rocked back and forth.

The front door slammed. Rapid, thudding footfalls came down the hall. Trey surged into the room, hesitated when he saw Chief Patrick, and then rushed to her, pulling her up and out of the chair into his arms.

"You already know," he said, stepping back to arm's length. "We're leaving. Don't bother packing. Just get your passport and come with me."

Trey's unexpected arrival and actions interrupted Patricia's shock, forcing her to look at him. The deep shadows accenting his ashen face, his urgency, jerked her back to the reality of her situation, her vulnerability. Alisa was dead. Her security was penetrated. No one was safe.

Trey grabbed her hand and tugged her toward the hallway. "Now."

He'd said passport? Yes. Escape the madness. Just the thought of leaving brought strength back to her legs. As she departed the room, she thought she heard him ask Chief Patrick for immediate transportation to the airport.

Amid her grief and misery, now muted by purpose, hope, and retribution, she searched with trembling hands for her passport in the hidden compartment in her dresser. She ached with cold. Her torso shivered uncontrollably. She rubbed her upper arms. Nausea rose. The contents of the hidden compartment went in and out of focus. Shapes shifted. Colors ignited. The room tilted. Panting, she staggered to the bathroom, doubled up over the toilet and vomited over and over until her stomach emptied.

Head whirling and disoriented, she sank to the cool tile floor and palmed sweat from her face. Or was it tears? Or both? Not that it mattered.

"Patricia, it's important we leave. We have to go. Now," Trey yelled from the other room.

She stood on trembling knees, retrieved the passport and determinedly stumbled back to the living room.

"Do you have your gun?" Trey asked.

She nodded.

He held out his hand. "Give it to me."

"Someone just killed Alisa."

"No guns allowed where you're going."

"What?"

"Just give me your gun."

She handed it over and he put it in the hall table drawer.

The night air was brisk as they left the house and made their way to Chief Patrick's windowless, black police van. The van took off once the three had settled.

"What about Hayley?"

"I called her on the drive here. She should be on her way to the Atlanta airport."

"Meredith?"

"She can't be moved." Trey let out a sigh. "We've stepped up her security."

"And Judy?" Patricia asked.

"She and Beau are leaving with us," Trey replied, his voice strangely coarse.

"Beau?"

"She wouldn't leave unless he went too."

They didn't go directly to Judy's home. Rather, they cut through alleys and circled back on themselves. Though Patricia didn't like the dark, congested alleys, she didn't say anything about them.

"Something about this has been bothering me, Trey."

"What's that?"

"With all the people looking into Mama's murder, the police, the Coalition, the church, even Willie Maye, why do you suppose the only people the killer seems to be after is my team?"

Trey shrugged. "Maybe Meredith got too close. And the killer doesn't know what she told y'all. You know, like he's trying to cover his tracks."

"But everyone knows where the money is now. So if that's a tipoff, why wouldn't the killer go after the other investigators?"

"Perhaps he doesn't know their identities."

"Yeah. Maybe that's it."

As she gnawed her lip, she glanced at Trey and envied his ability to remain calm and decisive at times like this.

"So how did the killer get our identities?"

"Meredith was talking to you when she was shot," Trey said. "Her assailant could have looked at her phone to get your phone number. Perhaps even your name." He nodded toward the curb. "We're here."

The van slowed and pulled up beside Judy's home. The house was dark. Judy and Beau emerged from the shadows and silently entered the van. Judy, her hair a mess and her face red, looked like crap, in strong contrast to Beau who, dressed casually in black, seemed groomed for a night on the town.

Patricia reached out and touched Judy's arm. "Are you okay?"

Her face scrunched. "Not really."

Judy opened her purse, found a pillbox, and lifted the jeweled lid. She removed one of the little white pills that crammed the box and popped the medication in her mouth. Judy leaned forward and offered the pills to Patricia.

Patricia shot Judy a look. She hated chemical crutches. "No, thank you."

"Are you sure?"

Patricia looked away, shaking her head. "I'm sure."

Of all times, this was a time when it was absolutely important to stay mentally alert and figure things out. She wished Judy would do the same even though their grief was so raw. First Mama, then Meredith and now Alisa. The answers to these crimes felt like they were just beyond Patricia's grasp, but she couldn't get there.

"Mr. Falcon," came a male voice over the van's intercom. "Your party has been approved for military transport."

"Military transport?" she asked Trey.

"Harder to track."

She liked that idea, felt comforted, but wondered how Trey had arranged for transport so quickly. She nuzzled him.

Trey massaged her neck, then the top of her shoulders.

The van slowed, then stopped. Ahead lay a long row of motionless cars.

"Go around them," Chief Patrick told the driver.

Emergency lights flashing, the van pulled onto the wide sidewalk, inched forward to an alley and turned into the darkness.

Patricia shuddered when she felt Trey tense.

Judy popped another happy pill.

"Is this safe?" Beau asked Chief Patrick.

"We do it all the time."

The driver seemed to know what he was doing, moving confidently past kitchen staff idling outside open doors and around rusted dumpsters.

"Trey, are we going overseas?" she asked, breaking the silence that saturated the van as it traversed the alley.

He nodded.

"Where?"

"Paris."

"Why Paris?"

"There's a Joint Operations safe house there y'all can use. If you and Hayley don't want to stay in—"

"I love Paris," Judy said. "We'll have a great time there, Patricia. Beau and I know some absolutely wonderful clubs with fabulous food and music. Trust me. We'll make sure you two have a grand time."

Patricia, guessing Judy's happy pills were kicking in, frowned. They were on the run and Judy was planning a vacation. How weird. "I just can't. It doesn't seem appropriate. Please, don't push me."

Judy nodded like a bobblehead doll. Beau seemed to have withdrawn into a world of his own.

"Is there somewhere else you'd rather go?" Trey asked.

Patricia shook her head, and it was settled. Paris was their destination.

Patricia's mind whirled as the van edged out of the alley into a street bright with colorful neon and an energetic club crowd. The only traffic jam was on the sidewalk as fashionable young adults surged between the clubs in search of who-knew-what. Paris with Hayley was undeniably much more inviting.

"How's the case coming for your team?" Patricia asked.

Trey turned to her. In the dim interior light he looked tired but commanding. "We made a breakthrough just a couple of hours ago. I think I know who shot Meredith."

Judy straightened. "How'd you find that?"

"My sources."

Instinct told Patricia there was more. "What do you mean 'sources'?"

"Uh ... a priest."

"A priest told you who shot Meredith?" Judy asked.

He nodded, then gave Patricia a long, silent, questioning look. "You and your friends," he motioned at Judy, "have clearly become the focus of the killer's game. This lead should speed things up, but you're both going to have to disappear until we put the killer behind bars."

She chewed her lower lip.

He took her hand and held it tightly. "Is there something you're not telling me?"

She shrugged. "I'm sure you know more than me. We got a license number on that truck and I gave it to Simon. And when I was at Judy's someone threw a brick over the wall that said, 'you're next'."

Beau turned to Judy. "You didn't tell me."

She shrugged. "I didn't want to alarm you."

Patricia frowned again. She knew their relationship was bad, but thought maybe with the current crisis they would become closer.

Trey held out a cell phone. "This is a secure international phone. If you *absolutely* need to call me, use it. Otherwise, no calls, no letters, no email, nothing. Just secure video conferencing from inside the safe house."

"You're not coming to Paris?"

"We're closing in on the killer and are all needed here. You'll be okay. It's a safe house."

"I'd be more comfortable if you came."

"You'll be more comfortable when I put the killer away."

She took the phone and placed it in her purse next to her passport. "So, who's behind all this, Trey?"

"I don't know."

"I thought you identified who shot Meredith, surely—"

"Her assailant is dead. We have his name. Herman Stockford. And we have an out-of-state address for him. It's a big lead. We're questioning his neighbors. One thing will lead to another. Believe me, we're close to identifying the person behind all this. I'll come to Paris for you as soon as this matter is wrapped up."

"I have complete faith you'll solve it soon."

But, despite being overseas, she wasn't going to stop looking for answers; she owed that to Alisa and Meredith and Mama.

CHAPTER 26

*P*aris
As soon as Patricia, Hayley, Judy and Beau got to the Paris safe house, Patricia arranged for a secure video conference with Trey to let him know they had arrived safely.

"Hello, Trey. We made it." Just seeing his face come up on the screen in the safe house communication room filled her with joy.

"How was your flight?"

"Spartan, but I'm not complaining."

He nodded. "Did the airport pickup go okay?"

"Very smooth. VIP treatment from French Customs on the plane and secure transport at plane-side."

"How's the safe house?"

She looked around the room, still awed by the extensive equipment. "Definitely not the Ritz, but it's nice not to be worried about being in the killer's crosshairs. Thank you, Trey, for arranging all this. How's your investigation going?"

He shrugged. "No change since you left. Lots of dead ends, but that's par for the course."

"Did you get Meredith set up so we can video conference with her from here?"

"Yes. She says she's looking forward to seeing your smiling faces."

"How's she doing?"

"She's Meredith," Trey said. "It would take more than a shot in the head to slow her down. How's Hayley?"

Patricia took a sip of spring water. "I think the jet lag has gotten to her. She didn't get much rest on the flight over, so she's sleeping right now."

"Judy and Beau?"

"Judy and her security detail went shopping. I don't know about Beau. He said something about video conferencing with the Coalition later today."

"Yeah. We have that set up for two your time."

"I'm sure the six-hour time difference creates some scheduling issues for y'all."

"We'll work around that," Trey said. "The biggest problem is that Beau doesn't have his case files with him."

"What about the cloud?"

"Beau's old school. Doesn't use the cloud. He's got the basic information in his laptop, and we'll feed him anything else he needs."

"Have you determined if the poison that killed Alisa was the same as the poison that killed Herman?"

"It was."

"The poison was relatively fast acting?"

"It is."

"Alisa was poisoned in her home?"

"She died in her home."

"Have you checked to see who had access to her home the day she died? Specifically, an hour or so before her death."

"Her husband doesn't think anyone was in the house the

hour right before she died, other than him. He'd only been home a half hour or so when she collapsed."

"Does he normally come home at that time?"

"No. He came home early."

"What about the contents of Alisa's stomach?"

"Why are you asking all these questions, Patsy?"

She let out a long breath. "I may be in hiding, but I'm still doing what I can to find Alisa's murderer."

Trey leaned closer to the camera. "I wish you'd stay out of this."

"I can't. I owe it to Alisa, Meredith, and Mama. Besides, the more minds working this case, the better. So, Alisa's stomach. Had she recently eaten?"

"No."

"Would the poison be stable in a beverage?"

"Possibly," he said. "I'll check. Good thinking, Patsy."

"Thank you. Are you still focusing on Herman as the key lead?"

"Yeah."

"What do you know about him?"

"All we have is his driver's license and vehicle registration. He wasn't carrying credit cards, and his cell was prepaid. No criminal record. No military service. No matches on his fingerprints or DNA. So far, we can't find a link between him and your mom."

"Any idea where he stayed in Savannah?"

"No."

"Would you send me your file on him?"

"Patsy, I'd like you to leave this business to me."

"I know, Trey. But I have to keep digging. Please humor me. The file, please."

"Okay. What do you have in mind?"

"Nothing yet. But if I find something new, I'll give it to Beau."

"OK. I just sent the file to you."

"Thank you, Trey. Talk to you tomorrow, if not before."

Patricia returned to her room after the video conference and exchanged emails with Meredith. Then she took a short nap, showered, and spent the afternoon reviewing the file on Herman. She and Hayley met Judy and Beau for an early dinner. Though the restaurant was down the street from the safe house their respective security details were close by.

"Whoever killed Herman killed Alisa," Patricia said to Judy. "Same poison. We need to find out who he spent time with in Savannah."

"No help on credit cards or phone records," Beau said.

Patricia nodded. "Trey told me. So, he used cash for everything. Where did he get the money from? Did he bring it to Savannah? Did he cash a check here? If she's well enough, Meredith could help us track that down."

"The killer might have hired him," Judy said. "You know, paid him off with cash."

"I still think we should have Meredith check her sources," Patricia said. "We can discuss that when we video conference her tomorrow morning."

CHAPTER 27

*A*t eight the following morning, Patricia and Judy met in the safe house communications room to video conference with Meredith.

"Good morning, y'all," Meredith said as her image appeared on the screen.

"How are you feeling?" Patricia asked.

"I have a little headache," Meredith said with a slight smile. "How about y'all?"

"Still jet lagged," Judy said.

"Meredith, did you get a name on that account where Mama's money is?"

"Yes. Herman Stockford."

"Was anyone else's name on the account?" Judy asked.

"No."

"We need to get everything we can on that account," Patricia said. "Especially the bank's internal security videos for the day the account was opened. They might show an accomplice or possibly Herman's boss."

"Will do." The tapping of keys came from Meredith's open microphone. "Okay."

"Have you had a chance to review the Herman file?" Patricia asked.

Meredith nodded. "Yes."

"Herman didn't have any credit cards in his wallet, and Trey says there's no record of any being issued to him. So we can assume Herman did everything in Savannah on a cash basis. I think our priority should be to determine where that cash came from."

"He might have a checking account in the city on his driver's license." More key tapping sounded from Meredith's end. "I'll check on that."

"Or someone in Savannah, perhaps the killer, was financing him," Patricia said. "Could you see if he cashed any checks in Savannah?"

Meredith dipped her chin. "Sure."

"I don't think the killer would be that stupid," Judy said.

"I'll still check just to eliminate the possibility."

Patricia glanced at her notes. "Another source of money could be a local job. If Herman had a job, they'd have to withhold taxes. We have his Social Security Number. Could you get access to his Georgia withholding?"

"Not officially," Meredith said. "But I have friends in high places. If Herman worked in Georgia and paid state withholding, I can find out."

"Wonderful." Patricia smiled her appreciation for Meredith's incredible resources. "Any more ideas, anyone?"

"Alisa was tracking down Sonny's local contacts when she was killed," Judy said. "It's possible she was getting too close to finding Sonny, so he killed her. I think we should keep an open mind that Sonny may be the killer."

Patricia turned to Judy. "Good thinking. Would you follow up on that?"

"Judy, if you need any help here in Savannah, let me know," Meredith added.

Judy gave a thumbs-up. "Will do."

"Okay, ladies, same time tomorrow." Patricia waved to Meredith. "Take care, Meredith. Watch your back."

"Y'all stay safe," Meredith said, returning the wave.

* * *

"I WANT TO DO RIGHT, MAMA," HAYLEY SAID OVER THE thrumming traffic noise on Avenue des Champs Elysees. She removed the linen napkin from the café table, placed it on her lap, and took a deep breath. "But I still don't have my heart in school. I'd like to delay school and spend a year here in Europe."

Patricia grimaced. "With that boy, Shawn?"

"No. He's only going to be here for the summer. After he goes back to school, I'd like to tour Europe. Please don't hate me."

Patricia reached across the small wrought-iron table, smiled, and took Hayley's hand. "Hate you? No. I love you more than anything. Go ahead. Take some time off. Gramps cavorted around Europe the summer before he entered Harvard Law School. He said it did him good. Once back, he settled down and graduated first in his class. You go ahead. See Europe, darlin'."

"I'm truly sorry."

"Nothin' to be sorry about, child." Patricia squeezed Hayley's hand. "I've learned a whole lot about how precious life is lately. Follow your heart. The path won't always be easy, don't you know. But your heart won't mislead you."

Tires screeched.

Patricia looked up.

A black sedan hopped the curb and came straight at their—

Patricia bolted up and grabbed Hayley's arm. Hayley's brown eyes widened as Patricia yanked her to her feet.

The car plowed through the empty table in front of theirs, scattering chairs.

Turning her back to the car, Patricia wrapped her body around Hayley, shielding her.

The sedan rammed the iron table into Patricia's back, knocking her down on top of Hayley. Terrible, mind-numbing pain tore through Patricia's back. The world spun. Brilliant stars filled her vision. She tried to scream. Nothing. The head-to-toe agony became secondary. Air! Air! She needed breath.

She inhaled, gasped from the stabbing pain, and sucked in the hurt with the air. Her mouth tasted of blood. The sickening smell of fuel registered. *Get up. Get up, get Hayley and—*

A bright flash exploded around her. Glass shattered. Hellfire scorched her back. She gulped foul air. Coughed. Choked. Her ears buzzed.

She forced her eyes open and looked back. Ten feet from her, huge orange flames engulfed the car. Black smoke billowed. Overhead, flames consumed the café's canvas awning. The quickly spreading fire would soon engulf them; they'd surely die.

No! She was still alive. She could survive. She put her palms flat on the ground and pushed up. Searing pain filled her back. Each life-sustaining breath was torture. Still, she persisted, finally standing on weak legs and helping Hayley to stand. Six, maybe ten, pain-stabbing steps later Patricia, shouldering Hayley, couldn't go any further. There was no air, no legs, no ...

* * *

PATRICIA RAN HER TONGUE OVER SLICK LIPS. HER PULSE

throbbed softly in her head. The air reeked of alcohol and pine disinfectant.

"*Madame* is a very courageous woman," a distant female voice said with a French accent. "Her quick action saved her daughter's life."

A shudder ran the length of Patricia's right arm. She forced her reluctant eyelids open to see who was speaking. Though blinding brightness registered, all she saw was a gray linoleum floor three feet below her. And why was she suspended in air? Where was she? Why couldn't she move? Her head spun. Her stomach roiled. She was going to vomit. She opened her mouth.

"She moved her lips," the voice said. "*Madame* Falcon. Patricia Falcon. Can you hear me?"

Patricia wanted to say 'yes' but her throat was numb. No words formed. No sound came. She nodded.

"*C'est bon*," the voice said. "Do not talk. You are in the hospital. Your back has been badly burned. You are in a special bed to keep you off your back, and you *must* remain calm. The medication will help you."

Patricia tried to smile her understanding, but her lips wouldn't move. She tried to raise her hand to her face. Neither arm would elevate.

"Do not struggle," the voice said. "You need to rest."

Her questions about Hayley's condition wouldn't rest until she knew the answers. Desperation raged, whipped, and tore through her head like a hurricane. Why couldn't she speak? Was it the drugs or her injuries?

Drool trickled from her mouth. Something refreshingly cool and wet wiped it away. Her face tingled where the drool had been. Someone was close enough to notice, to help.

If she made eye contact with them, maybe she'd get answers. Head throbbing, she squinted her eyes. Two slits. She scanned left and right for a body, anyone. Contact. She had to make contact. She twisted her head from side to side and searched the brightness. She could only make out an outline of what might have been a person. Good.

Darkness swallowed her.

* * *

Trey awoke from a troubled sleep as the Gulfstream eased down on the Orly Airport runway. His mouth was as dry as toast, and his bleary eyes itched. The jet shuddered as thrust was reversed and brakes engaged. The craft slowed. He yawned and stretched stiff joints, then watched the rain-soaked runway as they taxied to the General Aviation terminal.

As soon as the engines were shut down, a black Peugeot pulled up to the side of the jet. Still in a fog, he grabbed his briefcase, went to the front of the plane, and waited as the cabin attendant opened the door, deploying the stair into the rain. The wet tarmac glistened like black ice.

Two shadowy figures wrapped in black trench coats got out of the Peugeot, popped mammoth umbrellas, and scampered up the stairs.

As soon as the customs agent cleared him, they left the jet. Swirling, howling wind whipped rain everywhere. Together with his escorts, he cautiously clomped down the slippery steps and spilled into an idling limo.

Trey settled back onto the soft leather seat and breathed in the leather aroma wafting in the air. Normally, he would have been comforted by the familiar scent, but not today. He had too much on his mind.

As the limo left the airport and took the ramp onto the autoroute to the city, the gale picked up, sweeping the windows with sheets of rain as though the car had entered a violent car wash.

Patricia and Hayley were confined to an antiseptic hospital world where his incompetence had put them. He knew when your loved ones were in peril, you kept them close, guarded, and never out of sight. But he had gotten caught up in the chase for the killer, and the killer had been one step ahead in the chase for his family. A mistake. A God-awful mistake.

On the flight over, he'd been in contact with the French police, gathering information. The media was calling the car bombing at the café another terrorist attack, but no one had come forward to claim credit. Trey believed the attack was personal. The killer had followed his family to Paris. His throat constricted and he swallowed a choked breath.

The limo left the expressway. He looked out the window. Bleak, gray buildings with steep roofs came into view. No pedestrians. No one at the sidewalk café tables. The squall seemed to have sucked life from the city. As if to match his mood, *La Ville Lumière*, the City of Light, had morphed into the City of Gloom. Like a bar at closing, Paris had become inhospitable—lights off, everyone out.

Immediately on arriving at the *Hôpital Cochin* in Paris and presenting his credentials, Trey was shown to a small, tasteful conference room in the Burn Centre. The subdued incandescent lighting was warm. The absence of sound gave the place a solemn air.

An aide appeared and asked if he'd like coffee. Still under the influence of jet lag and a sleepless night, Trey was happy to say yes. The man left.

Haunted by concern for his family, Trey sat facing the entrance in one of the four leather chairs neatly arranged around a circular, polished teak table.

From what he had learned from his local contacts, the hospital was a level-one trauma facility, as well as the largest

Burn Centre in France. Fortunately for his loved ones, they were in the best place for their injuries.

He knew the basic details of Patricia's and Hayley's situation, but he had been advised the true extent of their injuries would take at least twenty-four hours to manifest. Frightful time he had partially spent crossing the Atlantic by private jet and sitting in a French government limo as it rushed through the streets of Paris.

Two men and a woman entered. The men wore suits and the woman wore a wrinkled lab coat.

Trey stood on unsteady legs. His hands quivered as he searched their somber faces for any sign of good news. Seeing none, his heart sank.

A tall, square-faced, white-haired male introduced himself as the translator. He had a vacant look that probably suited his occupation. Then the female doctor overseeing Patricia's and Hayley's care introduced herself, and, finally, the male head of hospital security. As might be expected, the security man's build was stocky and tall. The doctor seemed tiny and fragile beside the two huge men. Her short black hair contrasted sharply with her ghostly pale skin. They sat around the table.

The aide flitted in with coffee service and poured according to each person's preference.

The translator asked, "Shall we begin, *Monsieur* Falcon?"

Trey nodded, then took a sip of the harsh and hot coffee. The coffee jolted his senses to full awareness. This could be the most important meeting of his life. He needed to be totally in it. He took and a swig of fortification.

The doctor repositioned her oversize glasses, consulted her tablet computer, and lifted her sad brown eyes to fix on his face.

His jaw tightened. He wanted the truth, but he feared it as

well. He had no doubt the news would be devastating. A freight train of guilt returned.

The doctor spoke in French. The translator followed in accented English. "Your daughter, Hayley, faired remarkably well. Just a few superficial burns, some abrasions from her fall and smoke inhalation."

The doctor drew in a sharp breath. "Her burns are first-degree. Those wounds can be quite painful. Over the next two or three days the redness and pain should subside. Much like a sunburn, by the fourth day the injured skin will peel away."

The doctor's brow furrowed, marking her concern. "Sadly, your wife's injuries are more serious. Though her arm and back burns are largely second-degree, fortunately, the rest of her body escaped serious injury. No broken bones from being struck, but some torn ligaments. She too suffers from smoke inhalation. Her burns should, baring complications, spontaneously heal within two to three weeks without functional impairment, though she is likely to have long-term pigment changes. At this point, my primary concern is infection prevention and keeping further desiccation of the wounds under control."

"When may I see my wife and daughter?" he asked in a strangely weak voice.

"Immediately, if you wish."

"I wish."

"Pardon me, *Monsieur*," the security chief said. "About the Swiss Guard?"

"I want them to guard both rooms around the clock."

"Is there a particular reason?"

"Someone tried to kill my family with a car bomb. I don't want the killer to be able to have access to my family here."

The security chief nodded. "The papal guards will be no

problem, *Monsieur*. However, if I might be so bold as to make a suggestion, since the Swiss Guard has no police authority in our country you might want to see if the Holy Father would grant your family members diplomatic status during their stay. If diplomatic status were given, the Swiss Guard would have full police authority over all matters concerning them."

"An excellent suggestion, sir. Now, might I have access to my family?"

CHAPTER 28

*T*rey, dressed in cap, mask, gown and booties, pushed aside his trepidation. He sanitized his hands and stepped into the dim hospital room.

Patricia, arms swathed in bandages, lay facedown on the bed.

On seeing Patricia, his breathing accelerated and his pulse pounded in his ears. The image ... the love of his life reduced to *this*. He so wanted to be upbeat for her, but all he could think of was the reality of what he was seeing. The murderer had damn near killed her and Hayley.

Controlled by concern, he swallowed. Hard. Then he took a deep breath. He'd failed her. He'd failed to keep her safe. If he did nothing else the rest of his life, he'd never expose her to danger again. Never.

Though disconcerted, he did his best to push his worry aside so his agitation wouldn't taint his voice. His heart thudded as he watched the green line on her monitor beat faster, watched her respiration pick up. She'd been through so much. She had to be in pain. His voice was the only way he could communicate with her, and he wanted to give her hope, to lift her spirit.

"Patricia. It's me, Trey. Are you awake?" he asked, his words muffled by the thick infection-control mask he wore.

She nodded.

They'd told him because of her smoke inhalation treatment they preferred she didn't talk today. To minimize infection risk, they advised him not to touch her.

"The doctor says you're doing better than anticipated," he said quietly. "I told them to expect more of the same from you."

She nodded again.

"The doctor said Hayley is okay."

She nodded.

"I'm sorry I wasn't here for you. I was wrong to assume you were safe. If ... if only I'd stayed with you. Protected you." He took a deep breath to settle himself. "I love you, Patricia, more than life itself. I know I don't tell you that enough, but you are my bedrock, my foundation, my everything. And no one will come between us again, ever. From now on, I'll protect you. I'll be here for you. You can count on that."

* * *

TREY STEELED HIMSELF, STEPPED INTO HAYLEY'S HOSPITAL room, and froze. Afternoon sun streamed in through the windows. Hayley lay motionless, covered with a thin white blanket. She seemed so alone. So vulnerable. She slowly turned her head toward him.

He fixed his eyes on hers, looking for hope.

Her formerly bright eyes were sunken and dull.

His stomach tumbled. The doctor had said she was on some medication for smoke inhalation. Had the medication stolen her spirit, or had the tragedy? His pulse thundered in his ears. Trying to be strong for her, he forced as warm a smile as possible.

"You look good in white," Trey joked.

She exhaled an extended wheezy sigh.

"Your doctor says you're making good progress."

She nodded. "What ... what happened?"

"The French police think a terrorist was responsible. The car that jumped the curb was rigged with explosives and gasoline. They might be right. But there wasn't a corpse in the car. Whoever drove that car wanted to survive. Survival doesn't fit the standard terrorist profile. Plus, it was the wrong time of day. The café didn't have many customers. I think you and Mama were targeted."

"Did they capture the driver?"

"Not yet, but you're safe here. Your room is guarded by a special agent from the Vatican." He swallowed. "Sugar, you and Mama are the two people I care *most* about." He gritted his teeth. "I can't express how sorry I am for not being here. I made a mistake. A horrible, gut-eating mistake. I'm sorry. And though I so wish I could, I can't change what happened. But I can prevent any more harm from coming to you or your mother, and I will." He released a long sigh, hoping she'd reply, but she didn't. "Do you hate me?"

"No," she said, wheezing. "I don't hate you. I love you."

He squeezed her hand.

Hayley's eyes got hard. "So it wasn't a random attack?"

Trey swallowed. "I don't believe so, but don't worry. I'll never leave you or your mom again until this killer is caught. I'm going to do everything I can to stop the killer and bring him to justice."

"*We* are. I'm not afraid of him. I'll do anything I can to help, Daddy."

"That's my girl."

Her face transformed. Determination filled her eyes.

"Daddy," she said, "how's Mama?"

"She's doing better than the doctor expected."

"Exactly how is she?"

"Honey." He gently took her hand. "Her condition is serious, but not life-threatening. It will be two or three weeks before her wounds heal."

"Can I visit her?"

"Of course. Incidentally, I have someone I'd like you to meet."

"Who?"

"He's a person I've spent the last two weeks with. He's become like a brother to me. He's very smart about major criminal matters like this and has great contacts here in Paris. I trust him explicitly. It was his idea to have the papal guard in the hall." He stepped to the door and opened it. "He's just out here. Father John, would you please come in?"

Father John shuffled in and dipped his head to her.

"Hayley, allow me to introduce Father John. Father John, this is my daughter, Hayley."

Father John went to her bedside and peered down.

Hayley offered him her hand.

Father John took her hand. "Please call me John," he said in a kind voice.

"My pleasure, John."

"Father John will be here while I'm sleeping and—"

"You're ... you're going somewhere?"

"Just down the hall." Trey gave Hayley a pager. "Just a page away."

"Daddy, could I speak with you in private?"

"I'll just step outside." Father John inclined his head toward the door.

Once he left the room, Trey asked, "What is it?"

"He's an old, crippled priest. How's he going to protect us? Prayer? Divine intercession?" Hayley glanced out the window, where a mango sky was developing. "You know I'm a believer, Daddy, but Mama and I need a lot more than faith right now."

"I know, honey. Don't be deceived by appearances. Father John has keen senses, an exceptional mind, and is considerably more talented than anyone else I could find to protect y'all. And I'll be staying just down the hall. Trust me. What do you say? Are you good with this?"

"I guess so."

CHAPTER 29

Shortly before nine the next morning, Patricia opened her eyes and looked at her bandaged arm. Agitation billowed at being targeted. Targeted just like Mama, Meredith and Alisa. A shiver went through her, triggering sharp pain in her back. She let out a whimper, then clamped down her jaw and squeezed her eyelids tight, fighting to maintain control. If she showed too much agony, they'd restart the heavy-duty painkiller morphine. And she didn't want to go back into *that* foggy numbness again.

Despite the painkillers, the pain lurked, waiting for any movement. She took slow, even breaths. Calm, controlled breathing was hard. She wanted to gulp air, but she persisted with controlled breathing. As she calmed, the pain eased.

Her resentment toward her assailant was overwhelmed by her guilt. Her guilt over pulling her friends into the investigation of her mother's death, and then putting her daughter at risk. In retrospect, she should have done the investigation by herself, just her and Trey. Trey had better resources than her friends. But in her defense, at the time she was neither sure her mother had been murdered, nor did she know how maniacal the killer was.

She whispered a prayer for Meredith's full recovery, and for Mama and Alisa.

As for praying for her enemies? A sincere prayer for the perpetrator was going to take a while. Maybe after he was caught. Perhaps longer. At this stage, her anger overwhelmed forgiveness.

A knock sounded at the door. Her attention darted toward the entrance. When she saw Hayley shuffle in with Trey right behind her, Patricia's body tensed. Hayley moved ever so slowly, wearing a scruffy green hospital gown identical to the one shrouding Patricia. Hayley's ointment-slathered face was red and puffy like a bad sunburn. Patricia couldn't help but wonder what the rest of Hayley's body looked like.

As their eyes met, Hayley looked as stricken at seeing Patricia as Patricia felt about seeing her daughter.

Oh, Hayley, I'm so sorry. The words were in her head but she couldn't speak them.

Trey, straight and steady, walked to the bedside.

She dragged her gaze to him. Her man. Her dear husband. His gray-streaked hair shimmered in the bright overhead light that also accentuated his cheekbones above his mask.

He looked at her tenderly. "Thank God I have my girls back together again." He touched her hand. "How are you doing today?"

"Much better," she whispered, trying to maintain a sense of dignity. Her raw throat made speaking painful. But forced silence for two days made her want to speak her mind. "How are you taking this?" she asked, knowing his steely exterior hid emotions he'd only share when solicited.

His eyes pleaded for understanding. "I failed you and Hayley."

She squeezed his hand. "It's not your fault."

He paused, open-mouthed. His eyes gleamed, or were tears forming? He hung his head. "You don't know how much you treasure your family until they're nearly snatched from you and made to suffer beyond my comprehension."

She hated seeing him so pained, so exhausted.

He tilted his chin up a tad and rolled his shoulders back. "But, it is what it is." He put his arm around Hayley and added gently, "With God's help, we'll make it through this. We always have."

She knew his words, though spoken humbly, were no idle boast. They had survived disasters before, had been richly blessed, and were sincerely thankful.

A tear slipped down to the top of Hayley's mask.

"About your security," Trey said. "In addition to the guards, Father John's going to take care of things here when I can't."

Patricia's throat constricted. "You're leaving?"

"Just to sleep. Father John and I share a room down the hall."

"You can sleep here." She gestured toward the guest chair.

"They're still worried about infection and want you isolated as much as possible. Plus, I have a full bed in the other room."

"You don't look rested." Though talking hurt, the interaction lifted her spirits. And the more normal she acted, though exhaustion and the drugs were pulling her away, the more settled Trey would become. "You need to take better care of yourself."

"Me?" He shook his head. "No. I need to take better care of my family. Speaking of which ..." Trey opened a small duffle bag he carried and removed a handgun. "I want you to keep this close." He offered her the gun.

"They're concerned with infection. Is this sanitized?"

"One hundred percent." He handed her the gun.

"I thought guns weren't allowed here."

"They aren't. Your protection is more important to me than their laws. Besides, I'm working on securing diplomatic immunity for you while we deal with this."

"What about the guards outside?" she asked.

"This will hedge the bet."

"My last resort." She took the gun and checked it. The safety was off and a round was chambered. She slid the gun under her pillow, then wondered how she'd hide the gun when they changed her bedding. She'd cover that base when necessary. "Any progress on who attacked us?"

"The car was rented with a fake driver's license. The rental agency's security camera was broken. At this point the police are drawing blanks."

"So, since the French police don't have a clue, who's going to catch this madman with you staying here?"

"Father John and I have all our combined resources focused on catching this killer. Believe me, they'll catch him. Now, you just worry about getting better so I can have some of your hugs again."

* * *

TREY ENTERED THE HOSPITAL CAFETERIA AND SPOTTED JUDY sitting alone at a corner table, staring blankly with hands clasped in her lap. She was dressed impeccably in a beige silk suit with her hair pulled back into a ponytail.

He crossed to her.

She stood.

"Judy, you shouldn't be here. With the attack on Patricia, it's too dangerous for you to be traveling about in the city."

"How is Patricia today? When can I see her?"

"She's on the mend. In fact, she doesn't have to sleep on her front anymore. She's itching to get back to investigating."

"So, can I see her?"

"She's going through treatments right now. Maybe you could visit later today, before dinner. I know she'd like the company. Can you stay until then?"

"Absolutely."

Trey escorted Judy to a secure waiting room on Patricia's floor and told the guards to let Judy know when Patricia could have visitors. He then spun on his heels and strode back to his suite.

He was looking forward to getting on the video link with the other Coalition directors that afternoon. He hadn't communicated with them for a couple of days. He hoped they would have good news. If not the name of the killer, at least substantial progress. Was that too much to ask?

Fatigue gnawed at his senses. Trey pressed his fingertips into his temples. All he wanted was sleep, but he couldn't get his mind off one pressing issue—his near-fatal mistake of leaving his family alone in Paris.

He'd not been an attentive father or husband in the past. Between work and the Coalition there hadn't been enough time. He'd foregone so many family pleasures over the years for the sake of preserving the peace in Savannah. He'd missed countless vacations, school activities, birthdays and anniversaries. His stomach churned at the thought of how unfair his work focus had been to Patricia and Hayley. They deserved better.

He pinched the bridge of his nose. Truth be told, he wasn't critical to the Coalition's success. No one was. They had adequate resources at all levels. The directors could function without him. He supposed he could cut back on time spent on Cotton Coalition matters. But was that even possible? He lived to serve, and they seemed to own him. He would change that, today.

He crossed the beige marble lobby to the gleaming brass elevators. The elevator door opened before he could touch the call button—a delightful courtesy presumably triggered by the VIP concierge.

He glanced at his watch. He was right on time for his videoconference with the Coalition directors. Arriving at the door to the suite, he inserted his pass card into the electronic lock. He entered the quiet sanctuary and his feet and mind jarred to a stop. His hand darted for the underarm-holstered gun, then stopped halfway. Could his eyes be deceiving him? Was he that tired? He shook his head to verify what his eyes were seeing—Beau, Alton, Hempfield and Potter crowded around a circular table strewn with papers and laptop computers.

CHAPTER 30

The sight of his Savannah brethren filled his heart and eased some of the tension Trey had carried since learning of the attack on Patricia and Hayley. A good friend was hard to come by, and he had four of the best. This was a testament to why the Coalition owned part of him.

Beau, dressed in wrinkled khaki trousers and a pale blue dress shirt with the sleeves rolled up, stood and fixed his eyes on Trey. "How's Patricia?"

Trey ran his hand through his hair. "She's making remarkable progress, but she tires easily."

The faint lines at the corners of Beau's eyes crinkled. He tilted his head. "And Hayley?"

"Much better," Trey said as he crossed the terrazzo hall to the table and placed his briefcase at an empty spot next to Beau. He took a long moment to stare at his friends and slowly extended his arms. "I cannot express what this means to me, gentlemen."

"Did you see Judy?" Beau asked. "She's here to see Patricia and Hayley."

"Yes. I asked her to delay her visit because Patricia is getting inhalation treatments. Judy's in the secure waiting room. The guards will let her know when Patricia can see visitors."

Alton, wearing dark brown pants and a beige shirt, torso bent almost horizontal, trudged over and clasped Trey's hand. "How're you holding up?"

"Jet-lagged. Tired." He clung to Alton's surprisingly firm, surprisingly soothing hand. "Very tired. How are you holding up, my dear friend?"

"Still kickin'. Just started a new drug that seems to be working. Actually, it was invented over here. Don't that beat all?" Alton raised his bushy eyebrows. "Now, Trey, anything y'all need, anything at all, you be sure to let me know."

Thinking about how the killer might have tracked them, and knowing how much Alton needed to feel helpful, Trey answered, "Come to think about it, Patricia and Hayley could use new secure phones that operate in this country."

Alton's face brightened. He winked. "I'll get right on it."

Trey glanced around. "Y'all going to be here for a while?"

"We're here until we wrap up this nasty business." Potter came over and put his hand on Trey's shoulder. The dark stubble on Potter's face suggested he hadn't shaved for a while. It was quite unlike him to go unshaven. He was normally meticulously groomed.

Trey twisted his mouth. "That could take some time."

"Doesn't it always?" Potter said, stepping back. "But when we're working on something as important as this, time doesn't matter."

Hempfield stepped around the table and draped an arm over Trey's shoulder. "We'll take care of you, buddy. And we'll get that killer as well. Do you want to rest a spell before you join us?"

Trey glanced at the file folders and computers littering the table. "Rest? It looks like y'all started without me."

Smiling, Hempfield patted him on the back. "Started? We started on the flight over and never stopped. We each work for as long as we can, then sleep while the others continue on. There's always at least one of us online. We're open twenty-four hours a day."

"You got to be kidding."

Hempfield shook his head. "It was Alton's idea, and it seems to be working. We get information real time and immediately integrate it. We're beginning to have enough pieces of this puzzle that some parts are actually making sense." Hempfield gestured across the table toward Beau. "For example, Beau has figured out what poison the killer used and we're investigating distribution points within a day's drive of Savannah."

"Online?" Trey asked.

"No legal online sales permitted."

Trey looked down at the floor for a moment as a thought formed. "If the poison works in a half hour, have we been able to determine who was with the victims in that time frame?"

"Not yet." Hempfield ran his fingers through his unruly hair. "Henrietta was at her country club. Alisa was at home. We have no idea exactly where Herman was a half hour prior to his death, but the autopsy of his stomach suggests he was at a fast-food restaurant. Seventy miles per hour would back calculate to just west of Savannah. We're checking fast-food facilities for security videos."

"What was the time of death for Alisa?" Trey asked.

Potter straightened and tapped his keyboard. "Five p.m."

"Was anyone at home with her at that time?" The thrill of the hunt surged in Trey.

"Just her husband," Potter said, glancing at his monitor.

"Hmmm. Autopsy says her stomach indicated she'd just completed a light meal."

"So in each case the poison was administered with food," Trey said, pleased the puzzle was coming together so well.

"But Herman didn't administer the poison," Potter said. "It goes without saying he wouldn't kill himself. And Alisa died after Herman. The killer is someone else. Someone who hired Herman."

Hempfield keyed up an Internet site on his laptop. As traffic videos came on, he said, "Herman seems to be the key. We have a contractor going through traffic footage looking for Herman's truck. We've had some hits on his license number on the days prior to Henrietta's death. We're hoping to establish a travel pattern that would indicate where he spent his nights."

"What about parking garage footage?" Trey asked.

"We haven't started on that yet."

Trey sat down in an empty chair and keyed his laptop. "He had to park his truck somewhere when he was sleeping."

* * *

A SHARP KNOCK SOUNDED AT THE DOOR.

Patricia stiffened.

The door eased open.

Patricia tried to sit up, the movement causing pain.

Hayley came into the room with an easy gait.

"Hi, honey," Patricia said, relieved and sagging into a tension-free state. "Can you stay for a while?"

"About an hour. Until dinner." Hayley pulled a chair to the bedside and sat.

"How are your treatments going?"

"Fine." Hayley inclined her head a tad and raised her eyebrows. "Yours?"

"Mostly infection prevention treatments and so far no issues." She held up her right arm. "They took the bandages off my arms, uh, an hour ago."

Hayley's eyes widened. "That's great, Mama." Hayley leaned forward. "I remember when I was young you told me the Falcon women have always carried guns for protection. Protection from what?"

Patricia tensed again, sending stabbing pain into her back wounds. She willed herself calm. As the pain drained, she wished she could have avoided this conversation forever, that she could have continued to shield her lovely daughter from reality. But, since Trey had armed Hayley when she left for college and the killer had Hayley in his crosshairs, the time for the reality check had clearly come. Patricia hoped she would be able to help Hayley handle whatever distress the discussion would ferment.

"Do you have a dream for what you would like your life to be?"

An awkward silence followed, then Hayley said, "The future? The future is so distant. So much can happen. No. I don't have a dream like that. Do you?"

"Oh yes, sweetheart." Patricia's throat constricted. Tears welled. She brushed them aside and composed herself. "I dream of a better future. I dream that someday we—Daddy, you and I—can be truly safe."

Hayley looked at her expectantly. "From what?"

"Centuries ago, the first Falcon in Savannah, Moses, made a vow to protect the city of Savannah and ultimately the colony. Back then it was one of the few major ports, so it was an important patriotic duty. Our enemies are different today, but no less powerful, and each time one of them comes up against the Falcon family, we make more enemies. Corrupt enemies who would like nothing more than to see our family destroyed." Patricia took a long deep breath. "We don't know if this is what is at work here, but we have always been taught to protect ourselves and serve our city. You may not have noticed it, but all of your training from marksmanship to civic duty has been a part of that heritage. I'd hoped to simply let you enjoy college, but with your decision to travel, and the situation our family is in, it's time you knew everything."

"We're not savages. We're civilized folk. Civilized people don't act like that."

"Most don't, some do." Patricia studied her daughter's eyes, remembering when Hayley was a little girl shooting a pint-sized pistol for the first time. That gleeful girl had become a woman. A woman who, for her own safety, needed to know the truth. Patricia's heart fluttered. "But, darling, though you can't always see it, there is evil everywhere. And when evil becomes powerful in Savannah, it encounters your father and his friends. And it encounters the Falcon family."

Hayley nodded at Patricia's pillow. "Have you shot anyone?"

Patricia thought back to her hesitation that had almost gotten her killed when she was rescuing Faith from her abusive husband. Putting a bullet into another person was a terrible action to have to live with. An action easy to ignore at the practice range, easy to set aside when her gun was resting inside her designer purse. "Not yet."

"Could you?"

She let out a long, raspy breath that hurt. Could she maim, or possibly kill someone? Intentionally take a life? She shuddered. "I'd like to think I'd be able to do what was necessary to anyone who threatened to hurt my family or friends."

Hayley's eyes moistened. "Do you ever just want to run away from all this?"

"Not really. It's the same everywhere. You can't escape the

savages. And most anywhere we could go has more danger than we face in Savannah."

"Savannah's crime rate isn't that low."

"Honey, anyone who comes after us knows what the consequences will be. Our family has spent centuries teaching that lesson."

"Someone killed Grams."

"Definitely someone who doesn't care to live."

Hayley gave a shrug. "He's still out there after killing three people and evading apprehension on two continents."

"He's been lucky." Patricia took a deep breath. "But his luck will run out. It always does. Trust me."

"Daddy was talking about trust yesterday."

"I hope you heeded his advice."

Hayley nodded. "Mama, I've changed my mind about dropping out of college."

"Why?"

Hayley gestured to her face. "Recent events, and lying in bed feeling powerless."

Patricia nodded.

"I need an education. And I want it out of the way."

"So you're going back to school?"

Hayley smiled. "Summer school, if I can still get in. I'd like to try to get my bachelor's in three years. My Advanced Placement courses gave me a running start on it. And after summer school, I can take a maximum schedule this fall."

"Are you sure you can handle it?"

Hayley's eyes seemed to glitter with internal flames. "Of course I can. I'm a Falcon."

Oh my goodness. Hayley was finally claiming her birthright. "I can't begin to tell you how proud that makes me. And your father, well, he'll probably pop a few shirt buttons." Patricia looked at her hands and flexed her fingers.

"What do you say you and I put our heads together right now and try to figure out who this killer is?"

* * *

TREY'S SHORT NAP HADN'T DONE NEARLY ENOUGH TO REVIVE him, but there was a killer on the loose so he hauled himself up. After a quick shower, he headed back out to get an update from his Coalition buddies.

Beau, Alton, Potter, and Hempfield sat at the cluttered round table, eyes fixed on individual computer monitors, fingers tapping on keyboards.

Beau looked up. "There's some iced sweet tea on the end of the credenza. An orderly just brought it up. It's quite good."

Trey went to the coffee urn instead, eased the cup under the spigot and depressed the lever. "Since my mind's still a bit fuzzy, I think it best I stick with the coffee." He took his cup and sat in the high-back leather chair next to Beau.

Beau stood and, holding a hand to his stomach, shuffled toward his bedroom. "I'm just going to lie down for a moment."

"Are you okay?" Trey asked.

"Fatigued." Beau took a deep breath. "And some ... some heartburn."

"Oh my God." Potter's chair squeaked as he pushed back from the table. "You've got to see this video footage from a diner in Pooler."

Beau slumped to the alcove floor.

Startled, Trey shot up and ran to Beau. Trey's head swam with apprehension. He dropped to his knees and pressed fingertips on Beau's carotid artery. Beau's limp body stirred at the connection, then stilled once again. Weak pulse. Trey raised Beau's eyelids. Eyes glazed and unfocused. Trey placed his ear next to Beau's mouth. Shallow breathing. Not good. "Get a doctor in here, and don't touch that tea."

* * *

PATRICIA, EYES CLOSED DAYDREAMING, HAD BEEN THOUGH A lot in the past week. Dreadful experiences that made her stronger and better prepared to face adversity than ever before. And when she returned home, Savannah was getting a world-class burn center.

The door hinge squeaked. Patricia opened her eyes, squinting against the bright light.

Judy sauntered in and crossed to Patricia's bedside.

Patricia rolled to her side and smiled up at her visitor. Judy's hair was pulled into a ponytail. Her pale, drawn face seemed oddly hungry, older. Her wide, bloodshot eyes darted from side to side like an owl's.

"Thank you for coming," Patricia said. "How have you been? And would you mind going out and putting on a mask, gown and booties, plus sanitizing your hands? I'm sorry, but it's required."

"I'll only be minute, Patricia, just a minute. And how have I been? It's been a nightmare," Judy said in a harsh, hoarse voice.

"I know what you mean. But you need to—"

"I'm not putting on a damn gown or mask. None of that crap. And no, you couldn't ever know what my life is like." Judy narrowed her eyes and shook her head. Her cheeks glowed red. "You have everything, and a loving husband. I've got nothing ... and Beau. It's not right that you have it all. Not right at all."

Patricia swallowed and tried to think of something calming to say to her dear friend, who didn't seem to be making sense. "I know what you mean. God is gracious. He'll see us through this."

"Gracious?" Judy's eyes bulged. "Look at you. You're burnt to a crisp. How can God allow that?"

Judy's bizarre behavior tore at Patricia. "Hayley and I survived."

Judy rolled her shoulders back. "Unfortunately."

Patricia's mouth fell open. "Unfortunately? How can you say something so mean-spirited? Sometimes I just don't get—"

"No." Judy leaned forward until her face was inches from Patricia's. "You have no idea what a nightmare I live."

"Judy, what's gotten into you?" Patricia pushed back into the pillow. "I don't understand. Are you okay?"

"We all have personal agendas. Lord knows your family does. And over the years y'all have done very well exploiting others. Well, I have a personal agenda too." Judy opened her handbag. "And it's my job to tip the balance toward me." Judy pulled a syringe from her purse and stepped to Patricia's drip line.

An excruciating chill shot up Patricia's back. "Judy, what are you doing?"

"I'm finishing up my business, honey."

Patricia gasped. "What?"

"You won't feel a thing. At this strength, it'll be fast." Judy reached for the line.

Judy? The killer? Patricia dove for the call button.

Judy reached it first and dangled it just out of reach. "Uh, uh, uh," she sang, then tossed it into a corner.

The syringe in Judy's hand gleamed in the harsh overhead light as she inserted it into the port on the drip line, sending a shiver though Patricia. Adrenaline surged, strengthening her and making her senses hyper alert. Her heart raced. Swallowing her protest, Patricia ripped the IV from her arm.

Blood erupted. She clamped her hand over the wound. "Do you honestly believe you can get away with this?"

Syringe poised, Judy moved to the bedside and brought the syringe up.

Patricia's arm muscles spasmed. "Come on, Judy. You don't want to do that."

"You haven't left me much of a choice. You're smart. I made too many mistakes." Judy lunged for Patricia's arm.

Patricia swatted away Judy's hand.

Judy persisted and seized Patricia's forearm, pining it to the mattress. Patricia struggled to break free, but Judy was too strong.

"You would have figured it out sooner or later," Judy said, her eyes cold. "With you out of the way, I might have enough time to go somewhere. Hide. Start a new life."

"If I'm alive you can do the same thing. Go. Leave right now. I'm not stopping you."

"You're not stopping anything." Judy, a malevolent smile on her thin lips, brought the syringe down.

Patricia jammed her free hand under her pillow, jerked out the pistol, aimed to maim, and compressed the trigger. A single shot exploded from the barrel.

Judy crumpled to the floor. Her right hand was mangled.

Trembling violently, Patricia let out a long breath. "You killed my mother ... and Alisa. How could you?" She shook her head. "I should kill you." Impulsively, Patricia sat up in bed, ignoring the pain, and aimed the Glock at Judy, writhing and screaming on the floor.

Father John, his gun drawn, surged into the room. Trey followed.

Patricia dropped the gun and starred at her friend. "Why, Judy?" she whispered in horror.

The pain of betrayal that sliced through Patricia was worse than any of the physical pain she was in. Her friend.

Her mother's trusted friend. Alicia's trusted friend. Even as Judy screamed in pain, Patricia felt agony at the sound. Part of her wanted to leap from the bed and comfort her friend, because she couldn't believe the last few minutes had ever happened. It was inexplicable. And then Patricia began to shake uncontrollably as her body succumbed to shock.

CHAPTER 31

*P*atricia was moved to a new room so the police could secure the crime scene. Once everyone had left, Trey said, "They're going to detain Judy on attempted murder and charge you with firearm possession. We'll need to stay in-country until your case is disposed of. I'll see if I can get the matter expedited, but there will be a substantial fine."

"I hope they throw the book at Judy."

"The syringe with the poison is powerful evidence, and it's probably the same poison she used on Beau."

"Beau?"

"She tried to poison Beau an hour or so ago, but the doctors pumped his stomach before the poison could do too much damage."

"Thank God."

"Two counts of attempted murder should keep Judy busy for a long while."

"Three." Patricia grimaced. "The car bombing."

"Oh yeah."

"I can't believe she organized the car bombing on her

own," Patricia said. "Do you suppose there's someone else involved?"

"There might be. What with explosives and all. Well, the French police are very thorough. I'm sure they'll be able to get that one figured out and hang it on her."

"And I want her to pay for Mama's and Alisa's murders."

Trey nodded. "That's going to take evidence we don't have yet."

"I want justice, Trey. We *have* to make her pay."

"She hasn't admitted to killing either of them."

"She said I'd figure it out soon."

"At this point, it's a circumstantial case regarding your mother. I wish we could tie all the pieces together on how Herman relates to Judy and why your mother's money is in Herman's name."

"Bring Hayley and me laptop computers tomorrow morning and we'll get on it."

"The Coalition and the Savannah Police are on this, and they're much better equipped to gather and process the evidence that can convict Judy."

"Trey honey, she took my Mama from me. I owe it to Mama to do everything I can to bring Judy to justice for Mama's murder. I just *have* to be involved in this. Humor me. Please."

He sighed. "Okay. But you can't interfere with the police investigation in any way."

She nodded. "And would you send me your case file on Mama's murder?"

"Of course."

CHAPTER 32

The following morning, Hayley and Patricia had breakfast together in Patricia's room, then fired up their laptops.

"What do you need me to do?" Hayley asked.

"Have you read Daddy's case file on Grammy's murder?"

Hayley nodded.

"That was compiled before he knew Judy was the killer. I want you to extract whatever information he has on Judy's activities and arrange it chronologically. Then we'll look at the timeline and see what's missing so we know what to search for to fill in the blanks."

When Patricia's phone chimed an incoming email, she noted it was from Meredith and marked urgent. The message itself requested an immediate Skype videoconference.

Concerned something might be amiss, Patricia opened the video app and linked to Meredith's address. Meredith's image came up on the screen.

"It's the middle of the night there, isn't it?" Patricia asked.

"Just past two, but I didn't want to delay letting you know that I just found Sonny."

"Is he alive?"

Meredith smiled. "Very much so."

"Let's link Sonny into the conference. I have a bunch of questions for him."

"That's not necessary. I have his information. I'll brief you on what I have, then we can conference with him later if you have additional questions. So, Sonny has—"

"Hold it, Meredith. I have some big news too. Judy Simpson is the killer."

Meredith's jaw dropped. "Oh God. I was sure there was some mistake. I heard Sonny's information, but I—"

"It's true. I can hardly believe it myself." Patricia proceeded to tell Meredith everything that happened in the hospital room.

When Patricia finished, Meredith wiped her eyes and shook her head. "Well, that fits everything Sonny told me, I was just hoping it was a misunderstanding. But in the closed-circuit surveillance footage of the Hilton Head bank, Herman and Judy are together."

"The Coalition just found security footage of Judy and Herman in a diner on the day he died. Trey was coming to tell me when Judy came to my room. The diner video and the bank video should help the Savannah Police make their case against Judy." Patricia blew out a long breath. "So, what did you find out from Sonny?"

"Seems he's been in the Federal Witness Protection Program since before Henrietta died."

Patricia's breath caught as dread surged. "What on earth for?"

"Sonny was acquiring farmland in South Carolina on behalf of a Chinese businessman. Turns out the man's money was smuggled into the United States in violation of the

Patriot Act. Hundreds of millions of dollars of bulk currency."

"How'd Sonny know the money was illegal?"

"Sonny said he didn't know the money was bad. He'd investigated the situation before taking it on. The businessman was legitimate and provided solid references. The man's local bank confirmed the funds were available. By law, such large sums entering the US from a foreign country made the bank notify the FBI. Turns out the businessman was connected with the 14K Triad. When contacted by the FBI, Sonny helped them build a successful case."

"14K?"

"Second largest Chinese mob in the world. They've been trying to get a stronghold in the United States for years."

"But Sonny's out on the streets now, isn't he concerned with retaliation?"

"Apparently the feds were able to keep his identity out of the case. Secret trial. Special judge. National security and all that."

A chill went through Patricia. "Maybe it's best not to know. Witness Protection must have been a terrible experience for Sonny."

"He claims he enjoyed it." Meredith opened a bottle of water and took a sip. "They put him up in a high-end villa on Hilton Head Island."

"Did you ask Sonny about Mama's money?"

"Yes indeed. Turns out the Chinese businessman was acquiring the land for a major family entertainment complex similar to Disney World, only closer to the lucrative Northeast and Midwest tourists. Newer. Bigger. Planned to outdo Disney. Sonny reasoned that once the word got out about the project, all the land around the proposed complex would soar in value. So, he advised some of his biggest clients, including Henrietta, to buy the adjacent land. As he saw it, it was a sure winner."

"Mama never said anything."

"Sonny swore her to secrecy."

"Why did he have Mama transfer her money overseas, then back?"

"According to Sonny, Henrietta accidentally mentioned the investment opportunity to Judy. It was Judy's idea to move the money overseas to make it appear to others that the money was coming from China, to fool the local competition."

Patricia tapped her fingertips on the desk making a patter like gentle rain on patio umbrellas. "Why was Mama's money in Herman's name?"

"Once again to fool the competition. Henrietta was too well-known. Major land purchases by her would attract attention as soon as they were recorded. It's all public information. Judy suggested to Mama that Judy's cousin, Herman, make the purchases on Henrietta's behalf. Obviously trusting Judy, Henrietta agreed and had the money transferred into an account created for Herman. That kept her name out of everything." Meredith's eyebrows arched. "Of course, Judy had different plans for the money. Sonny feels terrible about what happened afterward."

"I imagine." Patricia shook her head. "But why did Judy have to kill Mama? She could have just taken the money and disappeared."

"When Sonny disappeared, she must have gotten spooked. Thinking she was going to be found out, she killed Henrietta."

"Thank God the feds froze the money before Judy got it out of the Hilton Head Island money exchange."

Meredith nodded. "Yeah. Once the feds started their

investigation, all recent large financial transfers from China to the Southeast became suspect."

"Sonny has sure filled in a lot of blanks. If his story checks out, I suspect that's going to be more than enough to put Judy away for the rest of her life."

"I feel so betrayed." Meredith brushed tears from her cheek. "And I really miss Alisa."

Patricia's throat constricted. "I miss her too. Big time."

CHAPTER 33

Two Months Later
    Savannah, Georgia

When Patricia heard the front door close and Trey's familiar footfalls in the hallway, she set aside her novel, Pat Conroy's last, and glanced at her watch. Five-thirty. Right on time. Since their return to Savannah, Trey had ceased working evenings so they could spend more time together. She took off her reading glasses and placed them gently on the table.

Trey entered the room.

She grinned.

His gray-lashed eyes twinkled.

He crossed the room and gave her a warm kiss.

A pleasant shiver went through her. Her cheeks heated. She reached up, wrapped her arms around his neck and deepened the kiss. My, oh my, what a guy. She was so blessed to have him in her life. So very blessed. She eased her lips from his and caressed his stubbled face. "I love you," she said.

"And I love you," he said as he stepped back.

Looking up at him, she reached out and stroked the outside of his thigh. "You're a fine man, Trey. The best."

"Why thank you kindly, Patsy. By the way, how did your lunch with Meredith go?"

"I can't believe how well she's recovered." Patricia took a tube of lotion from the end table and applied some to her forearms. "Except for her ever so slightly slurred speech, she seems the same as before. She says her weekly speech therapy sessions should have her speech back to normal in six months or so."

"I'm impressed how she was able to track the money trail."

Patricia nodded. "She's a talented woman."

"On the subject of talented women, Beau and I are going to support Alton's request to allow women to serve as Cotton Coalition members."

"Beau doesn't have children," Patricia said. "His seat will pass regardless. Why would he agree?"

"I suppose he now sees that the Coalition will be stronger with women in it."

"Isabel and Hayley."

"Isabel immediately. I'm going to wait a few more years to integrate Hayley. Let her finish college and law school. Let her get settled. And, if she decides to stay in Savannah, I'll see if she wants it. Though I hope to goodness she does. I'd hate to see almost 300 years of family tradition stop in this generation."

"I'm sure Hayley will appreciate that."

Trey stroked his chin. "I'm still bothered that with all the resources we and the church had on Henrietta's murder we never linked Herman to Judy."

"As a distant cousin who briefly lived with the family, the linkage was tenuous at best. He didn't take the family name and moved out right after high school. Other than census information, which no one thought to check, I don't know what other records might have tied the two together. We checked for criminal records and came up empty."

"And Beau said he'd never seen or heard of Herman."

"Well, the good news is that Meredith got the video of them together at the Hilton Head bank."

Trey picked up the *Savannah Post* from the end table. "Speaking of news, did you read this article?"

"Willie's story on Judy?"

Trey nodded. "Willie got most of our story right, but he distorted the terms of Judy's extradition. Contrary to the article, the prosecutor here isn't going to even consider asking for the death penalty. That's what he had to agree to in order to get Judy extradited from France. She'll pay for what she did, not by execution but with life in prison."

"I still can't believe what she did."

"It was terrible, but thanks to you, we've brought her to justice." Trey opened his briefcase, took out a black leather box and handed it to Patricia.

"What's this?"

"Open it."

She lifted the lid to see her Kimber 45. "This is the gun you gave me after we were married."

"Yeah." He nodded. "I took it from the safe for a few days. Check out the custom grip."

Engraved in the grip were the letters VJ. "VJ?" she asked, completely puzzled.

"Vigilante for Justice," Trey said. "That's what you are, and I'm damned proud. When others were ready to accept your mother's death as a heart attack, you investigated. And through your direct action in Paris, you brought Judy to justice. It's been a tough journey for you, but you did impressive work."

"We," she corrected.

"Okay. But *we* couldn't have done it without you." He leaned down, gave her a kiss, then straightened. "I'm impressed."

She nodded, then looked at the gun again. "Thank you, Trey."

"What do you want to do about the burn clinic?"

Memories welled up, pounding her brain. She shuddered. The nightmares she had experienced for weeks after the accident were gone, replaced by vivid memories no one should have to experience. But she had learned to endure the images. Though they came daily, they were the past. They existed merely to remind her of what she must do for others not so fortunate.

"I think we should move forward on establishing a burn clinic in Savannah. The feds recovered Mama's money. We could fund the clinic with some of the inheritance and name it after her."

He shrugged. "It's a noble idea, but I don't know if it's feasible. I don't have any idea how many burn victims we have in Savannah nor how many patients we'd have to admit to financially sustain a clinic. I suppose the Falcon Hospital Board of Directors could commission a committee to explore the possibility."

"I'd like that," she said.

"I'll ask Beau to head the committee."

"How's he doing?"

"Fine. His divorce is in the works and should be granted. He's petitioned the church for an annulment. Considering everything Judy did, he shouldn't have any problem there."

"I still can't believe she turned on us," Patricia said in a voice made strident by simmering anger.

Trey shrugged. "People do heinous things for money."

"She had plenty of money."

"Not of her own. She had a terrible marriage. She wanted

out, but probably knew she would end up broke if she divorced Beau."

"She'd get half in a divorce."

"I don't believe Beau is that well off. He's made some bad investments. Half of nothing is still nothing."

"But, to kill for money? Her friends? What good is all the money in the world when you're alone?" Struggling to make sense of it, she dragged her hands down her face. "Oh my. What happens to a person that makes them resort to something like murder?"

"Greed. Arrogance. Who knows?"

Patricia gazed at her hands folded on her lap. Judy had taken away her foundation, her Mama, as well as her great friend, Alisa. Patricia shook her head. "I don't understand Judy, but I pray for her salvation every day."

Trey's phone rang. He looked at the display, then said, "Excuse me, Patsy. I should take this."

She nodded understanding.

No sooner than he brought the phone to his ear did shock appear on his face. "What? What? No. No, get on it right away. Call me back as soon as you get the full story." Trey disconnected the call.

"What was that about?" Patricia asked.

"Judy escaped."

The End

Continue for a preview of

Savannah Secrets

Book Two of the Vigilantes for Justice series

Due out April 2018

SAVANNAH
Secrets

VIGILANTES
FOR
JUSTICE
BOOK 2

ALAN CHAPUT

CHAPTER ONE

$\mathcal{T}$rey Falcon left his law office at three o'clock and paused on the front stoop of the restored nineteenth century mansion to survey Falcon Square.

A breeze ruffled the Spanish moss hanging like tattered gray drapes from the ancient oaks. Foraging pigeons took flight as a young couple settled on a bench. Nearby, two children chased sun shafts filtering through the dense tree canopy.

As the air was unseasonably warm for September, Trey loosened his tie. A horse-drawn carriage filled with tourists clip-clopped past on the cobblestone roadway. Another ideal fall afternoon in historic downtown Savannah, yet his eyes scanned the entire square looking for anything out of place. His instincts, which had never betrayed him, warned that something was wrong.

He massaged the back of his tingling neck, pressing fingertips into tight muscles. It had been an intense day of depositions and, as usual, tomorrow would be equally brutal. He again glanced at his watch. Five minutes after three. A couple of hours until Father John and his daughter would arrive for dinner. More than enough time to meet with Trokev before going home to help Patricia get ready. The Trokev meeting was more than enough to make anyone jumpy. He released a sigh.

The dinner was a big step in Patricia's recovery from last year's attack. He swallowed a shudder and the chunk of guilt that erupted whenever her battle came to mind. That was history. Today was a new start for Patricia, for both of them. Everything had to be as perfect as possible.

Trey reached inside his jacket pocket and removed his phone. A little advance support for her big night couldn't hurt.

She answered after one ring. "Hey, I was just thinking about you."

Her voice sounded bright and self-assured. He hadn't heard much of that signature tone in the last year. Her full of life spirit had fallen prey to her trauma. Now her positive attitude appeared to be returning. A smile emerged, topping his reaction.

"I'm leaving my office for my three-thirty appointment and I thought I'd—"

"Check on me?" she inserted.

"Ah, yeah. You know me well; better than my mother. But you did toss and turn all night. Are you okay?"

When Patricia hesitated, Trey figured she might need an escape route. "You know, we don't have to do the dinner tonight. We can always postpone. Father John wouldn't mind."

"You're right, I didn't sleep all that well," Patricia said. "But, don't you know, I woke up feeling darn good. I'm enjoying getting back to cooking for guests, and I'm looking forward to a fun evening with Father John and his daughter. It's time, beyond time, to do this thing."

"I love your positive attitude," he said, glad she was taking the dinner in stride.

"I had a realization in the shower this morning after you left—I've shot people. Our enemies are the ones who should be fearful, not me."

"That's my girl." His skin bristled with pride. He glanced at his watch. "I have to go. I have one brief meeting on the way and should be home by four-thirty. I love you so much, sweetheart."

"I love you too, honey."

With a lingering grin, he stuffed the phone into his coat. Trey slipped on sunglasses and followed the slate sidewalk to the discrete parking lot adjoining his office. His Bentley sat at the back, next to Reva's car. A black SUV was parked closer to the front of the densely landscaped, private lot. Tourists, no doubt. He couldn't fault them. They were an important part of Savannah's economy, an economy his family had cultivated since the eighteenth century.

First one, then three more broad-shouldered bodyguard types in dark suits, day-old beards and aviator sunglasses poured out of the SUV and approached him.

Trey's stomach clenched. He'd seen the tactic before, like a wolf pack on prey. A slug of adrenaline cannonballed into his stomach, jacking his nerves. This was no Welcome-Wagon visit. And sending four meant they weren't here to talk. He should have listened to his earlier intuition; it had never steered him wrong.

He glanced at the thick-necked thugs, opened his jacket and brought his gun hand to his underarm weapon, poised to draw on the slightest provocation. Provocation he knew was coming, he just didn't know which of them would make the first move.

As they spread out trying to surround him, Trey jockeyed for position, but had no good alternatives other than to back up against Reva's car. The lead tough studied Trey like a coiled cobra deciding when to strike. The man's hesitation was good. He was likely considering his options. Would the man walk? Or would he—

Suddenly, the side of Trey's neck seared with a Taser shock, then another. His torso went rigid. His legs buckled. His mind imploded, then everything went black.

End of preview of *Savannah Secrets*
Coming April 2018

Sign up for my New Release Newsletter at www.alanchaput.com for an email note when *Savannah Secrets* is available

Or

Text CHAPUT to 31996 to receive a text notice when *Savannah Secrets* releases

ACKNOWLEDGMENTS

I am grateful to you for reading *Savannah Sleuth* and hope you enjoyed it. You are the reason I write. I appreciate your comments and support in email, in person and on social media. Your comments keep me focused.

Thank you to the reviewers and bloggers who've so generously spread the word about *Savannah Sleuth* and who've taken the time to give readers an opinion about it.

Thank you to my wonderful wife who has been by my side at each stage of bringing *Savannah Sleuth* to you. I'm so fortunate to have her support and unconditional love.

Thank you to my critique partners, Natasha Boyd and Dave McDonald. Without their relentless advice, you would have been reading a vastly inferior book.

Thank you to my editor, Elizabeth White, who further improved my writing, pacing, grammar, and punctuation. And who also meticulously fact-checked all things Savannah.

And finally, thank you to my cover designer, Fayette Terlouw, who brought Patricia Falcon so vividly to life on the cover of *Savannah Sleuth*.

As you can see, it takes a team to produce a book, and I'm very grateful to be on this particular team.

DISCUSSION QUESTIONS FOR SAVANNAH SLEUTH

Discussion questions for *Savannah Sleuth*

1. Who was your favorite character in *Savannah Sleuth*? Why?

2. What did the main characters in *Savannah Sleuth* want? How did they change through the story?

3. Who did you suspect murdered Henrietta? Why?

4. Do you feel the author gave you enough clues and let you fully in on Patricia's investigation of her mother's murder?

5. There's a big twist toward the end of the book. Did you see it coming?

6. Is there a message in *Savannah Sleuth*? What is it?

7. Did you feel this story was unique? If so, what about it seemed new and fresh to you?

8. Would you recommend *Savannah Sleuth* to a friend? Why?

Contact Al at al@alchaput.com for information on inviting him to Skype or FaceTime with your book club.

ABOUT THE AUTHOR

Alan Chaput writes Southern mysteries. His novels have finaled in the Daphne and the Claymore. Al lives with his wife in Coastal South Carolina. When not writing, Al can be found Shag dancing, pursuing genealogy, or interacting on social media.

BOOKS BY ALAN CHAPUT

The Vigilantes for Justice Series:

1. *Savannah Sleuth*
2. *Savannah Secrets* (coming April 2018)
3. *Savannah Justice* (coming July 2018)
4. *Savannah Passion* (coming 2019)

END NOTE

Thank you for reading *Savannah Sleuth*. Please consider leaving a review for this book at Goodreads and your favorite book retailer. Your comments will help other readers decide if they want to read *Savannah Sleuth*. It's a fact —reviews make a difference.

Please stay in touch. I love reading your messages and enjoy hearing what you want in future books.

Warmest regards and happy reading,

Al

LET'S STAY IN TOUCH

If you want to keep in touch with me between books, you can find me on social media at these profiles:

https://www.instagram.com/alan_chaput
https://www.goodreads.com/user/show/22658428-alan
http://www.facebook.com/alchaput
http://www.pinterest.com/alanchaput
https://twitter.com/alanchaput

And you can find me on the web at:
www.alanchaput.com